THE ROGUE SPY

DELHI CHAPTER | BOOK 1

KRITIKA SHARMA

KALAMOS LITERARY SERVICES LLP

Kalamos Literary Services LLP
Email: info@kalamos.co.in
Published in 2022
by
Kalamos Literary Services

ISBN - 978-93-91142-17-9

The Rogue Spy
Kritika Sharma

Cover designed and typeset in Kalamos Literary Services LLP

For my husband, Rajat
For my Sun and the Moon and all my stars, i.e. my beautiful children,
Vihaan and Vanya
And for my dearest friend, Anuj
Thank you to all of you.

A Canadian National.
Heiress to biggest
Mafia ring
Patricia Myers
A French National,
World's best hacker
Ava Paradis
Band of International Rogue Spies
Franc Ivanek
Samuel Guttman
A Slovak National.
World's best analyst
A retired Belgian
weapons expert
Adhira Shekhawat
An Indian.
Ex-military Rogue Spy

THE GIRL IN RED

"Well, isn't it as if I am standing in Madame Tussauds," she chuckled in an American accent as she looked around.

Wearing blonde hair, thick shades, a red knee-length dress and high heels, she was looking exceptionally out of place, and the occupants of the room sat frozen at her sight.

A woman in the Police uniform stood up suddenly and glared. There were two other men in the room, one in khaki kurta-pyjama and another in a black suit, and they just kept sitting, staring at her, too shocked to react.

"This is the Home Minister's office," the Policewoman shouted. "Who are you and how dare you barge in here like this?" The policewoman was not wrong in her display of anger, after all, the mysterious girl had entered the main chambers of Home Minister's office without any prior appointment or permission!

The girl in red just tilted her head and took off her shades. Her smile made the Policewoman gulp. The second man in a suit stood up, too.

There was a lot of commotion outside the office, and a few minutes later the entire security of the home minister's office was there.

"I would have to hurt you all if any of you touched me," the girl in red announced, still showing her perfect teeth.

Finally, the home minister stood up too, looking bemused. He gestured everyone to stand down and faced the girl with crossed arms.

"Well, I know I am early," the girl laughed. "You called me at 4, isn't it? Well, I am leaving the country for some work at 5, so, I came here at 11 to see what you wanted," she shrugged carelessly.

The entire demeanour of the home minister changed instantly. He pulled out his phone and called someone.

"She is here," the home minister spoke on the phone and disconnected.

"We shall continue our meeting later," the home minister spoke to the Policewoman and the man in the suit.

"But sir," the man in the suit was taken aback. Clearly he held some senior position of great importance but, at the moment, the home minister had attention for none other than the girl.

"Pankaj, this is far more important," the home minister announced and everyone cleared the room.

As now only the girl in red and the home minister were present, she looked around. It was a massive office with high-end furniture. On one corner was a big wooden desk and executive chair. Behind the table was the list of previous home ministers. On the other end of the room was a massive sofa set, where Home Minister was sitting with others minutes ago. The walls were decorated with photographs of historical people and many important framed documents.

As she walked around, soaking in the enormity of the room, the home minister took his seat.

"You can sit," the home minister addressed her politely.

"Thank you, Mr Home Minister," she laughed, still maintaining her accent.

He gestured her to a seat and she walked towards him.

"I understand you have called me for a job," she smiled as she sat down.

"Yes, your understanding is correct," he smiled back. "How do you want me to address you? Do you have a new name along with the avatar you are donning right now?"

She laughed again. "If you knew the reason why I have donned this avatar, you wouldn't believe me."

"Humour me," the home minister insisted.

She was considering him when there was a tap on the door and another man entered. And it was not just her whose jaw that dropped at the sight, even the man looked utterly shocked as he tried to recognise her.

"What is he doing here?" she spoke, finally ditching her accent and the fake smile.

"Dhira?" the man blanched.

"A-dhira.... It's Adhira Shekhawat," she growled at the man.

"Come Rudhir, come in," the home minister spoke, pointing at the chair next to her. Rudhir hesitated but took his seat. Adhira moved her chair a little away from him, a movement that didn't miss either man's notice.

"Ok, so now that Rudhir is here, we can start our discussion," the home minister pulled a file and opened it. "Firstly, my apologies, we have not been able to contact you before. I see that you have tried to work with us before."

A snort of unintentional derisive laughter escaped Adhira's lips. With her smile back in place, she asked, "Me, wanting to work with *you*?"

A frown appeared on the home minister's face.

"Meaning no disrespect, but I don't apply anywhere. People contact me because they need me," Adhira pointed at herself with pride.

The home minister now turned his glance towards Rudhir.

"I applied on her behalf," Rudhir spoke with bowed head.

Adhira snorted again and turned to the home minister.

"I have never applied to work with you, so, sir, with due respect, if this is what your file is saying, then please throw that away," Adhira pointed at the file in front of the home minister.

Home Minister shut the file and glared at Rudhir.

"May I know what is happening here?" the home minister demanded.

"She is the best, sir, believe me. You can see how well she has changed herself. Even I could not recognise her," Rudhir insisted.

The home minister didn't look convinced at these words so Rudhir added, "If you saw her real face, you will see why I am saying that."

The home minister shook his head, trying very hard to mask his annoyance. He was just about to dismiss her when Rudhir babbled, "She killed Butch."

Both the home minister and Adhira turned to him in surprise.

"Is this true?" The home minister asked Adhira, impressed.

"Yes," Rudhir interrupted. "I know your name was not announced but that's how you work, isn't it? In the shadows," Rudhir asked Adhira. "But I recognised your hand. Your signature kill style. I knew you killed Butch, who is the most wanted terrorist of the world."

"Well, he *was* the most-wanted terrorist at a time, yes," Adhira grinned broadly, "And I have no liberty to let you know but Americans may or may not have hired me to take care of their Butchy problem."

"You are hired," the home minister announced as soon as he heard her response. "Rudhir will be your point of contact and you will deal with only him and no one else."

Adhira raised her eyebrows at this.

"I do not accept this job," Adhira spoke. "No matter the money you throw, even though we have not talked about financials."

"Money is no problem, your demands will be met," the home minister brushed his hand carelessly. "Why are you not accepting this job?"

Adhira turned her face towards Rudhir. "I object to working with Mr Rajput here..."

"He is the head of R&AW, he will be your counterpart," the home minister dictated but Adhira's expressions didn't change. "This is a very sensitive mission, and I trust only Rudhir at present."

Adhira's eyebrows rose even higher at these words.

The home minister sighed and continued, "Not for money or anything, but do this job for them," and he pushed another file towards her.

Adhira opened the file as the home minister said, "I believe you know some of them…"

Adhira flinched as she recognised the faces of her former colleagues, but they were not smiling anymore, they were dead… bloodied, mutilated and very much dead.

Her eyes fell on the face of her friend and her eyes misted. "Bharat…" she whispered. "Bharat is dead?"

"Last night," Rudhir supplied.

"How? Who?" Adhira mumbled.

"I will let Rudhir fill you in," the home minister interjected, standing up. "I have to leave and wrap up my previous meeting. You both can discuss and finalise the details here. Remember, this is the most crucial project right now. Everything here is classified, and it should stay classified."

And with one nod at Rudhir, he left.

"Why are you looking like this?" Rudhir asked once they were alone.

"I may tell you, but then I may have to kill you," Adhira laughed and placed her legs on the table of the home minister.

Rudhir grabbed her legs and placed them down. She was about to kick him for touching her but stopped at his words, "You may not respect me, but at least respect this office and the man who holds this office. He is one of the best leaders we have."

Adhira shrugged and stood up.

"Do you have a file to give me?" Adhira asked seriously.

"Yes," and Rudhir handed her the file. "Also, take this," and he gave her a phone.

"I have a phone," Adhira stared at Rudhir in mockery.

"This is a secure line, it cannot be hacked," Rudhir informed.

"Oh, Mr R&AW," Adhira spoke sarcastically, "I can bet my life that I can get your unhackable phone hacked in seconds, but you cannot crack mine. Wanna bet? If I win, you are out of this case and will never bother me again."

Rudhir winced at the words 'Mr R&AW' but did not comment.

"So, you don't wanna bet?" Adhira screwed her nose, "well, it was worth a shot!"

"I—" Rudhir started but Adhira just raised her hand to shush him.

"I will study this," Adhira tapped the file and started to walk out.

"Dhira," Rudhir whispered, Adhira turned furiously.

"Do you have a death wish?" Adhira flared.

"I know you can kill me without blinking," Rudhir sighed. "I am well aware of what is strapped on your thigh."

"It's Adhira," she hissed.

"This is very important, please consider this a priority," Rudhir requested. "We need to bring justice to Bharat and all other agents. Please…"

"I am flying out to Brussels this afternoon; I will call you tomorrow evening. Then you can give me all the details and I can tell you how much this will cost you," Adhira informed.

"Why are you going to Brussels?" Rudhir asked suddenly.

"I think," Adhira spoke with raised eyebrows, "It is none of your bloody concern," and with one last look of utter loathing, she walked out.

XRS ATTACK

"I will land in two hours, I want you to pick me up from IGI," Adhira spoke quickly.

"What?" Rudhir asked, shocked.

"Which part did you not understand? I am landing in 2 hours, I need you to pick me up from the airport!" Adhira said scathingly.

"How are you calling from your flight?" Rudhir asked, still surprised.

"Why don't you ask your R&AW team to figure that out but I am sure that you will be just as successful as you were in hacking my phone…" the sarcasm was dripping from her every word. Adhira waited, but Rudhir didn't reply and she knew that Rudhir had failed to hack into her 'unhackable' phone. "I assumed as much, see you when I land. And I don't like to wait!" and she disconnected.

"Why can I never recognise you?" Rudhir asked in disbelief as a girl in a green business suit stood in front of him, glaring. "I can only recognise your smile, that too because this was the same condescending smile you were giving me yesterday."

Adhira shrugged and dropping her small bag in the back seat, sat next to him.

"Why are you dressed like this?" Rudhir asked as he stared at her.

Ditching her smile, she glared.

"Are you faking to be a Belgian?" Rudhir asked in disbelief as he stared at her pointed eyes and high cheeks. "How are you able to change your face so drastically?"

"Do you seriously want to know how I operate?" Adhira asked seriously.

"Well, yeah!" Rudhir replied, feeling hopeful.

"Well no! I won't answer you," she just shrugged.

"Dhira," Rudhir whispered as usual.

"A-dhira," she stressed.

"We have to work together, can you at least not hate me?" Rudhir pleaded.

"After what you did to me..." Adhira sat straight and looked ahead, "I don't think I can ever forgive you, Mr R&AW. Now drive, I need to understand what I am getting into before I accept this mission."

Rudhir wanted to ask so much, but her closed-off demeanour didn't allow him. Sighing, he twisted the key and the car started to move.

Adhira gave instructions and they stopped outside an under-construction building. Stepping out, she sat on the hood of his car and pulled out a cigarette.

"So, Mr R&AW," she blew the smoke in his face as he stood in front of her, staring at her with a befuddled expression. "What happened to our friend? Of late I was not a great fan of Bharat, but at a point he was my friend and his death is bothering me, not to mention the sheer gruesomeness of the crime."

"I agree, the attack has shaken up everyone, starting from the IB to the PMO. It is due to the gravity of this attack that the Prime Minister himself asked the home minister to take a lead on this. He does not trust anyone," Rudhir sighed.

"So, what were Bharat and his team up to?" Adhira demanded.

"It is classified," Rudhir exhaled loudly. "But I took special clearance to let you know all the details."

"Oh my..." Adhira exclaimed as she placed her hands on her chest dramatically, "Special clearances... My My... I must feel honoured."

"You don't have to mock the system, it is in place for a reason," Rudhir snapped.

"Yeah, I very well know the reasons for which your so-called system exists," Adhira snapped back. "Now, if you do not want to share it with me then fine..."

"I just said that I took clearance," Rudhir spoke in disbelief.

"Yeah yeah, before getting into this, tell me, do I need to ask for clearance every time I need some critical information because if that is the case, I don't think I can work and function properly," Adhira declared.

"Actually no, once you agree to work on this project, and sign the relevant documents, we will give you the highest clearance. I think your clearance would be higher than mine," and Rudhir laughed sardonically.

"I like the sound of it. What are you waiting for then, tell me what happened?" Adhira demanded.

"Don't you think that we should discuss this in some closed safe space? Somewhere I can show you the documents and the videos? We can go to my office," Rudhir enquired.

"Are you sure that your office isn't bugged?" Adhira demanded.

"Of course," Rudhir sounded a little offended by this question.

"Well, I don't trust the 'closed safe space'. If these agents were killed so mercilessly, then there is a mole. You can choose to believe it or ignore it, but someone on the inside is betraying you, and I don't like to be sold," Adhira crossed her arms and stared at him sternly.

"I believe you," Rudhir agreed instantly. "I don't know where, but there *is* a mole in our regime, there is no other way that these agents could have been attacked."

"So, a mole in which department?" Adhira asked suspiciously.

"It can be either IB or R&AW," Rudhir informed sadly. "There is an investigation going on, I am sure we will find the source very soon."

Adhira admired the hope in his voice.

"You don't believe in the investigations?" Rudhir asked as she stared at him with amused expressions.

"No, I don't believe in the fairness of your system's 'investigations'. Saw it first-hand, didn't I?" Adhira laughed.

Rudhir was about to retort but she raised her hand and interrupted him, "I am the least interested in fighting with you. So, why don't you just let me know what exactly happened so that I can be on my way and you can be on yours."

Rudhir considered her for a moment then closed his eyes to compose himself. She always had the tendency of getting on his nerves but that was how his Dhira was and he knew that she would never change. And a part of him never wanted her to change.

"It started a few months ago. An anonymous tip informed us that there was a new weapon called XRS and it was being imported in India."

"What the hell is XRS?" Adhira interjected.

"Don't know what it stands for, but it is unique and there are claims that XRS is the deadliest radioactive weapon at present. The black market was full of buzz and chatter about this. Everyone was making bids on it, even though nobody knew what it did or how it was operated or even how big it was... they only knew that it could kill millions in one go. A group of undercover agents led by Bharat were assigned on this," Rudhir spoke.

"Why Bharat?" Adhira interjected. "I mean if the weapon is so deadly, I am sure that US, Europe and everyone would be after it, isn't it?"

"The target was India… the buzz said as much so we took immediate action. I don't know who else was investigating but Bharat and his team were operating from here," Rudhir sighed.

"Okay," Adhira said, perplexed.

"Their job was to find the source of XRS, procure it and nullify it before it could hit our populous. The team started investigating and they had unearthed a lot of secrets regarding this weapon. This was a highly dangerous mission and because of the sensitivity of this project they all were holed up in a safe house outside Pune," Rudhir paused to draw a breath.

"Haven't you learnt a thing?" Adhira asked, confused, "You never put all your assets together. One aim and all are dead!"

Rudhir now knew that it was a mistake to put all the agents in one location but didn't want to admit it in front of her. Ignoring her comment, he continued, "Three nights ago was the engagement party of two of the team members."

"Oh my God!" Adhira exclaimed, "You put two love birds on the same mission? How come you are the head of R&AW? Don't you have any basic sense?"

Rudhir looked at her in disbelief. "They," he started with gritted teeth, "they got together after they started working on this project. If I had known," he clenched his fists in anger, "do you think I am that stupid?"

"I already know how big a stupid you are, Mr R&AW," Adhira glared. "Anyway, continue."

It seemed that fire would come out Rudhir's nostrils, but he resisted. "An invite was floated out with the announcement and it was sent to many people. The party went on till 11 in the night and as per the records, the team returned to the safe house just after midnight. They were still celebrating when they were attacked."

"How were they attacked? It must not be a physical attack... it would not be easy to take down six highly trained agents," Adhira wondered.

"It was not," Rudhir said dejectedly. "This is the recording of the day..." and he took out his laptop from the car and opened a video.

"Bharat always knew how to party," Adhira commented as they stared at the screen. Six people were dancing and drinking merrily.

"They were the newly engaged couple," Rudhir paused the video and pointed at a happy couple.

"They look so happy," Adhira spoke sadly.

"Now watch this..." Rudhir played and in the next few seconds, suddenly everyone present had stopped dancing and were choking. There was blood oozing out of their eyes, ears and mouths, and boils were appearing on their skins. The boils were rising and bursting rapidly as if someone was injecting the boils with an activator. Within seconds all six agents were on the floor, writhing in pain, and then after a while, nobody moved. They were dead.

"What?" Adhira gasped and replayed the video multiple times, repeating the frames where they had fallen.

"There must be more cameras in the safe house," Adhira spoke finally, "I mean, it cannot be the only footage."

Rudhir looked impressed and showed her another video.

"Show me all the videos," Adhira ordered and he opened the folder for her. She scrolled through all and analysed them seriously.

"I need a copy of all these," Adhira demanded. "I am sure we can pull out something critical."

"We have already analysed them, thoroughly. We couldn't find a thing, except—"

"Except the white blur, isn't it?" Adhira nodded. "Believe me, my team will find something."

"Your team?" Rudhir asked, flabbergasted.

"Seriously?" Adhira mocked him. "You think I managed to kill Butch, the most-wanted terrorist, the mastermind behind so many deadly attacks all over the globe *alone*? How do you think I did everything?"

"Where is your team? How do you operate? I need to know these details," Rudhir demanded this time. "I am handing the fate of my entire team, my department, my country in your hands."

"You will meet them when you meet them, okay," Adhira dismissed him. "Now, hand me a copy of the videos."

"First sign this, I will make a copy of the videos in the meantime," and Rudhir handed her a contract. "Home Minister has asked me to pay you the same amount you were offered by the Americans. I have assumed a figure, if it doesn't meet your expectations, there is a clause in the contract that will enable you to quote a higher price," Rudhir finished.

Adhira read through and appreciated the details.

"What will happen if I breach this contract?" Adhira asked as she signed each page. "And the amount is fine."

"Are you going to breach this contract?" Rudhir asked suddenly, he was engrossed in his laptop, making copies of the videos.

"Breaching contracts is bad for business and I don't do bad business, Mr R&AW," she smirked, handing him the contract.

"Here, I also copied the reports from the forensic department, NCDC, you know, National Centre for Disease Control and Defence department in here," he swapped a pen drive with the contract. Adhira pulled out her laptop and copied its contents. "Nice laptop," Rudhir complimented.

"Perks of being an independent contractor," Adhira laughed as she copied the videos on a server.

As she worked, Rudhir stared at her with a bemused smile.

"So, were you able to hack my phone?" Adhira asked, still staring at her screen.

"What?" Rudhir asked, surprised by the sudden question.

"My phone, did you manage to hack it?" Adhira asked as she chatted with someone in a foreign language.

"No, we could not," Rudhir informed simply.

"Of course… all my gadgets, including my phone, my laptop, are fortified. My data would rather wipe itself out than fall in the hands of someone else…" she finished.

Rudhir nodded without any interest.

"I will call you if the analysis reveals anything prudent," Adhira spoke, closing her laptop.

"Why do you disguise yourself? What happened to your true face?" Rudhir asked seriously.

"My work does not allow me to wear my true face. I don't think anyone except for my team has seen the real me for a long time now," Adhira shrugged.

"Dhira," Rudhir started.

Adhira pulled a knife out of nowhere and threatened Rudhir, "Mr R&AW," she snarled, "If you called me that one more time, I will kill you and I mean it. So, don't you dare think I won't?"

"I know very well what you are capable of Ms Adhira Shekhawat," Rudhir snarled back. "I know you can attack anyone, kill anyone… you can even hurt the man who made you for your selfish reasons… you are one woman who--who--" and he trailed off.

"I think that this concludes our meeting," Adhira fumed at him, but there was hurt in her eyes.

"Yes, it does," Rudhir stood back, he too had the same look.

"Thank you for the details. I will see you when I see you," and with that, she started to walk away.

"I will drop you," Rudhir said after her.

"I have become independent Mr R&AW, more independent than you can possibly imagine," Adhira replied with her back to him.

"I know that… I have not forgotten anything," Rudhir shouted at her retreating figure.

"Of course," Adhira shouted back as she turned to face him, "How can you forget me? After all, I am the one who shot her commanding officer in the back without any apparent reason."

THE BAND OF ROGUE SPIES

Adhira was now standing in a windowless room. The walls were painted white and they looked like a large blank canvas. There was a crescent-shaped table in the centre and on it were placed four large screens. Each screen was showing one of Adhira's team members and they all were discussing the case on a video call.

"It took me a while to study these, but I am finally done. Believe me, it was not easy… not easy at all. Someone only with my skills and eye for detail can–" Franc spoke from his screen. His thick Slovak accent always made it a little difficult for most people to understand him, but Adhira and her team understood him perfectly well.

"And when will you share that finding with us?" Ava asked from the next screen. Her French accent sounded very different in comparison to Franc's Slovak accent. "Will you keep on boasting about your rare skills or will you share the details? See, even Samuel is bored."

Samuel yawned broadly while Patricia laughed.

Adhira's team had a total of five members, including herself. Together, they were called 'Pentagon' or the band of Rogue Spies.

Franc Ivanek – He was a Slovak National and the world's best analyst. He could analyse any piece of information and could deduce things that no ordinary mind could. He was once part of British Intelligence but had to leave as his country was disgraced by one of the superiors. While retaliating, Franc had released some very compromising information about the British Intelligence, which had made him a wanted man. He was currently operating from his home country, Slovakia.

Ava Paradis – A French National and the best hacker in the world. There was not a single device on the planet she could not hack in seconds. And there was not a lock she couldn't undo. The longest she ever took to hack a machine was 98 seconds. She once worked for French Intelligence, but when she hacked into a Swiss bank on the orders of French Intelligence, she was thrown under the bus by the agency as they were forced to reveal their source. She was disgraced and thrown out and had been working as an independent contractor ever since.

Samuel Guttman was a retired Belgian weapons expert. He had dedicated his life to a weapon's manufacturing company in Belgium, and now worked to analyse enemy weapons and supply new gadgets to Adhira.

Patricia Myers was a Canadian national who was so resourceful that she could arrange anything and everything from her den. She was the one who arranged fake identities for her team; who provided Samuel with required parts for his gadgets; and made anything and everything available. She was part of a mafia family and used her ties to get things done.

"Franc," Adhira addressed him. "What are the findings, my friend?"

"The material used in the weapon is definitely radioactive. There is no other explanation for the rapid burns and boils," Franc informed. Even though Adhira was well aware of this, goose bumps erupted on her body.

"But the report didn't say a thing about any dirty bomb being present," Patricia asked sceptically.

"It is actually not a dirty bomb, it is something new," Franc sighed. "I have never seen a weapon wreak such havoc in seconds. It is like it came, wiped out any living beings around and went away. The half-life of the radioactive agent is extremely short, I am guessing minutes, so, by the time authorities reached the area, the radiation had died out completely."

"How did it happen?" Adhira asked curiously. "Something so deadly and quick to spread, but also so easily erased. What is this?"

"It is what your government and fallen agents were calling the XRS," Franc showed a few documents on the screen. "The XRS is a highly unstable and lethal material. I need to know who created it and how, we need to figure it out."

"Ava, can you put your hacking skills to use and do some research to narrow down a list for us?" Adhira asked.

"If I know what infrastructure, components and skill set is required to create such a weapon, I cannot just narrow down, I can give you a crisp answer," Ava assured with pride.

"We always show off," Samuel, the weapons expert chortled.

"Can you help, Samuel?" Adhira insisted.

"I cannot tell you the components as all of them were dissipated, but on the basis of the autopsy report, I can tell some main culprits that left their mark in the victims' bodies. I can also share other relevant details," Samuel agreed.

"Where do you need me?" Patricia asked promptly.

"I need you with me, Patty. Wherever Ava asks us to go, I need you to promptly arrange required logistics. The manufacturer could be anywhere in the world," Adhira smiled.

"Who will you be this time?" Patricia laughed.

"Whatever you would want me to be," Adhira winked "Thank you guys, as always…"

"Hey, we are *the team*," Patricia winked back.

"Or as I say, The Band of Rogue Spies," Ava added and everyone laughed.

"By the way," Patricia asked seriously, "Is it wise to work with… you know!"

"Well, there is a saying in India, *kabhi kabhi gadhe ko bhi baap banana padta hai,*" Adhira sighed "And it doesn't matter what our past relationships have been and what grudges we may hold, work always comes first, doesn't it?"

Everyone nodded solemnly and Adhira disconnected the call.

"Where are you?" Rudhir asked as he called Adhira the next day.

"Work," Adhira snapped and there was a moment's silence on the line.

"What are the next steps?" He demanded.

"I am flying to UK in a few hours, we have narrowed down the facility that created the weapon XRS," Adhira informed.

"What?" Rudhir blanched. "Why was I not informed about it? Didn't you think it was important to keep me apprised?"

"No, I did not," Adhira snapped again. "I am flying out at 10 pm tonight. And," she paused to gain some composure, "I don't keep anyone 'apprised'. I am not reporting to you or anyone," and she disconnected.

"Can I say something?" Patricia asked seriously. Adhira had forgotten that she was on a video call with her, discussing the plan. Adhira groaned.

"Sure," Adhira threw away the shirt she was folding and looked at her laptop to face her.

"I am your friend and your colleague," Patricia started.

"I consider you my closest friend, Patty. You and Ava both. Even though you are continents away, you are still closer to me than anyone in this whole country," Adhira wiped her face in agitation.

"So, listen to me and please, for your sake, do it. Tell him," Patricia insisted.

"Tell what to whom," Adhira turned and continued to sort her bag.

"You know what I mean Adhira, you know everything," Patricia sighed.

"I hate him and he knows it," Adhira snapped. "You will meet me outside London Heathrow Airport? Right?"

Patricia sighed, "Yes, everything is arranged. Just bring yourself, your gadgets, and your secret weapons. Your clothes, disguise and everything else will be ready with me…"

"Okay," Adhira nodded.

"And…" Patricia continued.

Adhira looked up at her serious tone.

"You need to bring your smile babe… you have to charm the heck out of someone there. See you in a few hours…" and with that, Patricia disconnected.

Adhira walked to the mirror and stared at her bare face. The smile she always wore for the world was not there. She was an agent, a spy who made the impossible *possible,* so she had to keep up appearances in front of the world. But alone, she didn't bother. Why should she? There was not a shred of happiness in her life at present. But she had learned how to fake a smile, through thick and thin, through suffering and pain, she had learned to smile in all situations.

"Do you know how much this ticket cost me?" Rudhir grunted as he stood behind Adhira to board the flight. "I see that you are travelling with your real face today," he commented, scanning her face. He couldn't help but feel a jolt in the pit of his stomach as he looked at her. He has been wondering for so long, even before she was hired by the home minister to work on Project XRS, how she looked now, and now it was answered, *just as beautiful as always.*

Ignoring his comment, she turned her back to him. She didn't know he would be here. If she had known, she would have changed her face, like usual. She always avoided recognition, it made her vulnerable.

"So, what's the plan?" he asked as the line moved at the snail's pace. "Who are we meeting? Where? And when are you coming back? You never told me so I couldn't book a return flight."

Grudgingly, she turned and gaped at him.

"Aa—" he started but the line moved and without sparing him a glance, she rushed ahead and when he saw her next, she was already sitting in her seat in the aeroplane, praying silently that he does not occupy the one next to her, which was mercilessly empty.

"I have boarded the flight and it is taking off," Adhira called and informed Patricia.

"Okay, see you on the other side. Take good rest, we will gear up the moment you land," Patricia spoke and disconnected.

Adhira pulled out the files collated by her team and started to read when the vacant seat next to her was occupied.

"It is an oddly empty flight," Rudhir commented as he stared around the first-class. Only four passengers were there. "I have never seen flights this empty before!"

Ignoring him as usual, she continued to read.

"I am not dying to talk to you, alright," Rudhir continued, slightly agitated by her behaviour. "I need to know what's happening on the case," he whispered. As it was night time, there was silence around them and almost everyone was getting ready to sleep.

"I prefer working on my own," Adhira commented as she flipped the page.

"You are bound by our legal contract to keep me in the loop," Rudhir stressed.

Rolling her eyes, Adhira pulled out another folder and shoved it in Rudhir's hands. "Now bug off, go back to your seat. I don't like company."

As fire was dancing in her eyes, he shirked slightly.

"Fine…" Rudhir sighed after a pause and walked away. He didn't want to fight her. He didn't know who she was now… He had fallen in love with a dedicated spy, the one who was once loyal to her country and its cause, but now she had transformed into a rogue one, who worked for the highest bidder.

"Adhira, how are you, my darling," Patricia hugged her tightly as she stepped out of the Heathrow Airport. "And who we do have here?" Patricia added, scanning Rudhir from top-to-toe.

"Unwanted tag-along," Adhira rolled her eyes as she gestured Patricia to lead the way.

"That's our transport," Patricia pointed at a vanity bus that was sitting idly across the road. "And we should head out right away, we don't want to attract London Police," she chortled.

As they made their way, Patricia talked to Rudhir.

"So, you are the ex, right, I am Patricia," Patricia shook his hand. Adhira turned furiously at Patricia, so she added, "What, he is your ex, isn't he?"

"Yes," Rudhir almost laughed. "I am *the ex*."

"God, we all hate you so much," Patricia spoke with narrowed eyes. "Well, not as much as Adhira here, but we do." Rudhir looked taken aback at these words.

"Well, I am here on official business, so I hope you people can keep your hatred inside," Rudhir commented sarcastically.

"We can try," Patricia laughed again as they entered the vanity bus.

Rudhir looked around the bus, confused. "An odd choice for travel, isn't it?"

"This is because of our star here," Patricia laughed again. Rudhir couldn't help but notice how bubbly and cheery

Patricia was, total opposite of Adhira. "She needs a makeover, doesn't she?" Patricia grinned.

"She does?" Rudhir looked confused. Patricia stared at him in disbelief, then turned to Adhira.

"Adhira," Patricia spoke as she pointed at a compartment, "Your disguise and gadgets are inside. The facility is approx. 3 hours away, so you have that much time."

"The Rudolf facility?" Rudhir asked, checking the file.

"Yes, the one which employs the scientist who developed your XRS," Patricia nodded.

"You have collected some amazing information in less than a day, how did you manage it?" Rudhir asked curiously.

"Am I allowed to tell him?" Patricia asked Adhira seriously.

Raising her eyes to the heavens in defeat, Adhira went behind the curtain.

"Well, because she allows it," Patricia tittered. "We have an expert hacker and analyst in our team. They are *the best* in the world. If they could not, no one could."

"So, there are three members in your team?" Rudhir asked. "Adhira, you and that hacker and analyst?"

"No, we are 5 in total. Franc is the analyst, he is like the brain. Ava is the hacker, she is our digital presence. Samuel is the gadget expert, he is our artillery. I am the provider of everything, so I am like the distributor and Adhira, she is our muscle. She is the one who executes operations and is always in front of all the missions. Together we are like a Pentagon. Each with our individual strengths and together, we are an undefeatable force," Patricia finished.

"And this Pentagon took out Butch?" Rudhir asked curiously.

"Oh, you know about Butch," Patricia laughed again. "Technically we are not allowed to speak about it, but yeah, we did…" she rolled her eyes. "Do you know what is harder than taking down world's most wanted terrorist?"

"What?" Rudhir asked quickly.

"Keeping quiet about it… It is so damn hard!" Patricia roared with laughter, Rudhir laughed with her too. "By the way, how did you find out about it?"

"I can recognise her style anywhere," Rudhir shrugged.

"Yeah, her style is unique, but I don't know if we would be able to leave her signature mark on this mission," Patricia wondered.

"As far as I know her, she always leaves her mark in one way or another," Rudhir smiled amusedly as he stared at the door behind which Adhira was getting ready for the visit to Rudolf facility.

"It's strange," Patricia spoke as she stared at Rudhir. "You don't look like a person who would betray her, and yet!"

"Betray?" Rudhir started.

"That's enough chit-chat," Adhira barked from the other side of the compartment.

"Time to close the chit and chat," Patricia nodded and went back to her laptop.

"Are you ready?" Patricia called after two hours.

"Nearly," Adhira replied. She came out after another thirty minutes and Rudhir gasped.

"Yeah," Patricia spoke as she looked at Adhira's disguise, "This used to be my reaction in the beginning, but now I have seen her change her face so often, I don't get surprised at all."

"How?" Rudhir asked as he stared at the face of a stranger. "Your eyes…"

"What about my eyes?" Adhira asked suddenly.

"Only they are unchanged…" Rudhir whispered. "They are exactly the same!"

"Well, not for long," Patricia interrupted. "With the right make-up, facial tape and a few more specialised equipment, we can change faces quite well. This was not easy before, but now it is like a piece of cake. Of course, if you have a pro like Adhira here…" Patricia chuckled as she placed a small kit in front of her.

"Blue eyes are his weakness," Patricia spoke as she handed Adhira blue contact lenses. "And these will be *our* eyes and ears while you are inside," she then handed her a pair of small blue-back opal earrings. "Put these on, we will do a test run."

Adhira obliged. Her earrings now were projecting the inside of the bus on Patricia's screen.

"How do I look?" Adhira asked Patricia in a whisper, but her voice echoed out of a speaker.

"Beautiful and stunning, as always," Patricia nodded.

"What is the range of these," Rudhir pointed at Adhira's ears.

"Not very long, hence we have planted several signal boosters all across the facility. We can hear them even if they are in the basement," Patricia informed.

"Aren't you worried that someone or something might interfere with the signal booster? And Rudolf facility is like a fortress, how did you manage to plant signal boosters all over?" Rudhir continued.

"We have people everywhere and, with the right amount of money, you can get anything done… And our devices are so small, no one will recognise them. You don't worry about our devices, just listen, observe and learn," Patricia finished with a wink.

"We are here," Patricia spoke as the driver thumped on the side of the bus. "Adhira, are you ready?"

"Like hell," Adhira spoke confidently, then grabbing a purse that was more like a prop for the investigation, she stepped out.

"Good luck," Rudhir spoke after her.

"Don't agitate her," Patricia scolded as Adhira slammed the bus's door shut.

Adhira waited at the entrance eagerly. It was five minutes to ten and as per Ava, their target was very punctual.

"Hello Sir," Adhira called a man in his late-thirties.

"Yes," the man stopped abruptly as he registered Adhira's appearance. She wore a fitting shirt and long skirt. Her hair was covered with a scarf and she wore sunglasses. She could see his pupils dilating as he registered her face.

"As-Salaam-Alaikum," Adhira raised her hand in courtesy and touched her forehead with her fingers, bowing slightly.

The man's eyebrows rose at the gesture, but composing himself quickly, he replied, *"Wa-Alaikum-As-Salaam."*

"I am Tabassum Khan," Adhira smiled as she took off her sunglasses. Everything from her fake name to her disguise was well researched and thought through.

He took a step back as he saw her piercing blue eyes.

"You—" he stammered, "You have blue eyes."

"Oh, are they distracting you?" she asked quickly, putting back her sunglasses. "My eyes often distract people," and with a tilt of her head, she gave him her most flirtatious smile.

A strong shiver went down the man's body and Adhira knew why. She was wearing a face similar to the poor man's dream girl. Ava, being the master hacker, had scanned through his browser history and had pulled out details on what kind of girls he liked. He preferred slender, fair girls with high cheekbones and blue eyes.

"You are Mr Iqbal Khan," Adhira asked in a honeyed tone, exposing her blue eyes again.

"Yes…" the man stammered again.

"Can I speak to you in private, please?" Adhira requested, batting her eyelashes flirtatiously.

"Yeah, come," he nodded hastily and led her inside.

Mr Iqbal Khan was the head of the R&D division in the Rudolf facility. This facility was like a fortress but with Mr Iqbal Khan by her side, Adhira gained easy entry without breaking any rules.

"How can I help you?" Mr Iqbal Khan asked as he sat in his chair, almost missing it and falling. Adhira grabbed his hand and steadied him.

"Thanks," he mumbled as he composed himself.

"I am a student of journalism and I was hoping to get an interview," she smiled shyly. Mr Iqbal Khan crossed his legs under the table to gain some control.

"Sure… but you don't have an appointment," he spoke thoughtfully.

"I know it would have been rejected, so, I took a chance," Adhira smiled bemusedly.

"Ahmm…" he placed his index finger on his chin and nodded.

"Please, this is very important to me and as you know how difficult it is for simple girls like me to, you know, get ahead, please can you help me?" Adhira pleaded.

"Fine, but you cannot record," Iqbal Khan ordered as he pointed at her phone and Bluetooth piece in her ear.

"Oh, sure," and she quickly turned off her phone and pushed it in her purse along with the Bluetooth piece. Then pushing her hair behind her ears so that the earrings broadcasted everything to Patricia's laptop, she smiled.

"So, what do you want to know?" Iqbal Khan asked.

"What do you do here?" Adhira asked with a smile.

"We develop many things here, most of our research is devoted to developing new radiology instruments. Our aim is to develop devices which emit the least amount of radiation and give the best and optimum results," he answered simply.

"Wow, that's amazing," Adhira nodded humbly.

"You can read all about it on our website," Iqbal Khan spoke and Adhira dropped her smile.

"Okay," Adhira sighed and pulled her bag. "I was hoping to know more, you know, get to know you better…"

"What do you mean?" Iqbal Khan asked quickly.

"Well, I like you, you are like my hero, my inspiration… I have been planning to come to meet you for weeks. It took me so long to find the strength to, you know," Adhira shrugged casually.

"What?" Iqbal Khan blanched as she stared at him with her piercing blue eyes. This was like a dream come true for him but his dream girl now looked disappointed.

"But, maybe you are not as I had pictured you to be," Adhira sighed, standing up. "I was hoping to have a long conversation, maybe catch up for a drink or something."

"I cannot share anything with you, they will fire me," Iqbal Khan wiped his forehead.

"There can be an anonymous source," Adhira insisted. "I swear I will never reveal my source, a journalist's honour. You are like my *hero*..." she stressed as she leaned on his table slightly. "I thought you were made of stronger stuff."

"I..." Iqbal Khan hesitated.

"Maybe some dreams are better than reality," Adhira scoffed, standing straight. "All my work has been a waste. You didn't even give me a line... and it's not just that, it seems you don't do anything exciting here. All you do is make boring equipment!" and she screwed up her face.

"My work is very exciting, who said I am boring," Iqbal Khan stood up, attempting to prove himself.

"Any regular company can make X-ray machines," Adhira rolled her eyes. "I thought you were into something more fun, more exciting and *more dangerous*."

"Dangerous and exciting like...?" Iqbal Khan asked seriously.

"I had heard a rumour, I can, of course, not reveal my source, but I heard that there was some radioactive weapon development happening," Adhira whispered to add mystery. "But it seems that your name is just a hype!" and she turned to walk away.

"Oh, we have developed a radioactive weapon," Iqbal Khan spoke quickly. Adhira was smiling now as she had accomplished what she needed – him to start talking. Adjusting her face to look surprised, she turned to face him.

"How do I know you are not saying this just to, you know, boast or you know, to impress me!" Adhira asked, cross-armed. "Many men claim they do many things, but..."

"Those men just claim, I can show you," Iqbal Khan said with a triumphant smile.

"Really?" Adhira asked with a sparkle in her eyes.

"Yes, but you have to promise that you will not tell another soul," Iqbal Khan whispered, moving close to her.

"Oh, I promise," and hurrying forward, Adhira kissed his cheek lightly.

A tangible electric jolt passed through his body, and she giggled.

"Maybe we can meet up for drinks later?" Adhira winked, standing back.

Licking his lips, he nodded and walked to the door.

"Remove this visitor tag and put this around your neck," Iqbal Khan spoke quickly as he peeked outside.

"Are we going to see something classified?" Adhira asked, super excited. She quickly removed the 'visitor' tag she had received at the main gate and placed an ID tag around her neck.

"I will lose not just my job but my head for showing you this," Iqbal Khan whispered as he handed her a mask. "Please put this on," and picked up his own mask.

"Why are we covering our faces here, in your office? Won't it be suspicious?" Adhira inquired.

"Not really," Iqbal Khan opened one of his shelves and pulled out a device. "I—" he paused to place the device on his desk and added a glowing metal on top of it.

"Wow, what is it?" Adhira asked, getting close to it.

"Just a prototype of a new chemotherapy machine," Iqbal Khan informed.

"So, is it radioactive?" Adhira took multiple steps back.

"No, this is just a dummy of my actual prototype. I am developing a device that will release ultrasonic waves to directly attack cancerous cells in human body. It is one of a kind, a unique idea," Iqbal Khan puffed his chest with pride.

"Wow," Adhira looked impressed.

"We will go down with this prototype in my hand. People clear the path when I am going down with my devices, they know better… and I always wear my mask when I handle my prototypes, so no one will question us," Iqbal Khan informed.

"You are a freaking genius," Adhira almost bounced on her heels and, ensuring that her earrings were not covered at all, she placed the mask on her face and looked at him.

Iqbal Khan, too, had placed his mask and only his bespectacled eyes and forehead were visible now.

"Good, no one can recognise you," Iqbal Khan looked at her seriously. "Now remember this – *omega alpha gamma 5213 beta G.*"

"What?" Adhira asked, perplexed.

"Just repeat it," Iqbal Khan ordered.

"Okay… *omega alpha gamma 5213 beta G,* did I say it right?" Adhira asked with furrowed brows.

"Yes. They will take us in one by one, and you have to finish the code, they will display the code with random things missing, okay? It is the protocol to only speak missing items and not the full code, okay?" Iqbal Khan explained seriously.

Adhira nodded.

"Are you confident you can pull this off?" Iqbal Khan stressed. He was sweating profusely

"*Omega alpha gamma 5213 beta G,* yes I am confident," Adhira spoke, squeezing his arm gently. "After you," she pointed at the door.

He stared at her hand that was still clasped around his arm and smiled weakly.

She pulled down her mask and revealed her perfect teeth, "I am confident, shall we go now?" Adhira asked, batting her lashes seductively.

Iqbal Khan rubbed his thumb on her chin, exhaled, pulled her mask back up and led her outside.

THE FACILITY

They walked together, with Adhira lagging a little behind to show that she was his subordinate. As Iqbal Khan had his dummy prototype in his hands, and they had their masks on, no one even turned their heads in their direction. They reached a door that read:

'ONLY SELECT PERSONNEL ALLOWED.
NO TRESPASSING'

Iqbal Khan sighed loudly and nodded at Adhira meaningfully as he entered. She followed suit. Inside was a small chamber, where two heavily armed guards stood. They were both covered in heavy plastic suits and wore gas masks. Adhira felt slightly worried but didn't fidget. She stood confident and tall, silently hoping that Patricia's signal boosters worked in this secret chamber as well.

Iqbal Khan entered first and then, after a minute, the guard pointed at Adhira to enter.

It was a small cabin, fully covered in dark wallpaper.

A man stood there. He handed her a card and stared at the one in his own hands.

The card read - ___________ *gamma* _____ *G*

She cleared her throat and spoke "*omega alpha*" she paused for a fraction of a second then continued *"5213 beta"*

He nodded and showed her the rack where she had to leave her purse. Once Adhira had deposited her purse, he allowed her to walk inside.

It was a huge room full of various types of equipment and files.

"Hurry, wear this," Iqbal Khan pushed a gas mask in her hands.

"What?" Adhira asked, taken aback. This was a problem, she didn't come all this way just to put on a gas mask and hide her only source of recording everything!

"It is very dangerous to breathe in the air here for long," Iqbal Khan's voice was muffled as he already had his mask on.

Reluctantly, Adhira placed the gas mask on, then thinking quickly. "Ouch!" She exclaimed and took it off.

"What are you doing?" Iqbal Khan asked, alarmed. "The gas here will kill you, believe me."

"My earrings are hurting me," Adhira moaned and unscrewed them.

"Put them there," Iqbal Khan pointed at a table, looking shocked.

"No, I would rather put them here," and Adhira undid the top two buttons of her shirt, exposing her pale, white skin and tucked the earrings in it, and buttoned the shirt back up.

Iqbal Khan looked at her exposed skin hungrily.

"These belonged to my late mother," Adhira lied very convincingly, "I cannot risk losing them at any cost. Besides, how would you explain if I forgot them here?"

Iqbal Khan nodded with an understanding and grabbed her hand boldly. She let him drag her to a shelf.

"See this," he was super excited now, "I developed this."

"What is this?" Adhira asked, picking up a glass bullet. It was empty.

"It is the shell," Iqbal Khan explained and taking it from her hand, he threw it violently against the wall. The bullet bounced off but was unbroken. "This is an unbreakable glass that can only be broken when thrown at a speed of more than 3000 ft. per second."

"3000 feet per second?" Adhira asked, shocked. "That's around 3300 kilometres per hour!"

"Kilometres?" Iqbal Khan looked confused. "Are you Asian?"

"My parents are," Adhira nodded simply. "Aren't yours?"

Iqbal Khan looked amazed at her words and demeanour.

"Normal guns are not that fast," Adhira quizzed.

"No, they are not. That's why these bullets can only work in a select few rifles. The bullet can fit in any rifle per se, but it won't break," Iqbal Khan continued.

"And what is this bullet supposed to contain?" Adhira asked, trying to mask her worry. If he created a bullet that needed such speed, it could not be anything good.

"This," and literally bouncing on his heels, he showed her a shelf that housed only one bullet and, from a distance, it looked empty.

He picked it up gently and shook it. It was not empty, instead, it was filled with a clear white liquid.

"The material changes colour when in motion," Iqbal Khan laughed.

It felt like someone had punched her in the chest. The liquid resembled a lot like what she had seen in the video where the agents working on XRS were attacked.

"What is it called?" Adhira asked, taking the bullet from him and twisting it in her hands. "And how many have you developed?"

She stared at the shelf which contained thousands of empty bullet shells, but none were filled.

"Well," Iqbal Khan started, taking the bullet from her hand, "I developed a material, it was a very difficult task, you know," and he slid his hand around her waist.

"What's it called?" Adhira asked again.

"I am not allowed to name it. Naming it will make it identifiable and the company wants it to stay quiet," Iqbal Khan explained. Though his face was covered, his tone was laced with anxiety.

"Why?" Adhira asked seriously.

"Because we tested it. And it was so deadly that the company doesn't want to associate its name with it. That's the reason we didn't mass produce it," he replied. Though Adhira couldn't see his face, she could tell that he was lying. He was clenching, unclenching his fists and fidgeting a lot.

"How many did you produce? And how did you test it?" Adhira asked, gently squeezing his hand as an encouragement.

"Only six," Iqbal Khan sighed as he looked at her thin fingers exerting pressure on his fluffy hand.

"And the test?" Adhira asked seriously.

"Well, it was unintentional," and he showed her a file.

Fixing the file in front of her earrings, which were now pinned to her chest, Adhira started reading. It was a thick file so, halting for a few seconds on each page, she just shuffled through, hoping Patricia would make a copy of each page.

"Are you done?" Iqbal Khan asked, now pushing his hand down her ass. "You know, this room is 100% camera free," he whispered seductively.

"Shouldn't you buy me a drink first?" Adhira asked, turning and pushing his hand away.

"But I thought," he was taken aback.

"I said let's meet for drinks later, I get in a good mood after a few drinks," Adhira raked her fingers on his chest. "This mask, this atmosphere is not romantic at all."

"Oh, I get it," he understood immediately. "Shall we?"

"No, first tell me how you tested it?" Adhira insisted.

"It was not intentional," Iqbal Khan sighed, "a team of scientists under me took the formula out of here, and they thought it was kind of a drug I was developing. They went to the parking lot and opened the vial."

"What happens when you open the vial?" Adhira asked curiously.

"This," he inserted a drive in a USB port and selected a video. There was no audio, but what she saw was horrifying.

And it also felt like Deja-vu. Three young men, laughing, holding a vial. One of them opened it and the moment the cork was undone, all of them started to choke. Big, ugly boils started to form on their bodies. Help came to them a few minutes later, but they were dead by then. However, the people who surrounded them were unaffected.

"Why are the others not affected?" Adhira asked, still staring at the screen.

"This is a highly lethal radioactive material. It gets activated the moment it is exposed to the air. In the vacuum of this bullet or any glass container with the right density, it will stay dormant. Once exposed to air, it starts to fade in thirty seconds and its deadly phase wears out in a maximum of two minutes," Iqbal Khan informed.

"Why bullets then? What happens if it pierces humans or animals?" Adhira asked seriously.

"Once mixed in blood, because of the presence of the red blood cells in the blood, it changes form. Iron fortifies it. So, once it touches blood, be it human or animal, its radioactivity will continue to multiply for at least twenty-four hours, and there is literally no stopping it. Its cooling down period drastically goes up, I have not yet tested it, but it will not be easy to control. You should know that it will be catastrophic if mixed in blood, and it can wipe out entire cities in a day. What happened to my scientists is just a trailer in comparison to what will actually happen then," he shrugged.

"You created such a deadly weapon intentionally?" Adhira asked, alarmed.

"Not intentionally," Iqbal Khan dismissed casually. "I wanted to make something new, and this is what I was able to create!"

"Who else knows about this?" Adhira asked and Iqbal Khan looked taken aback by her threatening tone.

"No one," Iqbal Khan shrugged. Adhira could tell that he was lying but didn't ask further. She knew she would get one more chance to interrogate him thoroughly.

"Where are the other five bullets?" Adhira demanded after a pause, determined to get as much information as possible at the time.

"Not here, this is the last sample," Iqbal Khan pointed at the shelf.

"One that killed your team of scientists?" Adhira demanded, pointing at the screen that showed the video.

"Yes," Iqbal Khan nodded.

"Where are the other four?" Adhira inquired.

"Err…" Iqbal Khan hesitated. "Why don't we go?" he spoke quickly.

"Yes, we should go," Adhira nodded, wondering how to take the sample. "But before we do that, can I, by any chance, get an empty shell?" she requested.

"Empty shell?" Iqbal Khan mumbled, confused.

"Yes, those," Adhira pointed at the shelf.

"Oh those, take five if you like," Iqbal Khan laughed. "They are useless. We produced shells first in hopes of making a fortune with the material but, well, they are useless now."

He moved forward to open the shelf but she grabbed his hand and said, "Allow me…"

Adhira picked up a handful of vials and started to walk.

"Okay," Iqbal Khan nodded and followed her. "They will give us medicines to prevent radiation poisoning, so do take them diligently, okay?" he informed as he took off his gas mask.

She placed the vials at a side and took off the gas mask too and replaced it with the normal mask.

"Let's go," Iqbal Khan smiled and walked out.

"Oh no," Adhira muttered as she followed him. "I will be back," and she hurried inside.

"What?" Adhira heard him speak from outside, but she had rushed to the shelf which held the bullet filled with XRS like a crowned jewel and swapped it with an empty one. Then pushing the filled bullet down her cleavage in one swift move, she rushed out.

"Sorry," Adhira panted. "I held my breath..."

"What happened?" Iqbal Khan asked. The guards present stared at them in shock.

"I forgot the shells," she showed them to the guards.

The guards checked each of the shells to ensure that they were empty, then handed her an envelope with medicine and her purse. And they headed out.

Adhira pushed the empty bullets in her purse and looked at Iqbal Khan. "I will see you later then," she winked at him.

"Where and when?" Iqbal Khan asked quickly.

"How about I pick you up at 1, I can meet you across the street?" Adhira suggested.

"I have never been picked up by a girl before," Iqbal Khan laughed.

"Everything has a first time, darling," Adhira traced her fingers on his chest, winked and walked out, still feeling his gaze on her.

"Oh my God, I am drained," Adhira complained as she entered the vanity bus where Patricia and Rudhir were waiting for her.

"Wow girl, you are a pro," Patricia high-fived with Adhira. "You had him wrapped around your finger like that," she flicked her fingers.

"Not so tough when Ava researches a guy, is it?" Adhira mock laughed as she handed Patricia the earrings.

"Yeah, he was acting so by the book in the beginning," Patricia rolled her eyes. "One touch and he was melting."

"Of course," Adhira sighed. She didn't like this part of her job, but she knew that sometimes she had to use her charms.

"Shame you couldn't find out about the other four bullets," Patricia pouted as Adhira disappeared into the cubicle to change. "Don't change the face, yet," Patricia reminded her.

"Arrange for a place to torture," Adhira called from behind the cubicle.

"Torture?" Rudhir finally spoke. He was sounding disgruntled and Adhira knew why but she didn't care.

"Duh, yes!" Patricia stared at him suspiciously. "How else do you think she will get the required information!?"

Rudhir just stared at Patricia with a dumbfounded expression.

"Can you stomach this torturer side of hers?" Patricia asked, patting Rudhir on his arm.

"I can stand her torturing someone," Rudhir barked.

At this, Patricia laughed so loudly that Adhira came out to see if she was okay. "She…" Patricia spoke between fits of laughter, "she is a worse torturer than Lucifer himself. She can make the devil feel ashamed."

"Very funny, Patty," Adhira slapped her shoulder. "Here," and she handed the bullet filled with XRS to Patricia. Rudhir raised his hand to take it but Patricia didn't let him. "This goes to Samuel," Patricia informed.

"This goes to Indian intelligence," Rudhir challenged.

"Do you want this case solved?" Patricia demanded, shaking the bullet and seeing the content turn shimmering white.

"Of course," Rudhir spoke, staring at the contents of the bullet.

"Then let us do our job," Patricia finished as she pulled out a very small cylindrical tube from a corner and placed the bullet inside it.

"You will leave it here?" Rudhir challenged.

"No," Patricia spoke as she pulled out a chain from inside the tube, put it in the loop that was on top of it, hooked it and placed the chain around her neck.

Rudhir stared at Patricia as she pushed the tube inside her shirt, adjusted the chain and looked up. "No one can take it."

"What if you are attacked," Rudhir demanded, still worried about the bullet.

"I would like someone to try," this time it was Adhira who replied, laughing.

Rudhir stared at her with baffled expressions. Adhira composed her laughing face and spoke, "Patty, this goes directly in the hands of Samuel."

"Who the hell is Samuel in your team? I am forgetting him," Rudhir asked, agitated. He never thought he would have to work like this.

"I told you, didn't I…?" Patricia sighed. "Samuel is our weapons expert. He makes gadgets and stuff. The earrings are his creation," Patricia reminded Rudhir. "You need to remember our team if you want to work with us," she scolded him. Rudhir fumed but didn't reply.

"Directly in the hands of Samuel," Adhira repeated, stressing the point. "This cannot change hands," she continued but Patricia stopped her.

"Of course, I am aware how dangerous this is," Patricia spoke strictly. "I will arrange for a meetup tonight."

Adhira nodded, "Good. I have to be out again in thirty minutes, can you arrange for some food?"

"Food, yes," and Patricia pulled out a packet and handed it to Adhira. "It's your favourite."

Adhira smiled and pulled out an egg sandwich from the bag.

"I will go and check on arrangements," Patricia spoke awkwardly as she stared between Rudhir and Adhira.

"What, Mr R&AW?" Adhira demanded, once alone.

"You use your sexuality to lure men and get answers?" Rudhir accused.

"Umm… no…" Adhira spoke, making a big O with her lips. Rudhir raised his eyebrows at this, "I use my brain, my smile, my cunning, my skills, my strength to get what I want…"

"Oh really?" Rudhir continued but Adhira raised her finger to stop him, "I also use," she pointed at herself as she spoke, "my mesmerising eyes, my smile, my boobs, my ass, my hands, my entire body to get what I want."

Rudhir stared at her in disbelief.

"I use and do whatever I need to get the work done, to get the information I need. Because based on my information, I am able to save millions. So, yes Mr R&AW, I use my sexuality to lure pathetic men like Iqbal Khan and get the desired information. Because that's what I am, and that's what my job is."

"You can use other things, not your body. You don't need to sleep with other men to get your work done," Rudhir barked.

"Firstly, I draw the line at sex. I don't even let men touch me inappropriately, I am a spy, not… well whatever! Secondly, it is none of your bloody concern with whom I sleep and not. It is my life, not of your girlfriend's, and thirdly, if a man uses his body to lure a woman then it is acceptable, but now when I, a woman, does it then it is objectifying…" Adhira laughed. "You are a typical ass and I am not yours to command, Mr R&AW, so keep your views to your own bloody self. I don't need your approval to do anything, and if you are going to run hindrances and object the way I work, then you can go fuck yourself," and with a scathing look, followed by a curt nod, Adhira walked out, leaving Rudhir stunned.

TORTURE

Exactly at 1 pm, Adhira, wearing the face of Tabassum Khan, waited for Iqbal Khan outside the Rudolf facility.

"Let's go," Iqbal Khan spoke from behind. Adhira was staring at the gate of the facility but he approached from the other side. His eyes were bloodshot and he was sweating profusely.

"Is everything alright?" Adhira asked, taking in his demeanour.

"Is this your car?" Iqbal Khan pointed at the red Vauxhall Corsa against which Adhira was standing.

"Yes," Adhira replied sceptically.

"Let's go then," Iqbal Khan spoke as he made to open the passenger door. "And hurry…"

Adhira quickly unlocked the car and he ducked in the front seat. "Just drive," he almost cried.

"What's wrong," Adhira asked as she turned the key in the ignition. "Why are you hiding here?"

He stayed low for a while and only sat back straight up when they were at least ten kilometres away from the facility.

"Would you tell me what's going on?" Adhira asked, worried. "You are scaring me, Iqbal."

His name from her lips acted like a trigger. He shouted, "Where is it?"

Adhira jumped at his shout, almost bumping in the next lane car. "Iqbal please, I am a simple girl, if you will shout like this, we both will end up dead!"

"Where is it?" Iqbal Khan demanded again.

"What?" Adhira asked, tears welling in her eyes now.

"Where is your purse?" Iqbal Khan asked, cursing under his breath.

"In the dash… dashboard," Adhira pointed with shaking hands.

Iqbal Khan opened the dashboard and pulled out her small purse. Upturning it in his lap, he looked at the empty shells.

"Where is the bullet?" Iqbal Khan snarled.

Adhira had just taken a left turn and was now on a relatively empty road.

Iqbal Khan pulled out a pistol from his pocket and pointed it at her head.

Adhira shrieked and stopped suddenly, with her hands raised.

"What – what are you doing?" Adhira asked, wide-eyed.

"Drive…" Iqbal Khan ordered as he looked around. There was an abandoned, under construction building visible up ahead, "Take the car there." He pointed at the building.

Adhira drove quietly, shaking in fear and stopped the car where he indicated.

"Get out," Iqbal Khan snapped as he undid her seat belt. With hands still raised, she got out.

"What is happening?" Adhira demanded. "I thought we were going for a drink."

"You stole it, didn't you? When you ran back inside, you swapped the filled bullet with an empty one. You took it, and now they are after my blood. They think that I stole it," Iqbal Khan cried.

"What are you talking about?" Adhira gasped.

"Give it back to me, I will not be fooled twice," he cursed. "Again! It happened again!"

"What happened again? You are scaring me," Adhira begged.

"A week after those stupid boys got exposed, a woman approached me. She was not as beautiful as you are, but she was very good looking. I had the five remaining bullets in my office then. She talked to me, made me show them to her, even had sex with me on the couch itself. And then… then…" he sobbed as he pulled at his hair.

"Then she stole the bullets?" Adhira finished.

"Yes, I tried to stop her, but she hit me hard on the head. One was left because when I stopped her, it fell and rolled under the cabinet. She had no time to take it out. She took four, and now you have taken the fifth," he loaded the pistol he was still pointing at her face.

"Why were those bullets in your office?" Adhira asked, crossing her arms and finally dropping the façade of a weak girl.

"I was studying them," Iqbal Khan replied, confused.

"After how many days did the woman approach you?" Adhira demanded, taking a step towards him.

"Exactly after a week," Iqbal Khan looked at her confused.

"So, Monday," Adhira recalled the day mentioned on the video of the exposure.

"Yes, Monday," his hands were shaking now.

"Who was she?" Adhira asked, now standing so close that the pistol he was holding was touching her shoulder.

"I don't know, the security tried to find her, but she had her face hidden on the security feed so no one could identify her," he replied, shaking violently now.

"You had sex with her, so you remember her face, right?" Adhira asked with raised eyebrows.

"Yes… I can never forget," Iqbal Khan stammered, "she is the most beautiful woman to have slept with me…"

"Who all know about this weapon?" Adhira asked seriously.

"Who are you?" He cried now.

"Someone who is feeling generous at the moment," and with one swift move, she took the pistol from his hand and unloaded it. "I think I will hold on to this for a while, shall I?" she asked with raised eyebrows.

"What?" He babbled; he was shivering violently now.

"Eh! I don't think I need to torture you at all. This scared form of you is all ready to pee in the pants," she taunted.

He looked baffled, tears now leaking his eyes.

"Answer me, who all know about the weapon? Your company is keeping it quiet, isn't it? How did the information get out?" Adhira demanded.

"I don't know, there are so many people in this organisation. Someone must have babbled," Iqbal Khan snarled.

"But a project like this, it would not be common knowledge in your company?" Adhira wondered.

"Why do you need to know it?" Iqbal Khan asked through gritted teeth. Adhira raised her eyebrows so he added, "The board members were way too confident about it, weren't they? They manufactured thousands of shells, they had talked to some people about selling it. So, I am guessing that's how it spread out!"

"How many people are on your board?" Adhira demanded.

"Twelve, maybe fourteen," Iqbal Khan groaned.

"Too wide to identify who leaked the info to whom and narrow down the potential buyers," Adhira wondered to herself.

"Who are you? Why is this happening to me?" Iqbal Khan cried, falling on the floor.

"This is happening to you because you are dumb enough to create a weapon that can eradicate the entire civilisation in seconds. And you are even dumber to let it fall into the wrong hands," Adhira groaned. "Now get up!"

"What?" Iqbal Khan stumbled on his feet.

"Arrange for the best sketch artist there is," Adhira spoke loudly.

"What? How can I?" Iqbal babbled, confused. "I don't..."

"Shut up!" Adhira barked. "I know that you are useless."

"Call me when the sketch artist is ready," Adhira spoke loudly again.

"Who are you talking to?" Iqbal asked, shocked. "Who are you?"

"Someone worse than your nightmares," Adhira grunted and grabbing Iqbal Khan by his collar, she dragged him to the car and pushed him against it. "I need the description of the woman who stole those bullets from you," she ordered as she loaded his gun and pointed it at his head. The difference was, her hand was steady as a rock.

"You will shoot me with my own gun?" Iqbal Khan almost fainted.

"Hmm," Adhira chewed her cheeks thoughtfully. "Your gun will make too much noise, won't it!" and with one swift move, she unclipped Iqbal Khan's gun and dropped it on the ground. Then, she pulled out her 9mm Beretta that was strapped to her left thigh.

"Now, where is my silencer," Adhira wondered dramatically, and pulled it out from a strap that was attached to her right thigh.

"Who are you?" Iqbal Khan stammered as he stared at her expertly handling the weaponry.

"I answered that, didn't I?" She asked with raised eyebrows.

Iqbal Khan was about to speak again when her phone buzzed.

"It seems like our sketch artist is ready," Adhira smiled as she answered the call.

"Are you okay?" It was Rudhir and he was worried. "Did he hurt you?"

"Hurt me?" Adhira laughed loudly.

"Are you okay?" Rudhir repeated, still panicking.

"Have you not been watching what's going on here? I was not scared of him, I was more frustrated with the act I had to put on. To pretend like a scared little girl," Adhira rolled her eyes and Iqbal Khan looked dumbfounded. "Now, get out of my ear and get the gang-banger on the line," Adhira barked.

"Gang-banger?" Rudhir asked, confused.

"That's me," Patricia's voice came from afar. "That's my code name… she cannot use my real name on a mission, duh!"

"I am here," Patricia's voice became clearer now as she spoke directly to Adhira, "and I have the sketch artist ready. You can connect."

"You," Adhira spoke to Iqbal, "Stand here," and she pointed at the hood of the car. She quickly pulled out her laptop from underneath the seat and connected it to the video call.

A blank paper and pencil were visible on the screen.

"Describe the woman to the artist," Adhira ordered Iqbal Khan.

"Why is it important? I already described it to the security of Rudolf and they could not locate her," Iqbal Khan stressed.

"They don't have our resources, now narrate," and shoving her gun in his back, she pushed him.

"Fine… fine…" Iqbal Khan agreed, scared for his life.

He narrated the face of the woman for almost two hours, and once done, he confirmed the sketch.

"That's the woman?" Adhira demanded.

"Yes, that's her," Iqbal Khan nodded.

"Looks like a disguise," Adhira spoke as she stared at the face. "I think we need to run some facial modification algorithms to identify the right person," Adhira spoke out loud.

"What?" Iqbal Khan asked, confused.

"I am not talking to you," Adhira rolled her eyes.

"Who are you talking to?" He demanded as he looked at her hands and ears. She had no phone or Bluetooth.

"You won't understand," Adhira sighed.

"I will leave now," Adhira walked to the driver's side of the car. "On behalf of the entire world, I thank you for your cooperation."

"Who are you?" Iqbal Khan asked again.

"Someone who can kill you, but is feeling generous today," Adhira grinned.

"What about me?" He almost cried, falling on the ground.

"You are alive, aren't you?" Adhira asked with raised eyebrows.

"Barely, they will kill me," tears leaked his eyes now.

"And after the stunt you pulled, you deserve it... Fooled by not one but two beautiful women, tell me how they are not justified in putting bullet in your skull," Adhira shrugged.

Iqbal Khan looked mortified. He stared at her for a second then spoke, "What will you do with the bullet?" he asked, eyes bloodshot and serious now. "It is lethal, it can kill hundreds."

"You should have thought about it when you created such a deadly weapon," Adhira fumed, "And you should have thought harder when you let it get stolen!"

"I—" Iqbal Khan started.

"Pathetic perverts like you, who fall for any girl that even looks at them, don't deserve such brains," Adhira scowled. "Do the world a favour and think with your brain and not your dick the next time a girl flirts with you. Do figure out if she is genuinely interested or just using you."

"That's what girls do with me," he was heartbroken. "They always use me. She did, you did..."

Adhira groaned and sat in front of him, "I... well, I am sorry to have used you. But my actions are driven by international security. Use your big brain next time."

"I am going to die alone," Iqbal Khan wailed.

Adhira sighed, got up and walked back to her car, "Better die alone than fall in love with a backstabbing bastard."

And before he could react further, Adhira got in her car and drove away.

THE TEAM MEET

"Tell me you got a hit," Adhira asked as she drove towards her team.

"Ava got one," Patricia announced and she sounded serious.

"Okay, so what is the trouble," Adhira asked seriously.

"Oh, it is a big *big* trouble," Patricia sighed audibly. "I have asked the team to recon here."

"Here? In London?" Adhira asked, feeling worried. "I wanted to fly home right now."

"You are not flying out anywhere. Ava booked flights for everyone the moment she got a hit," Patricia informed.

"Who the heck is this woman?" Adhira asked, agitated.

"I don't know," Patricia replied and Adhira could hear the exasperation in her voice. "Ava said she would tell when she is here."

"Why the suspense?" Adhira asked. "Ava can be too dramatic sometimes."

"Well, her exact words were, *I don't want Adhira to jump off the wagon and start killing randomly,*" Patricia informed.

"Why are we here?" Rudhir asked as he looked around. They were now standing in a house that looked more like a hostel facility. It was a big room that had eight beds placed in a circular pattern.

"We are to stay the night here," Patricia laughed as she threw her bag on a bed.

"Why?" Rudhir was confused. He was looking around, Adhira was already slumped in one of the beds. "We can stay in a hotel!"

"We, I mean our team," Patricia pointed at herself and Adhira, "Always stay together on a mission. "We usually work all night and day, stay in touch and bond."

"But," Adhira sat up in her bed, "you are not in our team, so feel free," and she pointed at the door. "Nobody will miss you, believe me."

Rudhir growled and took the bed opposite her. Adhira rolled her eyes and slumped back in her bed.

"Is this place safe to strategise?" Rudhir asked Patricia.

"Safer than any other place," Patricia assured. "Entire place was checked thoroughly and we will sweep it again once everybody is inside."

Rudhir nodded and looked at Adhira, who was staring at the ceiling, frowning silently.

"Do you need a moment?" Patricia mouthed to Rudhir.

He considered the offer but shook his head.

"You won't get another chance," Patricia whispered, "This operation is gonna get trickier with every move."

"Yeah I know and I don't want to rile her up," Rudhir whispered back.

"Your voice riles me up," Adhira barked from her bed.

"She has bat ears and dog's nose," Patricia laughed and Rudhir looked at her sadly.

"I think that I should take a walk," Rudhir spoke curtly. "I anyway need to catch up with my work and update the Home Minister," and without another look at Adhira, he walked out.

When Rudhir came back, it was daybreak and the room was unrecognisable.

The room was still the same but the walls were now covered with black paper and all the windows were boarded up. A big whiteboard, covering two beds, was placed at a side and there were many many printouts stuck on it.

The wall opposite to the door now had a big TV Screen hanging on it, and beneath it was a laptop and many unknown devices. There was a lot of commotion around, Patricia was standing by the whiteboard, pinning some new documents and Adhira was sitting on her bed with her back to Rudhir. A girl with flaming red hair was sitting on the chair in front of the laptop. She had her back to him and looked tiny. Two men were standing in the middle of the room, scanning and discussing the bullet that was filled with XRS.

"Ah, you are finally back," Patricia smiled at Rudhir. "The team arrived while you were out on your trip." Patricia winked and clapped her hands, shouting, "Okay, guys." Everyone except Adhira turned. "Meet Mr R&AW here," she pointed at Rudhir. "He is our point of contact in the Indian force and he is here in the official capacity. Mr R&AW, meet the team," Patricia pointed around.

"I am Ava," the girl with flaming red hair shook his hand. "I looked you up long ago, you are squeaky clean!"

Rudhir looked at her confused, so she added, "Oh, I am the hacker. I can hack into literally anything..."

"Oh," Rudhir looked exceptionally uncomfortable. "You are the one who looked up Iqbal," he asked.

"Yes," Ava grinned. "I searched through his porn preferences so I could get Adhira the look he truly, deeply desires," Ava spoke with such passion that everyone laughed. "What?" Ava asked comically. "You saw how he couldn't say no to her."

"I saw that," Rudhir sighed at Adhira's back.

"Mr R&AW, I have always found only one woman in your history though. You are really obsessed with her, aren't you," Ava continued thoughtfully.

"How often do you look me up?" Rudhir asked, shocked.

"Every time I get bored, so occasionally," Ava shrugged and walked away, leaving Rudhir's jaw hanging.

Franc walked forward and shook Rudhir's hand next. He was blonde and had a scarred face. He looked slightly dangerous at first glance. "I don't like you," Franc announced in his deep Slovakian accent. "So just expect professional discussions from me."

"I am Samuel," the final team member spoke. He was old, bald and had a kind smile. "I neither hate you nor like you. I believe there are always two sides to a story and I feel that you should get a chance to say your piece. Having said that, I am quite fond of Adhira, so you still are one of the least liked people on this planet."

"What the fuck did I do? What have you been telling people about me?" Rudhir demanded, fuming with rage now.

Adhira stood up and turned. "The truth,"

"And what is the truth?" Rudhir asked in the same tone.

"That you are a lying, backstabbing, unreliable, son of a fucking dog!" Adhira finished and walked to the whiteboard.

THE MYSTERY WOMAN

"We have identified the woman and it is our task to locate her and, well, do something about her," Patricia spoke loudly and a hush fell.

"So," Ava started as she pinned a photograph on the board. "This is the Duchess of the Rawyn Island."

"Rawyn Island has a duchess?" Adhira asked, intrigued.

"What the heck is Rawyn Island?" Franc said thoughtfully. "I have worked on many operations in the United Kingdom and I have never even heard of it."

"Oh, it is so tiny that nobody considers it of any importance. It only has one big mansion, few small fields and livestock and less than fifty people living there. Luckily this island is much higher than the sea level so it doesn't see a lot of flooding. Anyways, this tiny island is so insignificant that it is not even a part of any region or Duke/Duchess area," Ava informed.

"Where is it?" Franc asked as he stared at the map of the United Kingdom that was stuck on the board next to the woman's photo.

"Here," Ava pointed.

"That's water," Franc spoke, staring at the place where Ava was pointing.

"Yes, it is very small. The island is part of the Great Britain Kingdom but is owned and run by Mr Edwin Dawson. He is very rich, very influential and a Duke by birth, but is not interested in politics. He likes his calm and composed life," Ava pinned another photograph on the board. "That's Mr Dawson," she pointed.

"So, Mr Dawson owns the Rawyn Island and he is a Duke. Then this woman is Mrs Dawson?" Franc asked with raised eyebrows.

"Oh yes," Ava rolled her eyes. "And recently, Rawyn Island was declared a separate region with a duke and duchess."

"Why?" Franc asked suspiciously. "What happened there? That's a rather unprecedented move, declaring a small island a region with its own Duke," Franc asked suddenly.

"Yes, and this island is so small that it becoming a region didn't even make the news. Nobody is interested in it!" Ava rolled her eyes.

"What happened then?" Patricia asked, intrigued.

"Well, the first prince," Ava started as she looked at everyone, "The first prince is the crowned prince," she explained upon seeing Rudhir's expressions.

"I know who the First prince is," Rudhir rolled his eyes.

"Well, the first son of each generation is technically in the line of throne, so queen's son, her first son's son, the first son's son's son... and so on..." Ava continued despite Rudhir's comment.

"Ava, move on please," Franc groaned. "You always drag the matters and explain too much."

"Well, this great-grandson of the queen was in a deadly accident a few months ago," Ava continued, narrowing her eyes at Franc.

"It wasn't in the news," Adhira added, startled.

"They kept it hushed up, the queen wasn't happy that her favourite GG was almost dead," Ava rolled her eyes.

"GG?" Patricia asked.

"Great-Grand Son," Ava added. "Kind of a tongue-twister for me," she snickered. "Anyway, this woman," Ava pointed at the photo on the board, "She saved the GG and the queen was overwhelmed."

"Okay," Patricia stared at the woman's face sceptically.

"The queen wanted to reward her and asked the woman to demand anything," Ava laughed.

"Anything?" Franc blanched.

"Yup," Ava nodded.

"Mercy! I wish I had saved the GG," Franc scoffed.

"Touché, I also wish that. Because the woman asked for a place in the royal family. The queen, who never goes back on her words, picked up a small island, converted it into a region, named the owner Mr Dawson legally a duke of the region, and married the woman to him," Ava brushed her hands dramatically.

"Wow!" Franc nodded, impressed.

"And this woman is important because..." Adhira asked, peering into the beautiful face of the woman.

"She is the woman your Iqbal described," Ava laughed. "I ran the facial alteration algorithm a few times, you know the same I always run to identify her in the crowd," she pointed at Adhira, "And I got a hit."

"That's impressive," Rudhir, who couldn't help himself, complimented. "What is this software?"

"My own design," Ava shrugged. "Not for sale."

Rudhir's face fell at this so Ava added, "But I can lend it to you for some special searches," she winked and Adhira shot her an angry look.

"Anyway," Patricia cleared her throat loudly, "Why would she steal the weapon?"

"I don't know," Ava shrugged. "There is literally no trace of her before she became the duchess, so clearly her current identity is fake. And even after becoming the duchess, she keeps a very low profile. She is a diplomat now, but she just lives on the island, often travelling to the mainland for some sightseeing and random work."

"That's strange," Adhira spoke thoughtfully.

"Did you check her phone records?" Adhira asked.

"Yes, nothing suspicious, but I think she has a burner phone," Ava pointed. "Look here," and she showed them a video footage on the screen. "She crosses the ocean every other day, spends good amount of time on the Ocean bank and talks to people."

"No network on the island?" Franc asked suspiciously.

"Her regular phone does get the network, but..." she trailed off as she pulled up the call logs of the Duchess' phone.

"There is no overlap between the time she is on the ocean bank and her phone being used. She is talking, I can tell, but she is not using her own cell," Ava pointed.

"We need that burner," Samuel spoke for the first time. "I want to plant a chip in it."

"What chip?" Rudhir asked. "And how did you get these records?" he pointed at Ava.

"Mr R&AW," it was Adhira who spoke this time, "If you want to work with my team, you should know and remember three things. Firstly, *we don't tell how we do things* to anybody on the outside. We just do things. Secondly, *we don't follow any rule book or any law book*, we do things the way the mission demands. Thirdly, and very importantly, *we don't share or lend our developed tech*. So, if you want to give any expert opinion, which I seriously doubt you have, you can give, or else, please just shut up. We don't have space for 'so-called' moral high grounds here."

It seemed she had slapped Rudhir squarely in the face. Everybody was staring at them in shock.

"What is the name of the Duchess?" Adhira asked Ava.

"Mrs Pristine Dawson," Ava read the name from the file. "Of course, an alias," she added.

"Can anybody find me her real identity?" Adhira asked everyone present in the room.

Ava shrugged, Franc looked lost, Patricia looked apprehensive and Samuel just looked amused.

"I need her phone," Samuel repeated. "Only for a minute, that's it."

"And what if she changes the burner?" Adhira asked seriously.

"Well, then I need the new burner to plant the chip again," Samuel shrugged.

"What are you thinking, Adhira?" Patricia asked seriously.

"We need to pick her up," Adhira declared. No one reacted to these words, only Rudhir shifted uneasily.

"When?" Samuel asked.

"When she is on the ocean bank. That's the only time I found her alone," Ava supplied.

"She doesn't have security?" Samuel asked, intrigued. "She is a royalty now, she must have."

"Mr Dawson was kind of pushed into this marriage by the queen. As per the law, and by respect, he couldn't refuse her, but he doesn't treat Pristine as his wife. He was engaged to another woman before marrying Pristine and he lives with her in the mansion," Ava informed as she pulled up photos of the mansion on the screen. It was a massive villa, nothing short of a mansion, and it was stunning. Painted green, it had an aura of royalty.

"Nice," Franc commented.

"Pristine doesn't live in this mansion?" Adhira asked.

"She does, but separately. Dawson's fiancée, well, now mistress, lives with him and gets all the royal treatment and protection. Pristine only gets the title, this was kind of an arrangement between them before marriage," Ava supplied.

"So, why is she with him?" Adhira asked. "Just for diplomatic immunity?"

"Yep, looks like it," Ava nodded.

"How much is she travelling?" Patricia asked. "Do you have her travel records?"

"Here," and Ava handed her another document.

"In last six months, seventeen international trips to Iran, Iraq and Pakistan," Patricia read through. "No one found this suspicious? A diplomat travelling to these three nations repeatedly? Why has nobody checked her?"

"Maybe because she is a part of the royal family?" Ava shrugged.

"Can we point out where she goes in these countries?" Franc asked.

"As per my sources, she disappears. No camera is able to find her. Also, as the *burkha* is a necessity in these countries, I cannot run facial recog software either," Ava informed.

"I need her here," Adhira announced. "We cannot do a thing until we know why she stole those bullets filled with XRS and to whom she has passed them on. I need to know the details. And I cannot find details by sitting here."

"Let's pick her up tomorrow," Franc suggested. "I will work with Ava, so we can understand her pattern. I can figure out when she is travelling alone and we can nab her then."

"I will arrange for a safe house to keep her," Patricia nodded.

"What do you need from me?" Samuel asked, bored. "Mind you, I miss the comforts of my own bed," he added as he lied down in his own bed. "And not to mention privacy."

"I need an undetectable implant," Adhira spoke after a thought.

"Undetectable…" Samuel raised an eyebrow.

"Yep, she travels a lot, I need to know where she is going and when. I need to put a GPS tracker in her so that we can monitor her… so I need something stealthy," Adhira added.

"I know the reasons, I am wondering about the undetectable part, my dear!" Samuel groaned. "You know very well that no tech is undetectable. Sometime or another, it will bother her. I can make a miniscule chip, but it will be underneath her skin. She will feel it eventually."

Adhira twisted her mouth at this.

"Have you never felt the chip you have in you?" Samuel asked with raised eyebrows.

"I feel it all the time," Adhira flexed her shoulders, indicating her displeasure.

"So do I," Ava too screwed her face.

"I don't feel mine at all," Franc laughed.

"You all have chips in your bodies?" Rudhir asked, surprised.

"Yes, we do," Samuel nodded. "If you were part of our regular team, you too would have it. It is a necessary evil. The work we do requires tracking," he shrugged.

"So, I can track your whereabouts any day?" Rudhir looked at Adhira, then added, "I mean, any of you," he pointed around.

"The access is strictly restricted to our team, the Pentagon," Patricia informed.

"I don't understand you," Samuel added as he looked at Rudhir. "But maybe it's not my place to understand you."

"I need a tracker, maybe in her phone," Adhira suggested, agitation visible on her face.

"Given how inconspicuous she is… she will ditch her phone before she meets her handler or mate or whoever she is working with," Ava grunted.

"You figure it out with Franc, we will work with Samuel," Adhira nodded to Ava.

Ava and Franc retired to their corner full of gadgets.

"I need a chip," Adhira repeated. "It does not matter if it will eventually bother her, I need it. Because after getting made, her first instinct would be to run to her base," she stressed. "We all run home when we feel threatened. And that's what we want."

"I will work on a chip then," Samuel nodded and left.

"You will work on a safe house? And also, if needed, a place to hold her for a long period of time. We don't know how long it will take to break her," Adhira spoke to Patricia.

Patricia too nodded and left, leaving Adhira and Rudhir alone.

"I don't think you should do this," Rudhir spoke. "This is illegal."

"We are the band of international rogue spies, Mr R&AW. All we do is illegal," Adhira replied airily as she studied the files that Ava had left behind.

"Picking up a diplomatic woman is dangerous, maybe even suicidal," Rudhir continued.

"I am not scared of suicide, in my line of career, we all attempt suicides every day," she dismissed him.

"I am advising you against it," he stressed.

"It will happen like I want it to. We are picking up Pristine tomorrow, and that's it," she finished.

"Why is rule-breaking so easy for you?" Rudhir snapped back.

She stared at him with a bemused expression, "When the rules start to work against you, it is always better and safer to become a rule breaker."

PRISTINE

"Everything is in place," Franc spoke as they headed towards the ocean bank where Pristine was expected to arrive. They all were travelling via tourist bus, which looked like a normal bus on the outside, but on the inside it was full of their gadgets and other equipment.

"Timing is mapped?" Patricia asked.

"Oh yes! She tried to make it random, but using the security camera on the docks, I analysed her patterns, she arrives at different times every third day, but there is a routine. She repeats this routine every fifteen days to make it look random. But it is actually planned," Franc spoke with pride.

"That's amazing," Rudhir commented, impressed.

"Well, it wasn't that difficult," Franc shrugged with a careless attitude.

"So, today it is 6:40 PM?" Adhira interrupted. She was wearing blonde hair, black shirt and faded jeans. She was pretending to be British today, and her attire and face matched the people in the vicinity.

"Yep," Franc nodded.

"Everything ready?" Adhira looked towards Patricia, who nodded too.

As they arrived at the ocean bank, Samuel and Franc rushed to the edge and started placing listening devices discreetly. They were pretending to look around while in reality, they were planting bugs. "It is 6:20, she must already be on her way here," Ava spoke out loud as they all climbed down from the bus and strolled around like regular tourists.

"Adhira, I don't think you should kidnap her," Rudhir started but she threw him such a nasty look that he winced. "I am an officer of the law, I cannot," he tried again but she just shook her head in disbelief and walked away from him.

Exactly at 6:40 pm, a small boat stopped at the port and Mrs Pristine Dawson stepped down from it. The team stepped back in the bus to monitor the conversation while Adhira lurked around, clicking photos, and pretending to do sightseeing.

"The waves and the sea breeze is running interference," Franc's voice rang in Adhira's ears.

"We'll make do, will try to clear it back home," Ava added.

"Shush," Patricia silenced them as they were picking up random chatter from the public around. There were around a dozen people on the port now.

"Try device 3," Rudhir spoke from a distance. He was standing by the bus's door and staring at Pristine's back.

Franc did something and suddenly Pristine's voice came much clearly. She was talking on her burner phone.

"I know the risks," Pristine was saying. "Yes, I heard."

"And nobody knows who stole the last bullet?" she was asking on the call.

"Maybe you should take that fucker, it must be some beautiful girl, that fucker is a sucker for beauty," she laughed.

"Yeah, yeah, I know… the plan is all set bhai jaan, you don't worry about me. We will reach our target in a few weeks. We will eradicate their kind from the face of the Earth," she raved.

"Should we accelerate the plan then?" she spoke in a panic. "We need to make it happen before he draws his last breath."

"Fine… fine… how is the production faring, did you find what you need?"

"I will get him, don't worry. I am flying out next week, it will be done. Just keep the facility ready. We need to mass-produce it before the dawn of their time."

"Yes… Khuda Hafiz…"

And she disconnected.

"Oh my God!" Adhira spoke in her fake British accent, "You are Pristine, aren't you? The duchess," she exclaimed.

"Yes, I am," Pristine smiled as she quickly pocketed her phone.

"Oh – my – God…" Adhira exclaimed loudly. "Can I please have an autograph and a selfie," she requested.

"Uh?" Pristine looked confused.

"You are such a popular personality, do you know? My club is a fan of yours. You prove that any girl can achieve her dreams… Please, let me have a selfie, please… I will be such a star in my group… they will all be so jealous that *I met you…*" Adhira begged.

"Sure," Pristine hesitated and allowed Adhira to stand next to her.

"Smile," Adhira grinned as she raised her phone to take a selfie.

"Adhira, think about it, please…" Rudhir spoke in her ears.

"What was that?" Pristine spoke quickly.

Adhira was about to prick Pristine with a needle filled with a drug that would have made her dizzy, but she was interrupted.

"What's that in your ear?" Pristine demanded.

"My Bluetooth device," Adhira shrugged. "Selfie?" She requested.

"Why was the man calling you Adhira?" Pristine demanded. "You don't look like an *Adhira!*" she spoke with raised eyebrows. "Who are you?"

"I am a fan, ma'am," Adhira requested. "I just wanted to do some sightseeing and I got excited upon seeing you here. You have a kind of cult following, do you know?" she tried to manipulate.

"A cult?" Pristine raised her eyebrows.

"Yes, hard core fans," Adhira added, relaxing slightly that Pristine was buying the story.

"Oh really," and then, Pristine did something unexpected. She pulled at Adhira's hair, and the wig, which was tightly clipped to her hair, came out due to the sheer force with which Pristine had grabbed it. Adhira cried in pain as some of her real hair also got ripped from the roots.

"You must be the woman who fooled Iqbal or whatever his name is," Pristine barked a laugh as she threw the wig in the water.

"Only my cover stays blown, all the rest should stay hidden, no one else should be exposed," Adhira announced quickly as she heard a commotion in her ears. Her team was planning to come to her aid, but it was unwise.

"What cover? Who are you talking to?" Pristine demanded.

"Why did you steal the bullets?" Adhira asked, trying to divert Pristine's attention and get as much information as possible in the process.

"Where is the bullet?" Pristine asked with raised eyebrows. "You took the last bullet, didn't you?"

"Why did you want it in the first place?" Adhira asked seriously.

"Who are you?" Pristine asked.

"I am nobody," Adhira informed as she started to walk back.

"Take another step and you and your entire team will be killed. Especially the man who was whispering in your ears," Pristine threatened. "You seriously think I am alone and defenceless here?"

Adhira had no choice, she stood rooted to the ground. Though Pristine had no weapon on her, Adhira could sense many guns pointed in her direction... a lot of people roaming around the bank were not strollers or random sightseers, they were Pristine's acquaintances. However, there were some innocent souls as well and it was for their lives Adhira feared. Though she was rogue, she never spilt innocent blood.

"Come here," Pristine dragged Adhira to the farthest corner of the bank. "I can tell that you are an agent or a spy," she smirked. "Who do you work for? Americans? BI? Indians?" She practically spat the last word and Adhira knew that Pristine and her kind were the enemy of her country.

"Hand me your weapon," Pristine held out her hand. "Hand me your weapon or I will order the kill of everyone present on the port, right now. Everyone here will die today and it will all be your fault."

Adhira looked around, it was peak time and many people were arriving to witness the mesmerising sunset.

"Weapon, now!" Pristine demanded, flicking her fingers.

Adhira bent down and pulled out a knife. Pristine looked with raised eyebrows. "This knife?"

"Quiet, clean and leaves practically no forensic evidence," Adhira shrugged. "I know your kind prefers things that make a loud bang, but I prefer weapons that are quiet and have a personal touch."

"Personal touch, hey," Pristine spoke with a mad glint in her eyes. "Come," she grabbed Adhira's hand and dragged her to the boat she had arrived in. Adhira climbed first, Pristine followed.

"Do you want to say farewell to the man in your ears? Is he your team member or your lover, or both?" Pristine demanded as the boat started to move. She pulled out the Bluetooth from Adhira's ear, and spoke in it, "Say goodbye to your heroine now."

"Do you know what the most painful way to die is?" Pristine asked with a maniacal laugh. "Nick an organ and throw the person under water to bleed slowly. If the water is shark prone, which sadly this part of the ocean isn't, then the shark will come and rip the person away. The pain is immense, you know… I have seen people cry and writhe until their last breath was drawn," she paused to look at Adhira, "Hmm… maybe we will get lucky and a stray shark will find you…" she grinned, "But…" she tutted, "Even if the shark doesn't find you and you manage to swim, you will bleed. The more effort you put into swimming, the faster you'll bleed. And not to mention the strain and blood loss that will make you weaker by the second. Eventually, there will come a time when you will want to stop and drown but would the fear of what will happen if you stopped will let you? It takes a lot of effort to accept death and let go… only weak-minded people do it… and you, Adhira, don't look weak-minded. You will fight and you will lose and though I will not stay back to enjoy your struggle, I will know how you have ended and I will relish in the thought."

Adhira's whole body was now covered with goose bumps. Pristine's words had no impact on her, but her tone… the calmness behind her words wreaked havoc inside Adhira. It was as if killing someone, throwing them to sharks, was a regular affair for her.

"I hear a lot of commotion in your team," Pristine spoke as she pressed Adhira's Bluetooth close to her ears. "Your friends are shouting… is that them?" She pointed back to the ocean bank.

And even before Adhira could turn to see her team, in one swift movement, Pristine stabbed her just above her waist.

To Adhira it felt it was all happening in slow motion.

She saw the knife's blade glint in the setting sun, light bouncing off it as it touched her body; a slow, gradual pain spreading through her torso. Slowly, she turned to face the shore where she saw her entire team and Rudhir. Rudhir was on his knees, crying with his arms stretched. Patricia had her mouth covered in shock. Ava was in Franc's arms, sobbing. Samuel was standing aside, hands on his bald head… Her team was far away now… hopefully safe! Pristine's laughter brought Adhira back to her senses.

"Goodbye," Pristine mocked as she threw Adhira's Bluetooth and bloodied knife in the water. And finally, she touched Adhira's shoulder, pushing her back.

Splash… all was black.

NOSTALGIA

"Noooooooooooooo………….." Patricia and Ava cried as they saw Adhira's dark figure tumble from the boat.

Pristine waved them goodbye, her smirk evident from the distance.

"No-no-no…" Franc fell to his knees, crying heavily. "Adhira… no…!"

Ava, who had held Franc back from jumping in the water after Adhira, fell in Patricia's arms crying.

Rudhir rushed to a nearby boat and tried to undock it. But it was Samuel who reached him first.

Slap…

"You did it," Samuel, whose eyes were bloodshot from silent tears, spoke. "You killed her."

"She cannot be dead," Rudhir whispered, getting ready to jump in the water.

"She is in the middle of the damn ocean," Samuel pointed at the vastness of the water. "Even an expert swimmer like her cannot survive after getting stabbed."

"She is not coming out," Patricia wailed, who was looking out to the ocean hopefully.

"She won't, Patty. She won't," Ava cried heavily into Patricia's shoulder.

"Her GPS," Rudhir requested Franc. "Please check her GPS. Where is she? I can go and find her. I will find her," he insisted.

"After what you did?" Franc barked. "You killed her. You betrayed her, you backstabbed her, and now you brought about her death. You are the worst mother-fucker in the whole damn world. Get out of my sight, or I will throw you in this water as well."

"I—" Rudhir was speechless. He knew that they were right in cursing him. He deserved it. If he had not spoken at that moment, Pristine would not have heard him and Adhira's cover would have stayed intact. It was his voice that alerted Pristine. And now... now... Adhira... *his Dhira* was dead!

"Let's get out of here," Samuel spoke. Being the eldest of all, he was most in his senses. He dragged them all, one by one, to the bus and they drove back to their base.

Franc, tears still falling nonstop, slumped in the bed first. But it was not his bed, it was Adhira's. He put his face in her pillow and sobbed. Patricia, Ava, Samuel too laid down and remained still, silent tears falling. Rudhir just sat on a chair, staring at Franc as he rocked in Adhira's bed. Rudhir felt pity and offence at the same time. He didn't know what relation this team shared, but Franc clearly felt more for Adhira... the woman who is – *was* – Rudhir's.

It was Samuel who moved first. He quickly packed his bag and cleared his throat. "I can sense that this mission is over. I am going home."

"What do you mean?" Rudhir started. Even though he was devastated, his sense of duty for his country didn't leave him. "The mission is still on. We need to find that woman. We need to figure out who is behind all the attacks. We need to locate XRS."

"Without Adhira?" Patricia asked with tears-stained face. "This team is nothing without her, or should I say, it is nothing if any one of us is gone. Each member here plays a crucial role, we are handicapped if any one of us is out of commission," she hiccupped. "Interdependency, that's what made us unique. That's what Adhira wanted us to be, interdependent. Why do you think we have only one expert in each field? We are irreplaceable. All of us."

"Someone please throw this backstabber out of the building," Franc cursed.

"Franc please," Ava cried. "I understand you lost most, but still. We all loved her. I owe my life to her… I have lost my best friend."

"Why did you lose most?" Rudhir challenged.

Franc stood up, fuming. "Because I love her. We all owe our lives to Adhira at one point or another, she has saved our collective asses more times than we can count. But to me she is more… so much more… I have loved her from the moment I first met her. More than you can ever imagine loving her. I loved her so much that I – I did everything for her. Even though she never saw me more than a friend, a partner in crime, I still loved her."

"You moved on, Franc… you got married…" Patricia sighed. "Honour her memory and go live a happy life with your wife."

Franc didn't reply to these words.

"You loved her, yet you married someone else?" Rudhir demanded. He found it easy to accuse Franc, much easier to know about his life, this team's life in comparison to the pain he was feeling.

"Yes, I saw her hate *you* for years," Franc pointed at Rudhir, "But still she loved you. She only loved you, even though you are a bastard of the highest accord. So I moved on when I found a decent girl to settle down. But, but…"

"But you never stopped loving her," Rudhir sighed.

"Never… I settled only to bring peace to her mind. I love my wife, yes. I would never cheat on my wife, but Adhira…" and he cried again.

"How did you meet her?" Rudhir asked, interested. Hearing about her, talking about her was bringing him a unique sense of peace. He wanted to connect with her and hoped that the story of her meeting her team will help him do that.

Franc wiped his face and looked at Rudhir.

"She met me first," Patricia sighed with a smile. "And then together, we met Franc, then Ava and then Samuel."

"She was the glue who held us together," Ava smiled through tears. It was clear that talking about her, how they met, remembering those days were acting like a balm to their very fresh wound.

"She gave me reason to live," Samuel threw his bag down and sat.

"So, how did this team start? This band of International Rogue Spies, how did it begin?" Rudhir asked.

"It began on a breezy evening," Patricia sighed and closed her eyes.

Six years ago

Crashing waves always gave Patricia a calming sense. She grew up by Devonshire Beach in Alberta, Canada and water always felt like home to her.

Phwee wee! Someone whistled.

Patricia turned to see her audience, but it was way too dark for her to see anything or anyone. The moon was playing hide and seek with the clouds and she could hardly see anything. She dived in the water again and swam ahead.

As she came back to the shore, she heard raucous laughter.

She rushed to her things and wrapped herself in a long towel.

"Don't hide that gorgeous body in the damn towel, babe," a voice came. Patricia could tell they were very close to her. "I especially like the fluorescent colour of your bikini, baby."

Patricia had never felt conscious about her body before, but today she was. She had been wearing such bikinis since she could remember but she had never heard such a remark.

She pulled out a small gun from her bag but would it help? The laughter that was echoing suggested at least four men were there, but she didn't know where they were. She could easily be pointing her gun in the opposite direction like a fool. A part of her mind was shouting at her to run, but where should she? What if she landed right in their arms?

"I have a gun," she shouted in the dark.

"Ahhhh…." one of the men groaned with pleasure, "Her voice is just as honeyed as her body. Why don't you come and play with us? We can all enjoy in the water."

A gripping fear enveloped her. Patricia was a woman with multiple talents, but she had never learnt how to fight. She never needed to. She always had security around her, well always, except now!

"Show yourself," Patricia demanded. Even she could hear the panic in her voice.

"With pleasure," someone snickered and men approached her from all directions. "Drop your towel, let us also have the pleasure."

Yes, there were four!

"I will shoot you," Patricia shouted, though her hand was shaking.

"Try baby, try…" one of the men roared with laughter.

"Why don't I try it," someone spoke from behind. The voice was very soft but it sounded confident. It seemed like a very small girl was speaking but her voice was not shaking.

All four men turned quickly but didn't move. Patricia tried to see who was speaking but the darkness didn't allow visibility.

"One more… bro, one more…" one of the men whooped with joy. "Come, baby, come join your friend here. All of us can have fun together."

The clouds shifted and allowed the moon to shine its light on them. And finally, Patricia saw the girl who was speaking. She was a girl with the same physique as hers, the only difference was, she was much more confident than

Patricia felt. She was wearing all black and had her hair tied in an untidy bun. A small bag was strapped around her waist and she had no other possessions.

The girl walked casually towards Patricia, all four men let her pass.

"Are you okay?" the girl asked Patricia. Patricia shook her head, she was crying and shaking.

"May I?" the girl asked for Patricia's gun. Patricia shook her head again. She didn't wish to part with her only weapon.

The girl nodded and didn't take the gun from her.

"So, shall we?" the girl asked for Patricia's hand and together they started to walk away.

"Ooye, where do you think you are going?" one of the men asked.

"Home," the girl sighed.

"Take us as well, please…" one of the men spoke as he reached and grabbed the girl's shoulder. The girl grabbed his wrist, twisted it in one swift move, raised her knee and kicked him hard in the groin. The man fell on the muddy beach, howling with pain. The girl gave one swift kick on the man's jaw, and he slumped back, unconscious.

"Who's next?" the girl demanded.

All three men rushed forward, shouting in rage.

The girl snatched the gun from Patricia's hand and fired a shot in the mud. The sound of the shot echoed on the horizon.

"One at a time," the girl suggested as she gave Patricia the gun back. "Or maybe two. I have never taken three men in one go!" she spoke thoughtfully.

"Shoot him," the girl spoke to Patricia as she pointed at one of the men, "shoot him if he approaches me before the other two are down, okay?" she spoke to Patricia.

The three men considered the girl seriously.

"Come," the girl pointed at the other two. "Try and touch us."

Her confidence was threatening and overwhelming. The three standing men turned and ran away.

The girl smiled at Patricia and led her towards the light. "India is a beautiful place," the girl spoke quietly, "But as you can see, it is very unsafe. I suggest that you don't do anything adventurous after dark, okay?" she smiled.

"Thank you," Patricia almost choked.

"Should I drop you to your hotel room?" she asked.

"I—" Patricia was speechless. "Thank you, but I will find my way now."

The girl nodded, turned and walked back to the beach.

"Where are you going?" Patricia demanded. "Those men may come back."

"I am not scared of them," the girl shrugged as she sat in the sand.

"Can I sit with you?" Patricia asked.

"It is an open beach," the girl smiled for the first time.

"I am Patricia. This is my first visit to India and I must say, it is turning memorable!"

The girl laughed.

"What's your name?" Patricia asked.

"Adhira," the girl shrugged. "This is my first visit to Goa, but in my case, it is turning out to be not so memorable!"

"Why?" Patricia asked, intrigued.

"I was supposed to get married today, on this beach. He promised to marry me here, exactly the time he proposed to me last year, 8:15 pm, but he didn't show up..." Adhira sighed. "I knew things were not so well, but he was supposed to be here. He was supposed to stand with me, under all circumstances, but he betrayed me... I was so sure that he would come. I ran away, practically ran with nothing but this bag of necessities," she patted her waist which had a small pouch around it.

"Oh, that's too bad," Patricia cried again.

"I don't know what I was expecting from him. He didn't stand with me during the trial," tears leaked Adhira's eyes.

"Trial?" Patricia asked, stunned.

"I am Adhira Shekhawat, ex-military spy of India," Adhira said as she wiped her face.

"Ex?" Patricia asked with raised eyebrows.

"Freshly court-martialled…" Adhira closed her eyes and exhaled loudly. "How I wish to run away, but you know the salary of Indian spies does not do justice to the work we do, at least mine didn't. I used up all my savings in the trial and now I don't have enough money to even afford a decent room here," she laughed loudly.

"What?" Patricia blanched.

"I think I will find work in one of the hotels here," Adhira shrugged.

"Come," Patricia spoke, jumping up.

"Where?" Adhira looked confused.

"You saved my life, and Patricia Myers always pays her debt," and she literally dragged Adhira with her.

Present Day

Patricia laughed at the memory. "She saved me that day. My plan was to travel the whole of India, but she didn't want to stay there. So, I took her to Europe. I was on a world tour, trying to prove that I can survive on my own, to my parents, who run Canada's biggest mafia… failed horribly but found the best friend for life."

"I didn't know that she went to Goa," Rudhir whispered, he had tears in his eyes. "I didn't know!"

"Yeah, you don't know a thing, you bastard," Franc cursed. "You left her alone, penniless and broken. But Adhira was strong, she found strength in the pain that you inflicted on her."

"You don't know what happened," Rudhir shouted.

"We know enough, Mr R&AW," Patricia sighed. "On our way to the UK, she told me everything. Believe me, we know what happened."

"What did she tell you?" Rudhir asked seriously.

"You should have asked her," Patricia closed her eyes to compose herself. "I am not going to betray her trust. Never did while she was living, and will not do when she is –" she broke off suddenly.

"What happened next? Adhira met you next?" Rudhir pointed at Franc. He didn't want to break like Patricia did… not in front of the people who considered him a traitor.

"Yes," Franc wiped his face with his hands to gain some composure.

"Do you know who I was, you know, before joining this team?" Franc asked. Rudhir shook his head. "I was the top analyst in British Intelligence," he sighed.

"Really?" Rudhir asked, impressed.

"Yes, I am a Slovakian national but I was handpicked by the head of British Intelligence. They called me to work for them on a secret project and I was all for it. I love my country but Slovakia didn't use my talents well. Anyways, there was a coup in play, which British Intelligence was not aware of. Their own Prime Minister was at the centre of it. You must know about Brexit," he asked Rudhir, who nodded, "Well, there were certain plots in place which would have enforced Brexit back in 2016, but when I unearthed the coup, I was threatened. They asked me to let it go, but as everyone who knows me can attest I don't let things go. And while I was looking into this coup, I unearthed some dangerous plans. Plans to disrupt economies, take control of smaller nations, Slovakia included. I couldn't stay quiet, so I released all the documents on the internet and made sure that they were not erased easily. Well, it made me a marked man," Franc shrugged.

Only Rudhir gaped at Franc in shock, all the rest – who already knew this story – stared blankly at them.

"I was running for my life when I met these two girls," Franc pointed at Patricia, who smiled.

"Adhira and I bonded on our way to London," Patricia started, "We were visiting London's eye when we saw a man run haphazardly. I didn't care for him, I have seen many fanatics in my days, but Adhira, being her, followed him. She saw him hide behind a dumpster. Stupid place, he was clearly visible," Patricia laughed.

"Hey, you try and run from the authorities," Franc defended.

"Anyway, we saw a hoard of Police arrive… they were tossing and turning everything in sight and we instantly knew that they were there for him. So, Adhira did the most incredible thing," Patricia laughed.

"What?" Rudhir asked, intrigued.

"She…" Franc smiled at the memory, "She rushed to me and asked me to take off my coat and shirt. Her exact words were, 'if you want to live, take them off and put them in the dumpster,'" France laughed loudly. "Patricia shouted "hurry" from a distance, and I obeyed. Adhira dragged me to the middle of the crowd, made me stand in the queue, took off her scarf, wrapped it around my shoulders, pressed herself into me and kissed me. She kissed me like we were a couple. I was shocked for a second but then I held her and kissed her back. The police checked the crowd, people in the queue, but she had her hands on my face and no one suspected me to be so involved with a girl. I think she kissed me for hours, or I felt like it, and she let go only when Patricia informed us that they were gone… Ingenious really. I had never met a girl like her, she was so bold and daring. And I had never kissed a girl like that. I fell in love with her that day, but alas, she never reciprocated. I could tell that in her kiss as well, how she wished I was someone else, but it didn't matter to me. I joined them on the ride on London's eye where we talked. I told them my story and Patricia helped me run from the UK safely. And I became an integral part of this team that day…"

"She was indeed the boldest person I ever met," Patricia smiled at the memory as well.

"She never loved you back?" Rudhir asked seriously.

"No, she loved another. Who, of course, didn't deserve it," Franc sighed. "I tried to get together with her for three years, but then she made it very clear that she was not going to get entangled in any romantic relationship again, ever. So, well, I moved on. I met Kisha, my wife and settled with her soon after."

"So, you are a wanted man?" Rudhir asked.

"I was for a while, but Ava here wiped clean my records from all places. Now, I can travel freely," Franc shrugged.

"And how did you join the team?" Rudhir asked Ava, and she snickered. Her mascara was all over her face, and yet, she had a sheepish smile.

"I was following Patricia," Ava spoke as she turned red. "I am a hacker, as you know, I work behind the screens. And I have an alert with Patricia's details built in my system. When I saw that Patricia was in Paris, I had to see her in person."

"Why?" Rudhir asked curiously.

"Well, she is very popular," Ava shrugged. "You know she is an heiress, right?"

"I know now," Rudhir looked impressed.

"Well, she is very popular and so beautiful. I went to see her as I had hacked into her phone to track her location. I found her in the Eifel Tower. My heart broke when I saw her with another woman," Ava's face fell. "I didn't lose hope though, I searched on the woman who was with her and found the truth. I also found you in the search, such a bastard," Ava cursed.

"Hey," Rudhir retorted.

"Well, that's what I felt back then," Ava shrugged. "Anyway, I realised that Adhira and Patty were not a couple, so I planned to bump into them. I showcased my abilities to them, lured them into hiring me, and well, I have been on the team ever since," Ava finished.

"What? Why?" Rudhir asked, confused.

"Well, sometimes, some things are inevitable," Ava grabbed Patricia's hand and smiled. The look they bestowed upon each other said more than he needed to listen. They were a couple, just like he and Adhira were once!

His chest contracted as he saw the love in their eyes. Did he make a mistake by not going to her in Goa on their planned wedding day? Did he commit a crime by leaving her there all alone? What did she think really happened? She would never know the truth now, she is *gone*...

"I joined the team last," Samuel sighed from his bed. Rudhir looked at his bald head with leaking eyes. Samuel was lying in the bed with his hands on his face. "I liked that girl, she was very convincing."

"Why—" Rudhir choked. "Why did you join?"

"I am an inventor of sneaky things. I never could hold a permanent job because the company I worked with didn't like my techniques. I often used their own devices, the ones that I created, to spy on them. They only hired me whenever they needed something 'unethical'. They paid me well, so it worked for me. But it was never permanent. And I was always short on cash because what I build is not cheap! These girls approached me and I decided to join them," Samuel shrugged.

"Well, we approached him because Adhira figured that we needed someone who can make custom weapons for us," Ava added. "I studied the profiles of all the gadgets experts across the globe and he fitted perfectly. Freelancer, aloof, and a mastermind with a filthy record."

"Adhira did most of the talking, I offered incentives," Patricia smiled weakly.

"I wiped his record," Ava nodded.

"And I..." Franc sighed, "Well, I gave him the comfort that he was not the only man in the team."

"So, we became the pentagon, the band of rogue spies," Patricia choked. "Never complete without one other."

"But now," Ava closed her eyes. "Adhira is gone..."

"She is gone..." Franc cried again.

"Gone..."

"Gonee...."

"Goneeeee..."

SECRET ROOM

One Week Later

"Are you sure you want to do it?" Patricia spoke to Rudhir on call.

"I have to finish this mission," Rudhir sighed as he rubbed his eyes. He was staring at the computer screen, ready to take the next step.

"You are law and enforcement," Patricia voiced her concern. "We are lawless, seriously. You are using your position to spy."

"I am not letting this go. She gave her life, she..." Rudhir trailed off. Adhira's passing was still a sore subject for him. He swallowed the lump in his throat and asked, "What does the GPS say?"

Patricia sighed and a lot of clicking noise came from her side. "GPS tracker that was supposed to be in Adhira is still in the Atlantic Ocean. Now much closer to North America."

"It must be a big fish," Rudhir blinked back his tears.

"Oh, please don't," Patricia cried. "Please don't say it. I cannot even picture a shark or something tearing into *her*..."

"I—" Rudhir cried too. "I think I will call you when I get something. I need to finish the search of the entire R&AW department, then I will search IB and all the others. I will find the mole. Maybe that will bring us closer to the missing XRS bullets."

"Fine... and if they fire you, you can always join us. Without Adh... Oh my God!" Patricia exclaimed.

"What happened?" Rudhir jumped in his seat.

"Adhira..." she whispered.

"What now?" Rudhir asked, his heart thumping.

"Stay on the line," Patricia ordered, and putting Rudhir on speaker, she connected.

"Oh…" Patricia gasped.

"Hail Mary!" Samuel cried too. Rudhir could hear the entire team on call now.

"What is happening?" Rudhir demanded.

"Adhira?" Patricia sobbed softly. "Is it really you?"

"What?" Rudhir blanched.

"I just got a video call notification from Adhira's system. We all got it, but the screen is blank," Patricia informed Rudhir.

"Are you talking to Rudhir?" Franc demanded.

"Yes," Patricia informed.

"Ask the fucker to be useful and go to her house. Nobody knows the room, it must be her. Ask him to go and see if she needs help," Franc shouted.

"Text me the address," Rudhir was already running towards his car.

"Already did," Patricia spoke quickly.

Rudhir checked and stopped dead in his tracks. "This is not even a kilometre away from here," Rudhir whispered.

"Good, now hurry…" Patricia cried.

"Don't disconnect," Rudhir ordered. "Stay on the line."

"If I will disconnect, you cannot enter her apartment," Patricia informed.

Rudhir drove like a maniac and within ten minutes he was outside the apartment building.

"I am entering the compound now," Rudhir informed.

"Ok, give the address as following – 4B, urgent delivery with draft services," Patricia dictated.

Rudhir obeyed. The guard gave him a curious look then let him pass.

Patricia guided him where to park as if it was a normal routine. She then guided him about how to reach Adhira's apartment.

"There is a keypad on the door here," Rudhir spoke.

"You can enter by putting in the following code at the main door – A61DY8," Patricia supplied.

"I am in," Rudhir informed. He was amazed by the interior of the house. It was beautifully and elegantly decorated but it lacked human touch. It seemed more like a show house.

"She is not here," Rudhir announced as he searched the house. There were two rooms, a big hall, kitchen and three bathrooms in the apartment.

"Go to the master bedroom," Patricia asked.

"I am here," Rudhir spoke as he looked at Adhira's well-maintained room. "Nice!" He muttered to himself.

"Would you stop snooping around and look for her properly," Franc shouted, agitated.

"*I am looking,*" Rudhir growled.

"Do you see a big wooden panelled wall?" Patricia asked.

"Yes," Rudhir said.

"Now, stand facing it, with your right leg touching the foot of the bed," Patricia ordered.

"That's very specific," Rudhir spoke as he obeyed.

"Now, raise your hand, as per your height versus Adhira, your shoulder height and press your palm, exactly straight," Patricia ordered.

Rudhir did as he was asked to do. And as he pressed, a door opened.

"Adhira…." Rudhir shouted as he fell to the floor.

"Is she there?" Franc asked quickly. Rudhir looked up, Patricia, Franc, Samuel were staring at the room from big screens. The fourth screen said 'connecting…' Rudhir assumed that it must be Ava's.

"Yes, she is here," Rudhir called out. "Unconscious and hurt."

"Let us see her," Patricia spoke, getting close to the camera as if trying to jump out of the screen. And Rudhir lifted Adhira in his arms carefully.

"*Burkha...*" Patricia asked suspiciously. "She is hurt."

"Yes," Rudhir stared at Adhira's broken face.

"At least she is alive," Franc cried openly. "I knew she would be alive. If anyone can survive, it's Adhira."

"You take care of her," Samuel ordered. "Make sure she gets better. You call us if anything is needed."

"I will come to India immediately," Patricia spoke as she started calling someone.

Rudhir nodded and started to go out. There was a big TV panel beside the door through which he had come in. The panel showed each room of the house.

"Just press the button below the panel," Patricia informed him.

He nodded, smiled at Adhira's broken but alive face, and walked out.

THE SECRET MISSION

When Adhira came through, she found herself in her bed, with an IV line dripping some liquid in her veins.

"Dhir…" she whispered as she saw Rudhir sitting by her side. His heart skipped a beat as he heard her take his name.

"Dhira," he whispered back, gently caressing her face.

"Dhir…" she spoke again. "You left me…"

"I love you Dhira," he sobbed as he grabbed her hand and cried in it. "I love you so much, I would never leave you again…"

He looked up to see her response but she had closed her eyes again. She had drifted off to sleep once more.

"How are you feeling?" Patricia asked as Adhira opened her eyes once more.

"Sore," Adhira grimaced as she tried to get up. "Take this line out of my hand, Patty," Adhira ordered tugging at her IV.

Patricia sighed as she started to take out the IV line from her hand.

"Umm, where are my clothes?" Adhira demanded as she sat up and realised that she was covered in a sheet and was wearing nothing underneath it.

"Umm…" Patricia started but it was Rudhir who spoke, "Your clothes, under your *burkha*, were either torn or covered in blood. I had to take them off to…" he paused, then added,

"What the heck happened to you? I mourned you… we all mourned you. Why didn't you let us know you were alive?"

"Who gave you the authority to enter my house?" Adhira demanded, ensuring that her body was covered.

"I did," Patricia informed. "You had called us all on VC, but you were nowhere to be seen. I knew it had to be you, but I was with Ava in France, and Franc and Samuel were in their respective countries. We all were on different continents. Only Rudhir was near you, so I gave him the details. When he secured you, I flew from France last night," she sighed, then demanded, "Where have you been?"

"Since when do you call him 'Rudhir' and not 'Mr R&AW'?" Adhira asked with narrowed eyes.

"Since he saved your ass," Patricia replied simply.

"I don't remember anything since I arrived home," Adhira tried to remember.

Rudhir started, "I carried you to the bed. I took off your *burkha* and saw the state of you. To access your injuries, I took off your clothes and cleaned you. I even cleaned your hair as much I could. Then I called in a doctor to check up on you. The doc and her nurse came and gave you necessary medication. They were incredibly surprised to see the state of you. They confirmed that you were not raped, which gave me some relief. Then, after putting the IV line and instructing me to give you timely injections, they left. You have been under that sheet for the past twenty hours."

"I was not raped," Adhira informed with a twist in her mouth.

"I know that now," Rudhir replied simply.

"Nobody can rape me," Adhira growled.

"I knew that already, but I had to check," Rudhir shrugged.

"You let a stranger doctor and nurse in my house? In my safe haven?" Adhira spoke through gritted teeth.

"To save you," Patricia scolded her. "I'll be damned if you gave him a hard time for saving your life. Do you have any idea what we all went through…?" she glared at Adhira.

"It's time for you to leave," Adhira looked at Rudhir and demanded.

"Not until you tell me where the fuck you were for the past week," Rudhir declared.

"Can I get dressed first?" Adhira sighed, rubbing her bare shoulders instinctively.

"I see that you got rid of the tattoo," Rudhir hesitated.

"Yes, and it was a painful procedure," Adhira snorted. "But I am glad. Good riddance."

Rudhir's face fell.

"Why? Do you still have it? After everything, I would be surprised if you still had it," Adhira mocked a laugh.

In one swift motion Rudhir took off his shirt and there it was, on his left shoulder.

Ru-A-DHIR-a
Forever

Patricia leapt from the bed and looked at it closely. She was stunned to see the tattoo that was covering most of Rudhir's shoulder, however it was nothing in comparison to how Adhira was feeling. Was she shocked or emotional, even she didn't know.

"Nothing lasts forever," Adhira whispered, staring at his shoulder.

"Somethings do," and with one curt nod, he left the room.

Fifteen minutes later, Adhira, Patricia and Rudhir entered the secret room to do a video call with Franc, Samuel and Ava.

"Hallelujah, you are alive," Franc exclaimed. He had tears of happiness in his eyes. "I thought I would never see that smile again. God, I am so relieved…"

"I am very pleased to see you, dear," Samuel added.

"You are a bitch, you know that!" Ava cursed. "One week! We cried for one whole week. You should have seen Patty, she was devastated," Ava continued.

"I am sorry," Adhira replied weakly. Her ribs were still hurting, and even the small walk from bed to the room was taking its toll.

Rudhir brought a chair for Adhira and Patricia pushed her in it.

"Where were you?" Ava demanded, standing up and glaring down at Adhira.

"In many places," Adhira sighed.

"When Pristine heard his voice," Adhira pointed at Rudhir venomously, "Thank you very much for blowing up my cover and the entire operation by the way," she scowled. Rudhir shirked but didn't reply.

"We gave him enough hard time, love," Franc gestured Adhira to calm down. "Please continue."

"Well, while she was busy snatching my hair and stuff, I took her burner and pushed it in my fanny pack. Great thing it is absolutely waterproof, so I saved it," Adhira smiled. "She stabbed me, yes, but my protective vest didn't let the blade do much damage. There was a miniscule cut, that's all," Adhira shrugged.

"Your miniscule cut was infected," Rudhir informed sourly. "And—" he wanted to continue but Adhira raised her hand to shush him.

"Anyway, I swam underwater, you know that I am an expert swimmer," Adhira continued carelessly.

"I told them that you were one hell of a swimmer," Franc punched the air proudly.

"Yes, but when I came on the side of the ocean bank," Adhira continued. "I saw men observing you. While you were fighting and arguing, they were discussing. I heard their plan. If they realised I was alive, they would have killed you. And we don't know who they are or how deep their roots were, so I didn't come up to you all."

"I checked your GPS tracker, it was in the water," Franc spoke thoughtfully.

"Well," Adhira grinned naughtily.

"You cut it out of you?" Franc glared.

"Well, yes," Adhira nodded glumly. "When I scanned through Pristine's burner, I found out that she was talking to someone in Tehran."

"Tehran?" Ava exclaimed.

"Yes, and I know what goes on there and how I could reach the place. They believed I was dead but they were observing you, seeing how you were mourning and your daily activities. It was a perfect cover, so I used it and went to Tehran to check what was going on."

"You went to Tehran, alone?" Rudhir asked, shocked and angry.

"I did," Adhira shrugged. "Not the first time and not the last time."

"But you always have us as your backup," Franc added in Rudhir's tone.

"Do you boys want to know what I found out or are you going to bore me with your nonsense worries?" Adhira snapped. Both Franc and Rudhir retreated slightly, though they both looked scandalised.

"I took out my GPS chip, had to cut it out with a knife by the way," she winced as she twisted her right shoulder where it was once implanted, "and paid a fisherman to feed it to a fish and throw the fish deep in the water."

"So that's why your GPS tracker shows you are somewhere in the Atlantic, near America," Patricia wondered.

"Yes, I am guessing that some large fish ate the smaller one, well, never mind the fish," Adhira fanned her hands, "From there, I made my way to Tehran."

"Why did you take out the GPS?" Ava asked seriously.

"They were monitoring you. My movement would have alerted you and it would have tipped Pristine's men," Adhira shrugged again. "I needed a conspicuous cover and having a GPS implant, which would raise alarm all over, would not have helped my cause."

"I hate you," Ava growled. "I seriously hate you…"

"I love you too, darling," Adhira smiled at Ava affectionately. "And I am sorry for putting you all through this."

"You are not forgiven, *yet*," Franc spoke seriously. "What happened next? You took the help of Nikhar, as usual?" he asked with narrowed eyes.

"Yes," Adhira nodded.

"Who is Nikhar?" Rudhir interjected.

"Nikhar is the biggest smuggler in the Middle East," Patricia informed Rudhir. "He is in it only for the money and doesn't care if he is smuggling weapons, food items or humans. Till the time price is right, you will arrive where you want to."

"And is it wise to trust such a man?" Rudhir demanded.

"You can always trust men who want money. Only money is reliable because you can always pay more and buy them. They bend as per your will and you can get things done your way… however, emotions, relations are all rubbish," Adhira snorted.

Rudhir stared at her dumbfounded, seriously unable to comprehend her!

"Well," Franc spoke loudly. "You enlisted Nikhar to smuggle you into Tehran."

"Yes, and it was horrible there. It took me two days to reach the parts of Tehran where terrorist activities are at peak. Within hours of my arrival, I was picked up with other women," Adhira informed.

"What?" All of them shouted at once.

"Who picked you? What do you mean? What other women?" They all spoke in unison, making it incomprehensible for Adhira to understand what they were saying.

"One at a time, please..." Adhira laughed and gripped her chest as laughing made her every body part hurt.

Patricia and Franc repeated the questions one by one and Adhira obliged them with explanations.

"In certain parts of Tehran and neighbouring regions, terrorists are at full power. It is like there is no government there. The terrorist organisation at play is acting at will and local goons are supporting the lawlessness..." Adhira informed.

"And you landed smack in the middle of this lawless environment," Franc grunted.

Adhira nodded, "Yes, and they were rounding up women and little girls for slavery and prostitution. Beating them mercilessly to submit them to do their bidding. When I arrived there, well, I was straight away pulled into a van that was collecting women at the time."

There was a stunned silence at these words and Adhira was glad, because if their expressions were so deadly, she dreaded to think what their words would be.

Sighing, Adhira continued. "We were taken to some secluded place, it was full of cells, rows and rows of cages to hold women like animals. They were sorting women and putting them in respective cages. They liked me, found me incredibly beautiful, so after spending sometime in a cage like an animal, I was taken to the main hide," Adhira shivered slightly. Patricia placed her warm hand on her shoulder to calm her down. Adhira grabbed Patricia's hand and squeezed it. “Believe me when I say that it was the worst experience of my life, and as all of you know, I have seen so much on missions in the past years… this was by far *the worst,”* she shivered terribly and Patricia hugged her tightly. “It was awful there. From little girls to older women, all crammed together in holes as small as 4X4 room to be used and sold, it was devastating.”

“How did you escape?” Rudhir asked quickly. “And what is the main hide?”

“Main hide, some called it *aashiyaana,* is the place where the leaders of terrorist organisations live. People who are running all the ops in Tehran and neighbouring places,” Adhira informed.

“What organisation is playing there? We didn’t receive any intel about any new terrorist group rising since you took out Butch,” Rudhir spoke harassed.

“Maybe, if you give her space to speak, she will let us know!” Franc grumbled.

Rudhir chewed his tongue in agitation but didn’t speak. Adhira looked at Franc, who nodded at her encouragingly.

“They took me to the main hide,” Adhira continued after a pause, “and brought me to the men who owned the place, well, while I was waiting for their leaders to arrive and assess me, I killed two, injured four and ran,” she informed. “Got attacked, beaten, and dragged back to the hide. Stayed in an isolated hole for a long time, then again, dragged outside and was face to face with the leader of the group. I stabbed him and knocked him unconscious. I could have killed him but he made a noise and the guards were alerted. Ran again, hid in some ruins. The ruins got blasted, luckily I was in a house that once had a bomb shelter. They rummaged through the area, declared I was not there and left. I waited for the night to fall, then ran to the place I had agreed with Nikhar to meet. I had asked him to wait for me for one hour every night. I was already an hour late. Yet, hoping against hope that he hadn’t left me to die there, I ran. Found him at last. And he brought me back. I had not slept since the day we went after Pristine. Maybe that's why I passed out the moment I came in the safety of my home."

"Oh my God, Adhira," Patricia hugged her again and cried.

"I am fine..." Adhira patted her and looked at everyone and repeated, "I am fine."

"So, you undertook the most dangerous mission ever *alone*!" Franc screamed, "Did you find anything?"

"Yes," Adhira nodded.

"Ikhtiyaar Mohammad Ali," Adhira announced. "He is the leader of a faction that is emerging in Tehran. The group calls itself Ikhti-Baksh, and they are growing rapidly and nastily. Half of Tehran is under its influence. Men are throwing their wives and daughters at them for their cause. And what surprised me most is that ISIS is supporting them openly. I heard Ikhtiyaar talk to General Khuda Baksh, the current leader of ISIS, and it was as if they were closest of friends. And the name of the organisation tells tales about their bond too."

"Ikhti-Baksh," Franc spoke thoughtfully, clicking his keyboard haphazardly. "There is no news of it."

"I too cannot find a thing," Ava informed, she was also searching on the internet about it.

"They are very quiet as an organisation, they are planning something huge, incredibly destructive and they don't want any intelligence agency to get a wind of it," Adhira continued.

"Did you pick up anything else there? Anything to use?" Franc asked seriously.

"I picked up a lot of things, they thought I didn't understand their language, I am pretty sure they were speaking in Persian, but as I understand Arabic, Urdu and so many others, I picked up a lot of things there," Adhira sighed. "They are planning an attack on India. A massive one."

A ringing silence met these words.

Adhira turned to Rudhir as she spoke, "The Kargil War Memorial," she asked. He looked at her, feeling partially intrigued, partially scared. "The one that they are working on currently," she continued. "Is it on schedule?"

"Yes, its grand opening is on 26th July, the day we won the Kargil War in 1999," Rudhir nodded seriously. "Why?"

"The chatter I picked up, they were talking about a few things. Following words were often repeated in the conversations," she stood up and walked to the white board and started writing.

Kargil
Memorial
XRS
Bomb
Baksh
Ikhtiyaar
Haseena
Ola
Bullets
Production

"And..." Adhira strained. "There was something else, but I was too fazed to remember it."

"You can relax now," Patricia insisted.

"Ah yes," Adhira spoke as she scribbled a few more words on the board,

General
Border
Khan
Josh

"My hypothesis is that they are planning to attack India on 26th July, during the grand opening of the Kargil War Memorial."

"Here, in the heart of Delhi?" Rudhir rubbed his forehead to gauge the depth of the situation.

"Yes... Delhi is one of the most populated cities in India. If they unleash a weapon like XRS here, just imagine the havoc it will wreak," Adhira sighed.

"26th July is just next week," Samuel added.

"Yes, I understand that," Adhira winced as she took back her seat. "We need to move, and we need to move fast. Somehow, Ikhti-Baksh is working in conjunction with ISIS and Josh," she added.

"ISIS and Josh don't work together," Rudhir spoke with narrowed eyes.

"I know that Josh, being an independent organisation in Pakistan, don't see eye to eye with ISIS, but in this case, they are working together, or some factions of each organisation are, because I explicitly remember them mentioning 'Josh' once or twice," Adhira spoke seriously.

"This just got nasty," Rudhir grabbed his hair as he stared at the white board. "And who is Haseena?"

"She was not there," Adhira shrugged.

"And Pristine's name is not on the board," Ava supplied.

"Maybe because either she is not that important, or Pristine is just an alias," Adhira replied.

"Oh! She is important, I can tell," Ava spoke seriously. "You don't just put someone in such a crucial diplomat position for nothing."

"Maybe Pristine is Haseena," Rudhir shrugged.

"Maybe, maybe not," Adhira nodded.

"So, what is the plan? We need to act swiftly and quickly," Patricia spoke.

Adhira looked back at the board.

"We need to divide and conquer," she spoke.

Rudhir walked to the board and stared at it too.

"Can I make a suggestion," he asked Adhira, who nodded curtly.

"We need to identify where they plan to manufacture the XRS. It cannot be done anywhere. We also need to identify who this Haseena is," he paused to look around.

"Samuel," Adhira spoke.

"Yes, Adhira," Samuel spoke from his screen.

"You have a copy of the report that Iqbal showed me?" Adhira asked.

"Yes, I have it," Samuel nodded.

"Can you work with Franc to analyse what the facility needs exactly? Ideally, they would need two facilities. One to make bullets, which does not require anything specific, but the one to make XRS needs to have special requirements. From what I understood from Iqbal's report, they produced samples in their lab. The lab is underground, has walls to stop the radiation from spreading and to ensure that there is no contamination. Also, there was some specific lighting requirement… you know the heat, light, laser or whatever to merge the elements of XRS and convert it into its deadly form. Can you please study that, and Franc can help?"

Both Franc and Samuel nodded.

"Ava, can you hack into the chatter around the globe and look up these names- Ikhtiyaar, Baksh, Haseena and Josh?" Adhira requested. Ava nodded too.

"Patty, can you arrange a call with your most trusted sketch artist?" Adhira continued.

"Sketch artist?" Everyone asked with sudden curiosity.

"I saw Ikhtiyaar, I need to get his face down on paper before it is completely eroded from my memory," she tapped her fingers on the table.

"I can arrange that," Patricia nodded.

"You," Adhira finally looked at Rudhir. He froze suddenly. "Mr R&AW, you are going to use your network and connections to find me a way to delay the inauguration of Kargil War Memorial."

"That's impossible. The Prime Minister wants to give a statement through it. He will not delay it, not at any cost," Rudhir shook his head.

"This is going to cost him very much," Adhira gritted her teeth.

"I don't think he cares," Rudhir hung his head.

"Can you do something, anything useful in the least?" Adhira snapped.

"Hey," Patricia scolded. "He has been trying…"

"Then try harder," Adhira stood up angrily. "Find us the mole. There is a mole in one of your departments, I need to know who it is. I need them to feed wrong information to Ikhiyaar and General Baksh," Adhira shouted.

"You will open your stitch," Rudhir spoke calmly. "I am not all that useless, you know?"

"Yeah?" Adhira said sarcastically. "You got my cover blown. You delivered my real name into the ears of the enemy. It is good that I am an orphan and have no family whatsoever, what do you think would have happened if I had?"

"I am sorry, alright?" Rudhir retorted.

"Just go and find me the bloody mole!" Adhira limped forward and opened the door for him.

Giving everyone one last look, Rudhir stepped out.

"That was harsh," Franc spoke from his screen. Adhira shot him a dirty look and disconnected the call.

HARSHEST REALITY

That day, Adhira spent the rest of her time with the sketch artist. It took her really long because she kept on mixing the expressions of her captors with Ikhtiyaar. Luckily, the sketch artist was a patient man and worked at her pace calmly.

"Is that really him?" Patricia asked after good eight hours. "Thank you, Alan, I could trust only you with this."

Alan, the sketch artist, looked exhausted.

"If I am able to deliver then these eight hours are worth it," Alan sighed.

"I am really sorry," Adhira was way too embarrassed. This had never happened with her before.

"It happens when the victim is tortured by multiple captors. I have seen it happen before. The victim," Alan paused to read through Adhira's face, "I mean the person, who suffered at the hands of multiple bastards, keeps on confusing the faces. You need psychiatric help," he finished.

"I don't need help," Adhira retorted.

"Most victims of brutal kidnapping say that," Alan added. "But hey," he spoke again, reading Adhira's furious expressions, "I am just a sketch artist. I will send this to you and burn my copy. I don't want to be involved in whatever shit you girls get yourself into, okay?"

"Thanks, Alan, owe it to you," Patricia smiled.

"Anytime babe," Alan winked.

"I will wire you the money tonight," and with this, Patricia disconnected the call.

"I don't need psychiatric care," Adhira groaned as she laid back in her bed.

"What you need is to open up about what really happened there," Patricia sighed.

"I told you all what happened there," Adhira sighed.

"I don't believe that was it, okay," Patricia stressed. As Adhira closed her eyes, Patricia held her hand. "It's me… what happened there?"

"I—" Adhira started but Patricia's phone buzzed.

She quickly took the call and placed it down muttering, "I will call you in a while."

"Was it important?" Adhira asked seriously.

"Nothing is more important right now," Patricia sighed. "What happened to you there?"

Adhira gulped.

"Hey," Patricia wiped her cheeks.

"I was scared, Patty," Adhira spoke finally, "I don't remember being scared like this before. I think the last time I felt such deep dread was when I realised that Dhir had left me. When he betrayed me was the last time I felt such fear. But in that place," she shivered.

"Hey," Patricia hugged her and rubbed her back.

"You all thought I was dead, and this was the first time I felt I did something utterly stupid; you know. Faking my death, so none of you would come looking for me!" Adhira choked.

"We will come to that later," Patricia pursed her lips to stop herself from shouting at her.

"Nikhar put me in his truck as usual, our plan was to meet exactly twenty-four hours later. But I had a gut feeling, so I requested him to come and wait for me every twelve hours for an hour at our agreed-upon place. You know he likes me, so he agreed," Adhira smiled.

"Ok, so what happened when you came out of the truck," Patricia encouraged.

"Hell," tears glistened Adhira's cheeks. "Tehran is brainwashed by Ikhti-Baksh. Every man is selling his wife and daughter. They saw me and grabbed me too…" she choked. "I tried to run but someone hit me from behind and I lost consciousness. When I came through, I found myself in a cell. It was a 4X4 cell and at least two dozen girls were cramped in there. I realised that they had taken off my *burkha*."

"Really?" Patricia raised her eyebrows.

"Yes. These pigs, they would kill a woman if she steps out of the house without a burkha, but they had all these women there without it. Just in their bare essentials," Adhira replied. "They were sorting out the girls. Some were sent to slavery, prostitution, some were sorted to entertain the men in the pit and very few were chosen for a special job. They chose me for that special job, they literally dragged me by my hair to the main hide. I tried to fight, but they were just too many. I realised what my training lacks, Patty, it is fighting ten at a time," she exhaled to control.

"I don't think it is possible for anyone to fight ten at a time, well, outside stupid movies," Patricia rolled her eyes.

Adhira didn't reply to this.

"Why did they take you first? Weren't there many girls?" Patricia asked after a pause.

"I think because I was the different one there," Adhira replied solemnly. "No matter how hard I tried to gel with the crowd, a trained spy stands out. They were all staring at me, I don't know why, so the one who was sorting pushed me first in the main hide."

"They were staring because you are beautiful. Sometimes, such beauty is a curse," Patricia pursed her lips. "What happened in the main hide?"

"They pushed me in a dog cage, Patty, an actual dog cage. I couldn't even sit properly in it. I had to crouch all the time," Adhira whispered. "I was on the floor, with my back down. I felt I would die of suffocation," she cried. "I was praying to die because I knew that help was not coming in any form, but then *he entered.*"

"He who?" Patricia asked suddenly.

"Ikhtiyaar," Adhira gritted her teeth. "He was busy on the phone. And I understood what he was saying because he was talking in Urdu. He is not Iranian. I am sure he is a Pakistani who is using his charm and influence to brainwash the Tehrani population. He was talking to Khuda Baksh, I heard Ikhtiyaar take his name and I can never miss the name of the ISIS General," Adhira clenched her fists.

"When he was done, he came to me and removed my hair from my face. I pretended to be asleep," Adhira continued. "He left, ordering his men to clean me up for him. Four men came and dragged me out of the cage. I broke the jaw of two, killed two… and ran…"

"Oh thank God!" Patricia exclaimed.

"I was not even at the gate when they caught me," Adhira cried. "Ikhtiyaar was very angry. He tried to rape me and I stabbed him with his own knife. This angered him beyond comprehension. He decided to teach all women a lesson through me. He took off my clothes, leaving me in my underwear and bra, and beat me. He made countless men beat me black and blue, while he watched like a king on a throne. Then he threw me in an isolated cell. It was a pity on their part that they threw my clothes with me too or I would have died of cold, the cell was freezing."

"What?" Patricia cried.

"That was when the fear crept in, Patty. That was my lowest point… I wanted to die, kill myself. But another thought struck me, I had killed Butch, the world's most wanted man, who the fuck was this Ikhtiyaar."

"A good thought to keep you alive and sane in that place," Patricia nodded. She had goose bumps all over her body.

"No…" Adhira whispered. "The thought that kept me alive was of Rudhir."

"Rudhir?" Patricia asked, abashed.

"I don't know what I feel for him, maybe it was because he is the only person I have ever associated with as family… whatever maybe the reason but he was my anchor to sanity in that dark, dingy place. His face, only his face kept me awake. The thought of never seeing him kept me alive," Adhira cried again.

Patricia patiently waited for her to calm down.

"I don't know," Adhira continued as her sobs turned to hiccups, "I don't know after how long they brought me out of that hole, but they must have thought that the beating and isolation would cripple me. It was only one man there. I took his gun and shot him. The shot rang in silence. I shot another who came out at the noise and I ran… I ran and I ran like there was no tomorrow. Because I knew if I stopped, I would have no tomorrow. I hid in one of the abandoned houses. I stayed there even when I felt the house burning around me. It was hot, suffocating but it was a bomb shelter. Nothing penetrated the door, neither the fire nor the smoke. I stayed there for long, praying that Nikhar waits for me. When I felt it was safe enough, I stepped out in the dark. Nikhar was there. He gave me a *burkha* to hide me and, without any questions, took me back. He smuggled me to the border, but this time he didn't hand me over to another man as he had seen my injuries. He took care of me, treated me with compassion. He put me on a truck and assured me that the men will take care of me. But I didn't dare close my eyes. I travelled in the truck for three days and two nights, arrived in India yesterday. Found another truck heading to Delhi, and they dropped me off here, outside the apartment," Adhira finished.

"You should sleep," Patricia blinked back her tears.

"I want to go back, Patty," Adhira spoke through gritted teeth after a tentative pause. "I want to go back and rain fire on those men. I want to kill Ikhtiyaar with my own hands. I want to free those women. I want Tehran to be a women-free place. Let those men fuck each other… I will do it, Patty. I swear, I will free those women. After this mission, even if that is the last thing I do, I am gonna do it."

"I will help you, but we would need to make arrangements to keep those women somewhere, you know. They cannot enter India legally," Patricia sighed.

"I don't care, I will save them all," Adhira shouted.

"We will save them all," Patricia nodded.

"Thank you for being here for me," Adhira placed her head on Patricia's shoulder and closed her eyes.

"I am sorry but I cannot stay long," Patricia sighed.

"You will leave me?" Adhira asked, sadly.

"You know that I have to go," Patricia cried. "I have to be in Canada by tomorrow."

"I don't want to be alone, not tonight," Adhira sobbed. "I hate being like this but…"

"But you are a human," Patricia patted her hair. "I will ask Ava to come."

"I don't need Ava," Adhira closed her eyes.

"I know you don't need Ava," Patricia sighed.

"You need me," someone spoke from the door.

Adhira's eyes jerked open at the words.

"I am sorry, you didn't disconnect and I heard. I heard everything," Rudhir was crying too.

"How dare you?" Adhira blanched. "It was personal."

"Patricia, your flight leaves in three hours, you need to board," Rudhir announced without taking his eyes off Adhira.

Patricia nodded and walked up to him, kissed his cheek and whispered, "Don't you dare leave her again!" And walked out.

"I don't need you," Adhira closed her eyes furiously.

"I know that you don't need me… I am staying because I need you… and this time I am not going anywhere," Rudhir declared.

BACK TO HOME MINISTRY

Iran... Afghanistan... Taliban... Pakistan... Ikhtiyaar...

Aaahhhhhhhh!!!!!!!!! Adhira screamed as she woke up suddenly.

"What's wrong?" Rudhir demanded. He was sitting beside her in the bed and working on his laptop.

"Ikhtiyaar," Adhira panted.

"What about him?" Rudhir asked with narrowed eyes.

"He... he plans to destroy our country," Adhira spoke between heavy breaths. "He is planning something big."

"I gathered as much from yesterday," Rudhir sighed as he closed his laptop. "But first thing first, how are you feeling now?"

Adhira sat up, the pain was much less now in her torso. "I am better," she exhaled to calm herself.

"I must say, you didn't lie when you used to say that you have dense bones. The doctor was surprised you didn't break any ribs or anything. You just had bruises, deep cuts but no broken bones," Rudhir smiled but there was an angry spark in his eyes.

Adhira ignored his comment and looked at the clock. "Holy!" she exclaimed. "Is it really noon?"

"Yep, didn't want to wake you, but now seeing as you are up, we are due in Home Minster's office at 4pm today. I have already prepared lunch for you, so you can freshen up and eat," Rudhir informed. As he got out, Adhira noticed that he was fully dressed and ready.

"Why didn't you wake me up?" Adhira accused.

Rudhir considered her for a moment, and spoke rather professionally, "Because my asset was injured during a top-secret mission and she needed time to recover. You are no good to me or this country if you die of exhaustion and injuries!"

Adhira narrowed her eyes, but then accepted defeat. She got ready, then called her team to discuss the plan ahead.

"Where are we?" Adhira asked as, one by one, her team members connected. "Patty, you found your way back safely?"

"Yes, did you sleep well?" Patricia asked.

"Fine…" Adhira brushed her concern airily. "Were we able to locate the facility?"

"Not yet," Franc sighed. "Samuel is studying the XRS bullet. As it is so dangerous, he is being very cautious."

"Of course," Adhira nodded. "We don't want any casualties or spread in Belgium. Please be extra careful, Samuel."

Samuel nodded. "I have identified most of the elements, but I have a feeling that they have not disclosed the binding agent in their file. And that's what is causing me trouble."

"If it was missing in the files we have then I hope Pristine also doesn't know about it," Adhira said hopefully.

"If Iqbal was not stupid enough to let it out," Ava pouted.

"Yes, for the mind who created XRS, he is not very brilliant," Samuel nodded.

"Oh, he is brilliant," Adhira corrected, "Just not social enough to know where to open his mouth!"

"Yeah, like Samuel assessed. He is dumb!" Franc commented.

"Anyway, Ava, did you pick up any chatter about Ikhtiyaar, Baksh or Haseena?" Adhira asked.

"No, but there is a rumour going around about a deadly radioactive weapon. Many are wagering how to get their hands on it," Ava informed.

"I have no doubts about it. Not just terrorists, but superpower countries like America, China, Russia, they all would want such a weapon in their possession," Adhira agreed.

"Why is Rudolf so quiet about it? They created it, after all… well Iqbal did but as he is in the employ of Rudolf, so they technically own it, don't they? Why can't they simply manufacture and sell to them?" Franc wondered.

"If my hypothesis is correct, this was their original plan. They wanted to create and own the world's deadliest weapon and sell it to the highest bidder. But their plan went to drain when it was stolen by an unknown terrorist group. Given that nobody knows what this group wants, they simply cannot put their name behind it. It is way too bad for their business and reputation. I think they would rather have that group manufacture and claim it as their own creation, than say that they supplied a deadly weapon for mass killing," Adhira spoke thoughtfully.

"We need the location," Patricia added. "I want to bomb the facility."

"And expose the atmosphere to the horrors of this radioactive material?" Samuel raised his eyebrows sarcastically.

"Well, you know what I mean!" Patricia tutted.

"It is not easy to mass-produce, the materials involved are to be created with a unique fusion of multiple radioactive materials, and then there is the limit of supply…" Samuel added.

"Why don't you see if any of the required materials have gone missing lately from any facility or have been dealt with illegally? Can you pass on the list of materials used to the team? We all can pitch in?" Adhira requested Samuel, who nodded.

"I will help," Ava chirped from her screen.

"Your help is always appreciated, dear," Samuel smiled.

"Did you have a word with your Home Minister, Mr R&AW?" Patricia asked Rudhir, who was listening to everything quietly.

"Yes, is he smart enough to get the event postponed?" Franc demanded.

Rudhir shook his hand. "Adhira, we need to be in his office in less than two hours from now..."

"What does he want?" Patricia asked sharply.

Rudhir just shrugged.

"You go and have this meeting," Patricia twisted her mouth at the secrecy. "Update us in the evening?" she spoke to Adhira, who nodded.

"You really had to disguise your face again?" Rudhir shook his head as he led her into the Home Minister's office.

"What you do and what I do are two very different things," Adhira sighed.

"You never told me why you are in a disguise. The first time we met here, you had said to the home minister, 'if you knew why I had donned this avatar, you won't believe me...'"

Adhira raised her eyebrows. "Do you have the stomach to know the truth?" She asked seriously.

"Always," Rudhir nodded encouragingly.

"There is a hit ordered on your home minister and prime minister. And I am one of the people who were called upon to undertake the task," Adhira shrugged.

"What? Who?" Rudhir was taken aback.

Adhira twisted her mouth as if she didn't care about this. "There are many who want to kill these two men in this country. Anyway, my team are not assassins, so I declined the offer. Still, I don't want to give anyone any wrong impression, you know."

"Good to know," Rudhir couldn't believe her words.

"Are you seriously shocked that the Home Minister and Prime Minister can be a target?" Adhira mocked him.

"I know they are not very well liked... they are good people, strive to do right for the country, but to hire someone like you... it means that the people who ordered the hit are serious!" Rudhir spoke seriously.

"Good people. People who want to do right by others are always targeted. If they are allowed to do what they want, how would corrupt people survive," Adhira mused. "And yes, there are some people who are dead serious in eliminating your PM and HM and I don't want to take any risks by giving anyone ideas. You should also take precaution and never forget, you have a mole somewhere," Adhira pointed around as they entered the premises.

"I am sure it is not in the Home Ministry," Rudhir smiled at her expressions.

"Only time will tell," Adhira pouted as she entered the Home Minister's office behind Rudhir.

"Rudhir, finally you are here," the Home Minister's face lit up as he saw him enter. "I see you are not blonde anymore, Ms Shekhawat," he smiled as he saw Adhira.

Adhira nodded casually.

"Rudhir briefed me about your little *adventure* out there in the Middle East," the Home Minister sighed. It was clear he too didn't approve of it, just like Rudhir and her team.

"We all work differently, sir," Adhira nodded. "May I?" she pointed at a chair in front of him.

"Yes, I heard that you got badly injured while you were there," the Home Minister continued.

Adhira sat down, but not without wincing slightly.

"How are you really? If I could have avoided, I would not have called you, but I thought that you should witness what is about to happen. We are about make history," the Home Minister sparkled with pride.

"What do you mean?" Adhira asked seriously.

"You didn't fill her in?" The Home Minister raised his eyebrows at Rudhir, who shook his head.

"Let's go. It is about to happen," the Home Minister tapped his chair, got up and led the way out.

Adhira and Rudhir followed. Falling a few steps behind, Adhira demanded, "What is happening?"

"I informed the Home Minister what happened out there with you. All the details. He felt it was a perfect opportunity wasted if we didn't capture Ikhtiyaar while we still knew the location of his hideout," Rudhir informed.

"How do you know where he was?" Adhira demanded.

"Our agents there got in touch with Nikhar, paid a handsome price, got the location of your pick up and drop off, your description of ruins and bomb shelter helped. And, of course, the satellites," Rudhir shrugged.

"You are jeopardising the mission," Adhira hissed, looking scandalised.

"This is top secret," Rudhir assured her.

"What is the matter with you? How could you do this? Without consulting me?" Adhira raged on as they entered a room, and someone locked them inside.

"He didn't consult you because you were not well," the Home Minister interjected.

Rudhir relaxed at his words and added, "This is a top-secret mission. Only a handful of people know about it in this office. Ikhtiyaar is now the most-wanted terrorist for us. We have activated at least a dozen sleeper agents in the Middle East. It is a very-*very* discreet mission. Classified above classified."

"What is the plan?" Adhira spoke through gritted teeth as she stared at the black screen.

"Our team will get in, do the job and get out. Anyone who gets in the way is gonna get killed. Once Ikhtiyaar is dead, they will fall back," Rudhir informed.

"And you don't think that it would be wise to interrogate him first? Find out about XRS? Find out about his mission? Reasons to attack us?" Adhira demanded.

"If he is dead then his mission, his reason is dead," the Home Minister shrugged.

"What about XRS?" Adhira couldn't believe it.

"We'll deal with one problem at a time," the Home Minister huffed.

"And what about the women in there? Did you even consider them? What if they get in the way? Would your men kill them too?" Adhira demanded.

"Sometimes we have to consider the Greater Good," the Home Minister narrowed his eyes as he stared at the screen.

Adhira's jaw dropped at these words.

"I was one of those women just a few days ago," Adhira shouted. "Would killing me be for greater good, too?"

"Adhira, this is not up for discussion," Rudhir sighed.

"At least ask your men to not kill innocent women?" Adhira begged.

"I have already instructed them about it," Rudhir assured her but somehow she felt he was saying it just to keep her quiet in front of the home minister.

"Why are we doing this in broad daylight?" Adhira asked as she stared at the screen now, which was still black.

"Well, this is when we have observed no activity. We have been monitoring the area ever since you came back. This is the only window when it is quiet, I wonder why!" Rudhir spoke.

"That's when they enter the Harem or whatever you call it. That is one time they spend with their women," Adhira shivered at the thought. "They—the place is filled with shrieks and cries at the time and they take collective pleasure in it."

"I am glad that we have insider information," the Home Minister nodded.

A man in army uniform entered and locked the door again. As Adhira studied his profile, she realised that he was a General in the army.

"They are starting, sir," the General informed and suddenly the room was filled with the light from the screen. What they were seeing was the view of the camera attached to the head of one of the agents.

"Is this the right place?" the Home Minister asked Adhira. She, staring blankly at the screen, nodded.

"We have a confirmation," the General spoke on his phone.

"The chambers of Ikhtiyaar are there," Adhira pointed at the first floor of the house now visible on the screen. "As they will enter the house, there is a big sitting room, they call it *shamiyana*. They need to cross the *shamiyana* and they will see the stairs. On the first landing, they will see a long corridor with many doors. The first room is always locked, it houses their weapons. The second door is closed but it is linked to Ikhtiyaar's room. The third door is where Ikhtiyaar lives," she informed.

General relayed the information ahead.

"I should be there," Adhira whispered as she stared at the screen. "I know this place, I can get in and out in minutes."

"You just got out of that place, in no way are you returning there," Rudhir whispered back to her.

"I can take care of myself," Adhira retorted as she watched the agent walk forward.

"I have no doubt---" Rudhir started but froze as the sudden sound of firing, shouts and cries echoed the room. Everyone present jumped and cried as they saw the man wearing the camera fall to the ground.

The guns kept blazing for a few minutes and it was clear to Adhira and others that their agents had no time to hide or save themselves. The silence that followed in the room was the loudest of all.

Kamira... Kamira... they heard one of the men shout in Arabic.

"Camera," Adhira translated in shock. "He is pointing at the camera."

The camera that was relaying live feed to Adhira and others was now showing the ground, which was splattered red with the blood of their agents.

They heard a lot of commotion and suddenly, they were facing a man. His face was entirely covered but Adhira could see his eyes.

"Ikhtiyaar," Adhira whispered as she recognised him. Everyone present stared at her and then at the screen.

"Are you sure?" the Home Minister asked urgently as he walked closer to the screen.

"I can never forget those eyes," Adhira hissed.

"This is for you," Ikhtiyaar spoke in fluent English as he turned the camera and pointed it at a man crouching on the ground.

"Oh no! Nikhar," Adhira cried, clutching at her chest.

"We got your man," Ikhtiyaar shouted.

Nikhar was badly bruised and covered in blood. His one eye was oozing fresh blood and he was crying.

Rahma... rahma... min fadlik kun rahiman. li'awladi... bism allah... Ikhti—

Bang!

And Nikhar dropped dead on the ground.

"Have mercy, please have mercy... for my children. In the name of God. Please have mercy, Ikhti—" Adhira translated as tears stained her cheeks.

Ikhtiyaar kept dead Nikhar in focus for a while, then pointed it back to himself.

"First, witness this," and Ikhtiyaar pointed the camera around. At least ten agents were lying dead on the ground. A collective gasp echoed in the room as they saw the bodies of their trusted men sprawled on the ground, mutilated and bloodied.

"Liked the view?" Ikhtiyaar laughed as he pointed the camera back to himself. Adhira's blood curdled at the sound. "My favourite sight. Blood of Indians."

He paused for dramatic effect, then continued, "When I got to know that you are planning a silent attack, I realised it must be because of the whore who escaped last week… know this, when I come to you, which I soon will, I will find that whore and kill her myself," Ikhtiyaar barked and pointing his gun at the camera, he shot at the lens, making the line go dark.

PENTAGON

"This is horrible," the General whispered, falling on his seat. "Ten agents dead. One is either captured or missing," he wiped his face to gain some composure.

Adhira turned to Rudhir and swung a slap squarely on his face. The noise rang in the room.

"This is your fault," she barked. "You got them killed. And how dare you expose my asset? You got Nikhar killed, how are we going to work in the Middle East now? He ran an orphanage with more than twenty children, that's how he used the money that he earned by smuggling, to feed innocent children. What will happen to those children now? Do you think that Ikhtiyaar would leave them alone? You all just wanted to kill. 'Greater good' you said!" she shot a dirty look at the Home Minister, "Well, congratulations! You have just created at least fifteen more terrorists and you have thrown at least six little girls into the sex trade," Adhira barked.

"Adhira, we didn't mean for it to happen," the Home Minister started. "We lost good men today."

"And their blood is on your hands," Adhira snapped. "This is your fault," she pointed at Rudhir. "You exposed me in the UK and now, you have derailed my whole work in Tehran… This…" she pointed at the black screen and continued, "This is just too much…" and she walked to the door.

She was almost out when she turned and said, "And I hope you pompous fools have realised that there is a mole in your bloody Home Ministry, not in IB or any other agency.

If you wish to continue with my services, call me. But just know this, I don't want any government personnel, including you Mr R&AW, near me anymore."

And with this, she stormed out, tears still leaking from her eyes.

"Oh no," Patricia whispered as Adhira relayed the tragedy of the day to her team. "Ten dead…"

"And one missing or captured," Adhira added solemnly. "And Nikhar…"

"Oh Nikhar," Patricia cried.

"All because of me. He saved my ass so many times. He literally saved me this time, without him, I would have definitely been dead. And how did I repay him," Adhira sobbed. "All because of my intel."

"His children," Ava added sadly.

"Future brainwashed terrorists," Adhira shook her head in defeat. "All because of me!"

"Not you," Franc consoled. "You didn't give any potent information about him yesterday that could have helped your R&AW man to track him down. Nikhar was very popular, he had dealings with all sorts. If it is on someone, it is on him!"

"I gave the name," Adhira closed her eyes in grief. She could not erase Nikhar's scared, bloodied face from her mind. How he was pleading…

"Not your fault," Franc stressed. "And if you want to do something, work on avenging him. Find the man who killed him and so many agents there, don't cry and be miserable. Be yourself," he encouraged.

Adhira wiped her face and nodded.

"Where is Rudhir?" Patricia asked.

"We are on our own now," Adhira gritted her teeth. "It is all because of him."

"He is just following orders," Patricia tried to reason. "We all work as a team, we follow each other. He follows a different direction, that's all."

"Stop defending him," Adhira shrieked. "He is not part of this team. He is not in our Pentagon. He is out now and he is not coming back."

"Adhira," Franc started. "As much as I hate his guts…" he sighed. "First for getting you killed, well almost killed. Then this, but he is there on the ground with you. We always keep local support, it does not matter who."

"I will find some other support," Adhira snapped.

"There is a mole in your ministry and who knows where else. You can trust Rudhir, at least to the point that he would not betray you outright," Patricia exclaimed. "His love for you is his weakness, exploit it if need be, but stay safe."

Adhira's mouth hung open at her words. How could she! She was about to retort when her phone buzzed.

Adhira stared at the screen and spoke, "I am gonna put you all on mute, let's listen to this," and putting her team on mute, she took the call.

"When I heard that there was some trouble in the Middle East, I didn't expect you to be a part of it," a voice boomed from the other end of the line. "But when I heard some girl escaped, yours was the first name that came to my mind."

"Madam Special Ops," Adhira smiled as she addressed her.

"Well, yeah. Who else," Madam Special Ops laughed. "Did you miss me?"

"How can I ever forget working with you on Butch's case? The world's most wanted terrorist and America enlists my team to handle it. It was a mission to remember," Adhira laughed with her.

"I thought so too. It was fun to work on. But I had thought that after the money we paid you, you and your team must have retired by now… but it turns out you haven't,"

Madam Special Ops complained. "I don't feel so special anymore. You know, *the Pentagon* working only for me."

"Well Madam Special Ops, you know that we don't ever stay still," Adhira replied calmly.

'She is so pretentious,' Franc sent a message on chat. Adhira suppressed laughter.

"Did you really escape the clutches of Tehranis and that Ikhtiyaar?" Madam Special Ops asked very seriously.

"I can neither confirm nor deny that," Adhira responded. "But do you know something about Ikhtiyaar?"

"We have heard many things about him, but as his target is not us, we don't bother with him."

Adhira could hear the casual shrug in her voice.

"Okay, can you share some of these things that you have heard?" Adhira insisted.

"You know, I would if I could," Madam Special Ops chimed.

"Madam Special Ops, I know that you have not called me to discuss the time of the day," Adhira spoke dramatically.

"Of course, I didn't," Madam Special Ops huffed. "But first tell me, did you have something to do with Nikhar's murder?"

"I cannot say anything with regards to it," Adhira's face hardened at this.

"I thought so, you worked with him like we did. Now, you have gotten the best smuggler in the region dead," Madam Special Ops huffed.

"How can I help you, Madam Special Ops?" Adhira spoke through gritted teeth.

"I have called to help you this time," Madam Special Ops spoke very seriously.

"Okay," Adhira replied sceptically.

"I care for you, so I am telling you this..." Madam Special Ops started and Adhira laughed sarcastically, which didn't miss Madam Special Ops' ears. "Well, fine. You are a perfect asset and I don't want you dying of Ebola!" she corrected.

"Ebola?" Adhira blanched.

"Yes, it is a rumour that last week, post your miraculous escape, a few, not one or two, but a good number of bodies had been dug out of the ground in West Africa," Madam Special Ops informed. Goose bumps covered Adhira's body as she turned and looked at her team. Her shock was reflected on their faces. "Congo, Liberia, Guinea, these three are known to have missing corpses. I don't know if you know but Zaire ebolavirus is the deadliest strain of all, and that's what these corpses were infected with. Its fatality rate was nearly 90% and once infected with the original virus, there is no cure for it."

"Where are the bodies?" Adhira asked sharply.

"On their way to India," Madam Special Ops sighed sadly, and Adhira's jaw dropped.

"Miranda, are you sure?" Adhira finally used her name.

"I am so sure about this that I am not offended that you just took my name," Madam Special Ops stressed.

"When is it coming to India? Which route? Is Ikhtiyaar behind it?" Adhira asked quickly.

"If it is on schedule, it is due to arrive in Pakistan on a private plane tomorrow. And enter India via Ladakh," Madam Special Ops informed.

"I hope you are aware how wide Ladakh is," Adhira cried. "How are we supposed to stop this?"

"This cannot get out and you cannot take support of the border control. Half of that area is filled with terrorists disguised as locals, I think you know that," Madam Special Ops continued.

"I know," Adhira groaned as she wiped her face.

"But," Madam Special Ops sighed, "one of my informers have told me which route they are possibly taking."

"Which one?" Adhira asked quickly.

"It will be an unmarked truck that will contain corpses. It will enter via a small dirt road. I have it marked on a map, well, rough coordinates. In no circumstances, you are to open that truck without a hazmat suit. If exposed, you are dead, you hear me," Madam Special Ops ordered.

"I hear you," Adhira sighed.

"I will email you the coordinates," Madam Special Ops spoke stiffly. "But be cautious Adhira, this is not going to be easy. One whiff and you are gone."

"I hear you," Adhira nodded, feeling disturbed. "This is entering India tomorrow?"

"I am pretty sure that Pakistanis are not going to keep rotting corpses infected with Ebola in their hanger for long. I think they will be transported immediately," Madam Special Ops sighed.

"Wow, thank you. What can I do for you in return for this information?" Adhira asked.

"Oh, you will owe me one," Madam Special Ops laughed.

"I would rather do your bidding now," Adhira rolled her eyes.

"No, you will owe me one. And make sure that your Home Minister and Prime Minister know about this too. I would like to have an ace up my sleeve as leverage in future some time," Madam Special Ops laughed and disconnected.

Adhira stared at her phone for a while then looked at her team.

"What is the plan?" Franc asked, unmuting himself.

"I…" Adhira was still speechless.

"This changes everything," Samuel groaned. "A bioweapon? This is ridiculously dangerous."

"That's what I am thinking…" Adhira nodded. "Why would anyone do something so dangerous? I mean, digging out corpses, multiple corpses. For what?"

"An act of terrorism, what else?" Ava added.

"I know, but why? Why are they going to such lengths?" Franc wondered. "First XRS, then getting that Pristine woman a diplomat position, then this… What is their ultimate goal?"

"Beats me," Adhira shrugged. "When I was held as a prisoner there, Ikhtiyaar didn't say a thing about why he was doing it. Only that he was planning to go to Afghanistan in coming days."

"Why didn't you tell us this before?" Patricia scolded. She shuffled through her notes and cried, "Not once did you mention that he was due to arrive in Afghanistan."

"Seeing the present condition of Afghanistan," Adhira sighed, "You think that we can activate any asset there? With Taliban in power now, I highly doubt any of our assets will work with us now, or even if they are alive."

"That's true, and none of us can now enter Taliban. It is very volatile at present," Patricia agreed. "You will *not* enter Afghanistan at any cost Adhira, is that clear?" she glared.

"I know… I am not *that stupid!*" Adhira rolled her eyes at Patricia. "My disguise as a man has been blown many times there, and I have always resorted to using a *burkha* to protect myself. But now with the Taliban in power, I doubt that poor women there are even allowed to see the sunlight. I cannot risk it."

Patricia, Ava, Franc and Samuel stared at her in shock.

"I…" Samuel hesitated as he spoke. "I would love to see your disguise as a man. I have never seen it. I mean, how are you even able to pull that off?"

Adhira smiled at his question. She knew that he was only saying this to lighten the mood.

"If I survive this attack on my country, I promise I will show you my disguise," Adhira laughed.

"Don't be ridiculous," Franc scolded. "You will live… if anyone can survive it, you can."

"I like your confidence," Adhira grinned. "Now, for tomorrow…"

"What is the plan?" Patricia asked seriously. "And what do you need?"

"I need a hazmat suit. Can you arrange one for me at the airport? And a car, of course," Adhira thought. "And, I think I need Ebola Vaccine, just to be safe."

"Yes, it will be arranged. The vaccine, we need to see. Didn't you get it done last year?" Patricia asked.

"I did, but as I am about to face the deadliest strain, I think I need a booster at the least..." Adhira nodded.

"If they pulled out the corpses from the very first strand of the Zaire strain, then the vaccine will not save you," Franc spoke sadly. "It doesn't matter how many doses you get."

"Wow, you are so hopeful," Adhira screwed up her face at him.

"Flight booked for tomorrow at 6 am," Patricia informed.

Adhira nodded.

"What about Rudhir?" Patricia asked.

"I am not taking him," Adhira closed her eyes as her nostrils flared.

"You need backup, if not him, then pick another asset," Patricia insisted.

"I have lived in Ladakh for four years, Patty. I know that place better than Delhi. I can even predict which dirt road Miranda is going to show me on the map. Ladakh was my favourite place during my tenure in the Indian Military, I will be fine there."

"It was six years ago, and don't forget that the place ruined your life," Patricia growled.

"Ladakh didn't ruin me, your Rudhir did. I am not taking him with me. And as I have to wake up tomorrow at 3 for the flight, I think I would go to sleep now," Adhira spoke irately.

"Fine. You take your sleep now. We will make all the arrangements. I will also arrange for a vaccination at the airport itself. Hazmat suit, car, and the vaccine will be there for you at Ladakh airport when you land at around 7 am," Patricia spoke.

"Thank you, Patty. You are so resourceful," Adhira smiled.

"We all serve at the pleasure, darling," Patricia winked.

"We all do," Adhira agreed.

"Any weapons needed?" Samuel asked.

"I need information on the rifle that can fire the XRS bullets. Maybe we can narrow down the location of XRS via the rifle," Adhira spoke thoughtfully.

"On it, then," Samuel nodded.

"Thank you," Adhira replied.

"What about us," Ava asked.

"Can you and Franc dig a little more into this Pristine?" Adhira spoke suddenly. "Scan through Pakistan's, Afghanistan's and Iran's newspapers if need be. Look for Ikhtiyaar and Pristine. What if some news had covered their faces at some point? These countries have good media support. Try and find something on Pristine. I want to know, why the hell did they go through so much trouble to put Pristine in a diplomat position? Was it just for the XRS bullets or something more sinister? They must have a wider agenda. Please look into it," Adhira spoke quietly.

"I will help you," Franc spoke to Ava.

"Thanks," Ava nodded. "This is gonna take me a while on my own."

"Serving at pleasure," Franc laughed.

"Whose pleasure are we talking about actually?" Adhira asked her team with narrowed eyes.

"Each other's," Patricia chimed. "After all, we five are the *Pentagon*."

She laughed and everyone followed. Adhira bade farewell to her team and went to bed. Tomorrow was going to be a huge day.

LADAKH

"Hazmat would be in the boot of the car," Patricia informed as Adhira stepped out of the plane on Ladakh Airport and felt the fresh air breeze across her face. "And once this mission is done, can we all go and enjoy Ladakh? I saw images on Google, it is heaven."

"It is indeed heaven," Adhira smiled as she looked at the stunning horizon. The beautiful mountains were visible from the dense cloudy sky, and as the clouds shifted, she could see ice-capped mountain peaks. The air was chilly and Adhira hugged her coat close to her body. "But, by the time this mission will be done, it will be too cold to visit."

"Duh! I live in Canada, I can handle the cold!" Patricia rolled her eyes.

"Yes, but the rest of us cannot," Adhira felt a chill as the cold air brushed her face.

"Fine…" Patricia accepted defeat. "I am so jealous of you right now."

"Jealous?" Adhira laughed. "I am about to hunt down a truck full of Ebola corpses," she whispered. "I would gladly swap places with you."

Adhira walked out of the airport and stopped dead. "I seriously wish to swap places with you right now," Adhira gritted her teeth. "What is *he* doing here?"

"You hate him, but we all love you. And you are not going on another mission alone, ever," Patricia snapped. "Rudhir stays, else…" she threatened.

"You are so resourceful but you couldn't find me another lackey?" Adhira groaned. She didn't care if Rudhir heard her.

"Lackey?" Patricia shrieked. "Adhira, he is the head of R&AW, he is not your servant!"

"Whatever," Adhira rolled her eyes. "So I guess there are two hazmat suits in the boot?" she asked as she opened the rear end of the car.

"Yes. We cannot have him infected either. And he already got vaccinated so he can tell where the vaccination guy is so that you too can get your shot," Patricia continued.

"Fine," Adhira snapped. "Gotta go."

"Good luck Adhira, stay in touch and be careful. We can take hundreds of missions, but there is only one of you," Patricia stressed.

"Yeah, yeah… bye now," and Adhira disconnected and glared at Rudhir. He gestured a man to come forward.

"You need a shot for Ebola?" The man asked.

Adhira nodded. The man did his job quickly and left.

"Shall we?" Rudhir spoke as he walked to the driver's side. He was visibly nervous.

Adhira sighed and got in. She really didn't want to, but one thing that she never did was disagree with her team. After all, it was her team who always kept her safe.

Rudhir drove in silence. Before meeting Rudhir here, Adhira had planned to relish the scenic beauty of the place while looking for the unmarked truck, but now she was forced to relive some memories that she had so painfully pushed back in her mind.

"So…" Rudhir started awkwardly. "How did you find out about this bioweapon?"

Adhira chewed her lips as she stared out.

"Fine, I realise that you won't be interested in sharing the secret source," Rudhir nodded curtly.

"Actually," Adhira started acidly. "My source wants your Home Minster and Prime Minister to know that it was *her!*"

"Really?" Rudhir raised his eyebrows at this. "Who is it?"

"Miranda Jones, head of Secret Services Ops, United States," Adhira replied flatly.

"Oh really?" Rudhir looked impressed. "I didn't know that you had such highly placed sources."

"You don't know hell about me," Adhira snapped. "You didn't bother knowing... you just – you just... never mind," Adhira sighed. She wanted to scream, she wanted to punch him and she wanted to kill him. But it was not worth it.

"What I just?" Rudhir demanded as he parked the car at a side.

"We are on a time-bound mission, or have you forgotten that, Mr R&AW?" Adhira scolded him.

"I haven't forgotten anything, and I haven't forgotten this place," Rudhir pointed outside. Adhira looked where he was pointing and her heart thudded to a stop. It was their spot. A small, stunningly beautiful lake with sparkling blue water. This lake was not listed on any tourist site so it was still untouched and pristine.

Tears leaked from her eyes as she gazed at it, unwanted memories pouring in. He raised his hand to wipe her face but she slapped his hand rather harshly.

"You lost your right to touch me when you betrayed me," Adhira snapped.

"For the life of me, how did I betray you?" Rudhir shouted back. "After what you did. You shot your commanding officer, damn it!"

Adhira stepped out of the car, slammed the door shut and walked to the side of the lake. Rudhir followed her quietly. As they stood exactly in the spot they used to, years ago, she spoke.

"You didn't ask," Adhira whispered. "You didn't ask me once why I did it!"

"I know that you had an argument with him," Rudhir informed. "Something about a posting!"

"And you thought that I had suddenly gotten mad? Lost my mind? For how long did you know me back then? We were together for eight years by then. We even knew each other's breath. Why didn't you ask me why I did that?" Adhira asked with fisted fingers.

Rudhir didn't respond to this. He just stared at her.

"What do you think happened all those years ago?" Adhira asked tersely.

Rudhir looked at her uncomfortably.

"Well?" She demanded with raised eyebrows.

"You had a row with Commander Seth and you shot him in anger," Rudhir commented.

"And why do you think that happened? What could be the possible reason for such actions? Didn't you consider this once? Didn't you bother checking for it?" she was turning red with anger.

"I was told that you disagreed, you lost your temper. You are, well were, known to lose it in anger!" Rudhir looked scared now.

Adhira was breathing like a dragon, the only missing thing from her nostrils was actual fire.

"I helped you, you know," Rudhir added. "I begged dad to save you. I even cut a deal with him. He promised me to ensure that your life is spared, in exchange–"

"In exchange of what?" Adhira asked in disbelief.

"If I never contact you again," Rudhir looked apologetic.

"Why are you here now?" Adhira demanded. "What about your deal?"

"This case took precedence. You are the best, there is no doubt about it," Rudhir made an excuse.

"Your dad is dead. Isn't he?" Adhira asked shamelessly.

Rudhir nodded solemnly.

"So, it was all because of you?" Adhira spoke through gritted teeth.

"What?" Rudhir was shocked.

"You and your asshole dad," Adhira cursed.

"ADHIRA" Rudhir shouted. "I will tolerate anything but I will not accept you insulting my father. He is dead, for God's sake."

"How did he die?" Adhira asked quickly.

"Heart attack, died in his sleep," Rudhir whispered.

"Damn! The fucker didn't even suffer," Adhira cursed again.

Rudhir grabbed her shoulder and pressed her against the car.

"You…" Rudhir paused to gain some composure, "You will not insult my father. How dare you? He is dead. You are alive because of him. Are you truly as insane as they said you were? Have you no respect?" He was fuming.

Adhira pushed him back.

"Insane, am I? If I am so insane then get the fuck away from me. You are just as pathetic as he was. Like Father, like son. What else could I have gotten, getting mixed with your kind," Adhira shouted.

"Shut up. You have no idea what he did for you," Rudhir screamed back.

"I know very well what he did. He took my life. My honour. My career. My love... Well, you and your love were never mine, so that's one thing I can never blame him for," Adhira snorted.

"You think I didn't love you?" Rudhir couldn't believe her. "I still love you, you dumb woman. Despite your insanity, your tantrums, your insults for my poor father."

"Love? Where was your love when they accused me of being a cold-blooded murderer? Did you consider asking me even once? Asking me why I did it?"

Rudhir was speechless.

"You just ran off to daddy and cut a deal. What did you think happened? I suddenly lost my senses and shot my own commanding officer? Why would I do it? You knew me for years, yet you believed it when they said I was mad? Shot a man for no apparent reason?"

"My dad saved you," Rudhir repeated.

"Your dad," Adhira scowled, "was the one who ordered my court-martial."

"No. You are wrong," Rudhir shook his head. "He assured me that he saved you."

"I didn't need saving. Had you asked me once, you would have known. I was innocent," Adhira whispered.

Rudhir was stunned by this. "What?"

"I was innocent, I had all the proof in the world. The entire panel was in my favour, but suddenly Colonel Singh was replaced by your father and everything went haywire. Colonel Singh was my mentor, he was like my father, and *your father* replaced him giving the reason that Colonel Singh is always biased towards me. Instead, it was your bloody father who was biased. And all because of you!" Adhira shrieked.

"You didn't shoot your CO?" Rudhir asked, shocked.

"I did shoot him. Of course, I shot him," Adhira shook her head.

Rudhir rolled his eyes and Adhira punched the car to control herself. She wanted to punch Rudhir but didn't want to live up to the reputation of being crazy and impulsive, at this moment at least.

"If you had bothered asking me, you would have known," Adhira spoke again.

"Okay, I am asking now. Why did you shoot your CO?" Rudhir glared at her.

"Do you know what my first thought was when I walked away from the incident? After I shot him?" Adhira whispered sadly and Rudhir just stared at her.

"That you will support me. No matter what, you will stand with me. But you didn't. So much happened to me post that incident, but your betrayal, your lack of trust, that's what broke me… when you didn't show up for my trial, that was the moment I realised how terribly alone I was, but…" Adhira sighed as she paused. "But it was worth it, wasn't it? I was a simple military personnel with you and now I am an international spy. I earn millions, have all the luxury that anyone can dream of. Russians, Americans, everyone want me. I have a team who would die for me. I have friends who accept me for who I am, no matter how crazy or on the verge of 'losing it'… I am free, yes I am rogue but I am free. So, thank you, Mr R&AW, well, you and your bloody father."

"Yes, you should thank us, you are alive because of us. Because of my dad. Your actions would have resulted in lifetime imprisonment or death," Rudhir scathed.

"Oh, that's what your dad said, did he?" Adhira asked in a mocking tone, now smiling broadly. "You gave up on me to such an extent that you didn't even bother reading the court script of my hearing?"

"Court scripts are confidential," Rudhir stated the obvious.

"Since when do you care about confidential?" Adhira mocked.

"Since always," Rudhir stared at her in disbelief.

"Meh!" Adhira shrugged. "You should read them though."

"Why?" Rudhir demanded.

"Because, then you will know the true face of your devious father. It was he who asked for the death penalty. It was him who forced the jury panel to do my court-martial. It was all because of him. And why? Just because you asked him to…"

"No, you are lying. Why would he do that?" Rudhir demanded.

"Because his only son, his legacy, his pride, fell in love with an orphan. A mediocre girl who had 'no standards'. A girl who didn't suit his stature," Adhira laughed at her own words. "Your dad once said to me, *Boys in Rudhir's age like to experiment and do time pass. You too are just that, so don't get your hopes up. You too shall pass. Enjoy him while you can girl because you and he are never happening.*"

"Why didn't you say anything?" Rudhir asked, shocked.

"*He was your father.* I had no family. I was not going to drive a wedge between you both. Well, now that I think of it, it would have been better if I did…" Adhira laughed again.

Rudhir was about to speak when Adhira's phone buzzed. She raised her hand to quiet him and took the call.

"Why are you and R&AW dude stationary for so long?" Ava asked on the call.

"My mistake. Anyway Ava, why were you calling me?"

"First to know that you are okay. And to inform you something important and interesting," Ava chimed.

"And what is this important and interesting thing?" Adhira asked.

"I found Pristine. Your idea worked. I searched through all websites and found a photograph that resembles Pristine. It is actually a partial photograph but my face recognition software matched it 60% to Pristine," Ava informed.

"Partial? Why partial?" Adhira asked confused.

"It was not on any news site, it was on Facebook. We ran an algorithm across profiles in Pakistan, took a while, but we got a hit," Ava informed.

"That's excellent," Adhira exclaimed. "So, you have something concrete for me?"

"It was a newspaper clipping that someone had posted on FB, it was an obituary so I am guessing it is of Pristine's mother or close relative as the face matches so much. There was an address and I could make it out on the newspaper clipping," Ava informed. "I have already sent you the address. The clipping was old but it is a start. I am hopeful that you will find something there," Ava informed.

"Yes. That's an amazing job, Ava," Adhira complimented. "Only you could have done this."

"I know, right," Ava chimed with pride.

"Yeah, super proud of you," Adhira smiled.

"I also picked up some chatter," Ava spoke seriously now. "There is also a possibility that there is no bioweapon entering India today," she continued.

"What do you mean?" Adhira looked confused now.

"It might be a ruse to throw off their scent. You know, create a scenario to distract us from the main plot. While we hunt for this bioweapon, they attack as per the original plan," Ava wondered. "Now, I am not 100% sure of this, but Adhira it is highly likely that this bioweapon is not real."

"But Miranda is the head of the United States Special Ops team. She is not easily mistaken," Adhira whispered.

"That's why I am not sure," Ava groaned.

"What should I do then? Chase after the bioweapon or Pristine?" Adhira asked.

"We took a poll," Ava spoke quickly, "You know, like we always do in such cases."

"Obviously," Adhira nodded.

"We think you should go after Pristine. Because Pristine is, for sure, involved in this. And by getting to her, or knowing her agenda, you may find out the entire truth… if we know the reason, maybe we stop the attack after all."

"Ok, if this is what the Pentagon wants," Adhira nodded.

"And I have also started on a new approach towards finding about XRS mass production,"Ava added.

"And that is?" Adhira asked, pulling out her laptop from the car to check the address Ava had sent. "But before you tell me that, ask Patty to arrange for transport for me to get to the other side, please. You already have my location."

"One sec," Ava spoke and Adhira heard her quickly type something on her computer. "Patty says that transport is already arranged and is on your way now. ETA 18 minutes."

"Thank you. So, about this XRS," Adhira spoke as she pulled out her bag from the trunk of the car and started to undress.

"What are you doing?" Rudhir blanched as she took off her jeans.

Adhira glared at him as she strapped something on her thigh and wore a loose-fitting bottoms.

"I am tracking all the scientists capable of making a weapon as deadly as XRS. I have narrowed them down to 17 across the globe. I will screen them all, do a thorough background check, and if anyone fits the pattern, we will pick the person up," Ava spoke.

"Sounds like a plan," Adhira appreciated her work. "I should get prepped now. I will see you later then," Adhira spoke and disconnected the call.

Turning her bag upside down, she opened a secret compartment and pulled out a thin strip that looked and felt like skin.

"What?" Rudhir asked, shocked. But Adhira didn't pay heed to him. Taking off her shirt in the middle of the road, she strapped the skin just below her breasts. She then took out her Indian passport, money in various currencies, and pushed them in the skin like strap. She then put her shirt back on. Then taking out a *burkha*, a Pakistani passport and money, she started working on her face.

She worked quickly on her face for ten minutes, while Rudhir just stared at her, open-mouthed.

"Where are you going?" Rudhir demanded.

"Change of plans, you can go to hell if you like. I am going on a mission," Adhira spoke as she put on the *burkha* and placed the passport and money in her small pouch. "My bag and the things it contains are precious. You must ensure that it is not lost. Can I trust you enough to not lose my bag?" she demanded as she thrust her bag on his chest.

"I want to come too," Rudhir spoke quickly.

"This is *my mission.* My team and I designed it. You are not a part of us. You never will be, so do what you do best, and run away like a good boy," Adhira mocked as she started to walk away.

"Where are you going?" Rudhir demanded.

Adhira didn't reply, just stood at a distance, waiting.

"Are you going inside Pakistan?" Rudhir demanded, grabbing her hand tightly.

"I am a spy and I will go where the job takes me."

Rudhir pushed her burkha aside and grabbed her face, "I love you. I won't lose you again."

"You lost me when you left me," Adhira pushed him.

She saw a 4X4 approach from a distance.

"Stay out of sight. Just keep my bag safe for your own sake," Adhira pushed him.

"You shot your CO in the back. You paralysed him for life. He didn't attack you, you shot him in the back," Rudhir shouted.

The 4X4 was approaching but it was still a few miles away. Adhira turned and faced him.

"I shot him because he was raping a 9-year-old Kashmiri girl. He dragged that girl into his cabin. I saw him. I tried to stop him but he pushed me out. I heard the girl's cries. She was begging for mercy. I banged the door, but he didn't stop. So, I took an aim from the window. I shot him because he was raping a 9-year-old. Your dad knew this. The entire jury knew this. I have statements from the girl's parents. From that little girl, I had proof. No one accused me. No one except your pervert father. He said, 'no matter what the CO was doing, shooting a superior, especially in the back is highly disgraceful.' He called for my court-martial. He forced the hand of others using his seniority. He did this. *You did this.* You didn't even ask me once, you didn't come to me and say, 'Dhira, I know you. You must have a reason. Tell me why you did it.' You just went to your dad and ruined everything... I know you won't believe me even now, so go to Ava. Ask her for the court records. She has them. Read it all yourself. You will know the truth. Read it, Mr R&AW, and you will know what kind of men live in your family. You are like your dad... bastard in, bastard out."

And with that, she put back her burkha on.

The 4X4 stopped in front of her.

"The sky is blue," a man spoke from the driver's seat.

"No, it is purple, look again," Adhira replied.

The man nodded, satisfied with the code words.

"Who is he?" The man asked, pointing at Rudhir who looked as if Adhira had stabbed him mercilessly.

"Just another bastard," Adhira shook her head.

"Bothering you?" The man gave Rudhir a dangerous look.

"I am on a schedule, let's go," and without sparing a look towards Rudhir, Adhira got in the front seat with an unknown man, and drove away.

THE TRANSPORTER

"You have the address?" Adhira asked as she took off the Niqab and exposed her face. "I feel so suffocated. Mind turning up the AC?"

"Sure," the man did the needful. He glanced at her face and nodded appreciatively.

"What?" Adhira demanded, not liking the appreciative smirk.

"General is a ladies man, he is going to be very happy," the man snorted.

"What?" Adhira asked, shocked.

"You are one beautiful woman, it will please him," he gave her a sly look. "You should rest, it will be a long drive till there and longer over there," and he laughed.

"What are you implying?" Adhira asked, partly shocked, partly irritated.

"I am not implying anything, lady. Just rest, it will be more than eight hours ride," and he sat straight and continued to drive.

Adhira called Patricia and spoke, "*qu'as-tu dit à ce conducteur?*"

"Umm… why are you speaking French?" Patricia asked suspiciously.

"*En raison du conducteur… Maintenant répond moi,*" Adhira insisted.

"I just asked the driver to drop you off at the mentioned address. He is the transporter. His job is to get people over the border. He is very efficient," Patricia informed.

"Alors, pourquoi me traite-t-il comme une putain de pute?" Adhira hissed.

"What? He is treating you like a prostitute?" Patricia repeated the question.

"Je demande la même chos," Adhira rolled her eyes.

"I know you are asking the same to me..." Patricia translated and Adhira hissed furiously. "Well, he is just a transporter and knows nothing. Let him do his job and ignore him. And well, if he knows anything, I think it would be wise to get some info because we are sailing through unchartered waters here. Ava is finding more details on the address though. Her focus is divided. She found Pristine's address and then started to look for the scientists as the idea clicked her at that time."

"Well, thanks then, I guess. *Au moins, trouvez-moi des détails sur ce pilote,*" Adhira groaned.

"Yes, I will get you the details of the driver," Patricia sighed and disconnected.

Adhira closed her eyes wondering what to do when the driver spoke, *"Moi French, Madame."*

"What?" Adhira laughed as she looked at him quizzically.

"Well, I know French, madam," he laughed with her. "Of course my accent is not as good as yours, but I transport people of all nationalities here. Many Europeans and Americans come to me to cross the border illegally. And if they pay handsomely, I oblige. So yes, I know French and many other languages. I can't speak that well, but I understand it all."

"Oh ok," Adhira replied, feeling embarrassed.

"And if I am not wrong, you just asked your friend to find details on me in the end there, didn't you?" he asked.

Adhira nodded.

"Why don't I give you my details so you can validate them when your friend comes back with more information?" he offered with a laugh.

Adhira turned to face him, intrigued.

"I am Arth Bhatia, well, that's my real name…" he grinned. "Feels so weird to give it to someone unknown these days." He laughed loudly. "But seeing how you were talking to your friend, I am sure you would find that out soon enough…" he shrugged.

"What are you called otherwise?" Adhira asked, amused by his casual demeanour.

"Well, here I am called a 'cabbie' or 'transporter'."

Adhira nodded and studied his profile. He had a long, tanned face with a stubble. His cheeks were slightly pigmented but his cheekbones were sharp, hiding the imperfections of the skin. He had a straight face and full lips. Overall, he was handsome and kind of attractive.

"What are you called?" Arth asked seriously. "Your real name, please."

"Adhira Shekhawat," she laughed too.

He gave her a sharp look and whistled. "Oh, so the prodigal daughter has returned."

"Prodigal daughter?" Adhira asked, shocked.

"I have heard of a girl named Adhira who had balls bigger than most men in the entire world. Shot her CO to save a teenager from getting raped. Got court-martialled and disappeared from the grid," Arth looked at her with high regard.

"That's me," Adhira nodded, silently wondering why Rudhir had never heard of this.

As finally she had a chance to listen to Rudhir's side, for the first time in years, the thought of Rudhir didn't envelop her with hatred. He didn't betray her. Yes, she lost everything because of him but his intentions were good. All he did was protect her, even if his bastard of a father had royally screwed her up.

"How old was that teenage girl exactly?" Arth asked, bringing her back to her surroundings.

"She wasn't a teenager. That poor girl was barely nine years old back then," Adhira sighed. "It was not a good day…"

"Wow, only nine," Arth whistled. "Of course, it was not a good day but you did an amazing thing back then. And, I am honoured to drive you to your destination," Arth looked impressed.

"So, have we established that I am not a hooker?" Adhira asked seriously.

"Yeah, but then why are you going to the General's residence. You know why girls go there, right?" Arth asked with a quizzical look. "That old hog will jump your bones, I tell you. He looks at any girl and wants to, well you know, bang her."

"I have some work there. Need some information. Do you know this General?" Adhira asked curiously.

"Every military person in the area knows the General," Arth laughed.

"I am ex-military of the area, I don't know him," Adhira wondered.

"Well, you are young so you won't, but every military person who was here during the time of Kargil war knows him. He was the mastermind that caused the Kargil War," Arth scoffed. "So many dead, just to fuel his hatred," he gripped the steering wheel tightly.

"Were you in the War too?" Adhira asked him, trying to gauze his age. He didn't look old enough to be in the army to witness Kargil War.

"I was in the final year of NDA, barely twenty years old when the Kargil War broke. I remember the night we got the call, where all final year students were assigned duties and shipped to the respective locations to fight. I was scared, but I was trained for it. I fought them, I killed them, I protected our motherland, but what I wasn't trained for was the bloodshed of my own brothers. I had to carry torn, broken bodies of my co-cadets from the field. The blood, the broken bones, the pain I felt during the war was nothing in comparison to what followed," Arth shivered.

"What followed?" Adhira whispered, her body was covered in goose bumps.

"The nightmares, PTSD, living and re-living the war all over again," Arth quivered again.

"Hey, I am not weak, okay" Arth defended himself. "It's just that I was..."

"Young," Adhira added.

"Yes, barely twenty. Now I think I can stomach all that, but back then, it got..."

"Difficult," Adhira gave him an understanding nod. "We all grow with time and experience."

"Yes," Arth relaxed a bit.

"So, you left the army after the war?" Adhira enquired.

"Yes, many did. Preparing for war and actually fighting one are two very different things... the loss and stress gets too much to think sanely. I stayed home for a while but it was too much. You know family drama, societal pressure and stuff. My parents passed away the year after the war so I came back here, but didn't join the army. Just stayed here, explored the land. I roamed this area for more than a year, discovered many, *many* secret passages. Soon I decided to work as a 'transporter', and well, here I am," Arth laughed.

"Why didn't you re-join the army?" Adhira asked.

"Something broke in me, that feeling of sacrifice. I am not proud of it, believe me. But I saw too much during the war and I don't think I can do it again," Arth sighed.

"I get it," Adhira nodded. "After my court-martial, I just didn't feel like working for the government. I mean I don't do anything against our nation, but I just can't work for them..."

"Yeah, when you are employed with the army or something, you cannot bend the rules as per your requirements," Arth agreed.

"Bend?" Adhira mock laughed. "I don't have any rules, let alone bend them."

"Me neither," Arth laughed with her.

"I like you, Mrs..." Arth asked with raised eyebrows.

"Miss, always and forever Miss," Adhira smiled.

Arth beamed.

"I like you, Ms Shekhawat. You are a badass," he grinned. "How can I be of assistance to you?"

Adhira hesitated. Stories and all aside, Arth was a stranger and she always preferred to thoroughly study a person before trusting them.

"Well, given that you are reluctant, let me tell you a bit about your destination," Arth smiled. "General was the prime reason Kargil War was fought."

"Am I going to the house of one of the four Generals termed as 'Gang of four', who were responsible for the war?" Adhira blanched.

"Yes and no. General is not one of the four, instead, he was the one who instigated them," Arth informed. "Hayat Khan—"

"Hold on," Adhira interrupted, raising her hand. "Hayat Khan, as in Josh. The leader of the extremist wing of Pakistan, who is hell bent on ruining India, Hayat Khan?"

Arth grinned at Adhira's stunned expressions.

"Glad to see that you are realising the depth of the pit in which you are putting your leg," he laughed.

Adhira pouted nervously. This was new and dangerous, even for her... She had heard briefly about Josh and Hayat Khan, but as she was always dealing with ISIS or terrorist organisations rising and falling in the Middle-East, she never directly dealt with Josh organisation.

"Okay, continue," Adhira spoke. She wanted to gather as much information from Arth as possible. He looked at her curiously for a second, then spoke, "Hayat Khan was a teenager when India and Pakistan were divided. He blames India for many things, for all the horrendous things that happened in those days..."

"Teenager in 1947?" Adhira's jaw dropped.

"Yep, he is an old bat now. Must be 85 plus in age, still kicks ass like a young man though. And hops from one girl to another like one too..." Arth screwed his face. "Often, girls are transported from India for his pleasure. He sees them as 'Indian pride' and undressing them gives him unique pleasure..."

"What? Why do girls go there in the first place? And why *do you* make it happen?" Adhira was shocked.

"Poverty Adhira, poverty. They pay so much that poor girls agree... and if I won't do it, someone else will. I at least ensure that the girls are safely returned home... which, mind you, others won't," Arth scowled. "Anyway, I pray he dies soon... I hate him, seriously!"

"Okay," Adhira understood his reasons for transporting girls, but couldn't understand the edge in his tone. "Why such hatred?"

"He is the real reason behind Kargil war, won't you hate him too?" Arth asked in disbelief.

"I would, I mean I do... but your hatred sounds personal," Adhira added.

"It was because of him that I lost so much in my early years. Hell yes, my hate is personal. It is personal for everyone who fought in the war... personal for all the family members of the soldiers who fought then, dead or alive!" Arth snapped.

"I am sorry," Adhira shook her head. "I have seen many things, I have seen fights, and I have seen death up close. But I have not seen actual war, I was too young back then to understand it."

"How old are you?" Arth asked.

"I am thirty-three," Adhira informed.

"Hmm, then you must have been barely ten or eleven, securely wrapped up in your mumma's arms, watching the news of the war on the telly," Arth laughed.

"No television," Adhira smiled ruefully.

"Whatever. You seem well off, so your parents must have protected you from the horrors of the war, a good decision too," Arth summarised.

Adhira didn't reply, she just turned her face and looked outside.

"Hayat Khan was the mastermind behind Kargil War, and it is his address that we are going to," Adhira whispered to herself.

"Yes, and have you heard they are creating a Kargil War Memorial in Delhi? Calling it the biggest event of the century," Arth snorted.

"Yes, I am aware. It is not very far away from launch," Adhira dismissed casually, lost in her thoughts.

"I wonder why they are doing it in Delhi. We already have one here," Arth spoke.

"To honour the warriors of Kargil. To honour you..." Adhira smiled.

"Remember me when you visit it, okay?" Arth joked.

"I will," Adhira smiled.

"Take your parents there and ask them what they made you do when the war was going on," Arth added.

"Okay," Adhira replied flatly.

"I am sorry, when did they pass?" Arth apologised sincerely.

"How?" Adhira was shocked.

"I can read people," Arth spoke.

"Long ago," Adhira whispered.

"How long ago?" Arth stressed.

"Too long for me to end up in an orphanage at the time of the war... no one to hold me when we heard the horrors of war, just me and my own arms..." Adhira smiled.

Arth was speechless and there was a long silence in the car post this declaration.

"Who else is in the family of Hayat?" Adhira asked after a while.

"He had a son, who died in the war. His daughter-in-law ran away with someone else after the war. His daughter passed away too, in the early days of her life. It is rumoured that she was the victim of some riot in Pakistan. He has two grandchildren, a girl and a boy. It is said that the old man had brainwashed the children thoroughly… raised them to hate India and groomed them to ruin our country," Arth finished.

"How old would these grandchildren be?" Adhira asked suddenly.

"In their twenties, I guess," Arth shrugged.

"Have you seen these grandkids? Are they in Pakistan? Do you know their names?" Adhira asked, excited.

"Not seen them, haven't heard of them for long… old man had big plans for them. It is also rumoured that they ran away when they realised that their grandpa was a whack job," Arth laughed again.

"Now…" Arth spoke suddenly. "Look at the mountain there?" he pointed as he parked the car on a side.

Adhira looked ahead. It was a small hilltop, partly covered with ice. She nodded.

"We will get into Pakistan as soon as we cross that top," Arth spoke. "Which passport are you carrying?" he demanded.

Adhira raised her eyebrows at this question.

"I—" Arth spoke as he pulled out Pakistani, Chinese and Indian passports from different corners of the car, "have all 3." And he threw them in her lap.

Adhira looked at each, they were all valid passports.

"I don't have a Chinese passport," Adhira informed, handing him back his passports. He hid them in their spots again.

"Word of advice, always carry Chinese in these ranges. You never know which military you will encounter here… these are dangerous waters," Arth looked around for some movement.

"Give me your passports," Arth demanded. "I need to put them together with mine. You cannot risk getting caught with the wrong passport, or even worst, both passports."

Adhira sighed and handed him her fake Pakistani passport. Then, she lifted her *burkha* and pulled out her Indian passport from the skin pouch attached to her chest.

"Nice abs," Arth complimented.

Adhira glared at him, so he sat straight.

"For a girl with your courage and boldness, you are way too uptight, you know that?" Arth spoke as he hid her passports in their respective places.

"For a girl with my courage?" Adhira asked with raised eyebrows as Arth started to drive.

"Well yeah, entering Pakistan alone. With no backup, whatsoever," Arth shrugged. "What happens if you disappear?"

"Then I disappear," Adhira shrugged carelessly.

"Your French friend won't come looking for you?" Arth asked carefully.

"She is in Canada… so no, it would be very difficult for her to come looking for me," Adhira smiled.

"And your friend, who escorted you to my car?" Arth continued in the same tone.

"He is not my friend," Adhira twisted her mouth. "I have no friends… so if I am lost, if I die, I don't think anyone in the vicinity will even mourn me… Well, my team will, yes. But they are all internationally based."

"Seriously?" Arth was shocked.

"Yeah… I never realised this… and it pinches a bit to say it out loud but I have no one, and that's my truth," Adhira pouted. "Who do you have?"

"My brother, his family, my friends and other relatives…" Arth narrowed his eyes at Adhira.

"Good… when you are dumped at an orphanage at an age you don't even remember, you don't have any relatives," Adhira shrugged and Arth just gaped at her in shock.

They drove in silence as they crossed the hilltop.

"I knew we wouldn't be caught," Arth laughed as they safely entered the soil of Pakistan. "I know the border patrol's routine by heart, I even know when they do random rounds…"

"That's good," Adhira spoke, disinterested.

Arth drove to an isolated spot and stopped.

"Wait here and keep your head down," Arth ordered as he hopped out of his car and opened the back door. Adhira saw him slightly lift the car seat and pull out new number plates.

"Pakistan's number plate?" Adhira asked curiously.

Arth nodded and rushed outside.

He swapped the number plates on the front and back, ensured that he was not watched, then hid the Indian number plates under the back seat and drove again.

"You are smart," Adhira complimented.

"Smarter than you can anticipate," Arth winked.

"Have you heard of XRS?" Adhira asked suddenly.

"What?" Arth looked confused. "Is it a video game or something?" he sounded genuine. Adhira stared at his expressions for a while, reading him, trying to understand if he knew anything about XRS. But it was clear that he didn't.

"Nothing," Adhira sat back.

"Now sit straight, the ride is gonna get bumpy," Arth spoke as he started driving downhill.

"Whoooooaaaaaaaaaaaaaaa……..hahahahahahaha…" Arth laughed heartily as the XUV rolled down, uncontrolled at full speed.

"What?" Arth asked Adhira after good ten minutes of jumps and jacks. She was sitting comfortably, looking neither scared nor amused.

"I am used to worse shit," Adhira replied with an attitude.

"You are not easily pleased, are you?" Arth asked as he parked the car at a side, turned off the headlights, pulled out binoculars and looked around.

"When you live a life like mine, no..." Adhira rolled her eyes. "What are you looking for?"

"We are in Pakistan now and there are two check-posts in each direction," Arth pointed towards his left and right. "Border patrol will pass us in some time and once it passes us, we will fly... literally fly before the next one arrives and spots us."

"Okay," Adhira too looked around. "Won't the Pakistani number plates help us?"

"It will but I really don't want to get caught. Better safe than sorry," Arth shrugged.

"True," Adhira agreed.

"It's funny, I often get bored by the time I arrive here, but six hours with you, and time just flew by," Arth snorted. "Didn't even feel hungry."

"I could do with some food though," Adhira massaged her stomach.

"We cannot stop at any restaurant on our way. I have some food in the cooler box behind your seat, help yourself," Arth pointed.

Adhira pulled out two sandwiches from the cooler box and gave one to Arth. "It has beer too," Arth added.

"You want a drink?" Adhira asked as she started to pull out a beer.

"No, for you. I am driving..." Arth rolled his eyes at her.

"I am good with water," Adhira sat straight back. On a mission like this, she needed her alertness and wits at hand.

"How far?" Adhira asked after a while. "I need to use the loo."

Arth pouted at this.

"I can hold a little longer," Adhira added as she saw his expression.

"Here they come," Arth spoke as he pointed at the road and Adhira saw two jeeps pass them in slow motion.

They waited for a few minutes then Arth started to drive very slowly with the headlights still off. Once he crossed the road which had the patrol monitoring, he pressed his foot hard on the accelerator and it seemed to Adhira that they were literally flying.

"How are you driving in the dark?" Adhira gasped.

"Daily practice," Arth laughed. "By the way, there will be a *dhaba* or two up ahead, but it won't be hygienic, I must tell you," Arth spoke. "I mean for us, it is all okay, but for a lady..."

"This lady," Adhira laughed at his concern, "Travels across the globe on missions. I have been to remotest, dirtiest, smelliest bathrooms... I mean, some were so foul..."

"Fine... I get the picture," Arth laughed with her.

"I can't believe you are an international spy," Arth added as he looked at her with admiration. "Why are you a spy?"

"Girl's gotta eat," Adhira winked.

Arth snorted and continued to drive.

"Here," Arth parked the car at a side of a small shack. "Bathroom for you."

"Thank you," Adhira smiled, covered her face with the *niqab* and went to the washroom.

While waiting, Arth refuelled the car using the petrol filled canisters he had in the trunk.

"Shall we?" Adhira asked as she came back.

"The sky is blue," Arth spoke seriously.

"What?" Adhira asked, lifting the *Niqab* to show him her face.

"The sky is blue," Arth repeated very slowly.

"No, it is purple, look again," Adhira replied, confused.

Arth nodded, opened the door for her and she stepped in.

"So, was it clean?" Arth asked as he took his seat and started the car.

"What was that? Did you forget my face in a few minutes?" Adhira demanded.

"I don't take risks. Every time you step in this car, you have to say the code. No code, no entry," Arth shrugged. "And though I know that this is not your real face, I can never forget how you look presently."

Adhira's body got covered with goose bumps with the intensity of his gaze.

"How do you know that this is not my real face?" Adhira asked curiously.

"You are a spy, aren't you…?" Arth spoke thoughtfully and it confused Adhira. "And, well, you have a different face on your Indian passport."

Adhira laughed at this. "You are so pathetic!"

"Well, thank you," Arth laughed with her, staring at her face with the same intensity.

"I don't do hook-ups, you know," Adhira clarified.

"I am not looking for a hook-up," Arth too clarified.

"And I don't have time for a relationship in my life," Adhira added.

"Everybody has time for relationships. Some people just don't want to open their vulnerable side to someone else," Arth shrugged.

"It is already dark, when will we reach the address?" Adhira changed the subject.

"Tomorrow morning," Arth spoke automatically.

"What?" Adhira blanched. "It was supposed to be eight hours journey."

"It is… but it is no good to go to that whore-house in the middle of the night. You won't get your information, he will just push you in his bed. Morning, post breakfast should be the ideal time…" Arth replied.

"Are we in Islamabad yet?" Adhira enquired. The dark outside was making it difficult for her to get her location.

"No, will reach in an hour," Arth informed.

"Fine…" Adhira sighed and pulled out her phone to check her messages.

Arth drove in silence for a while.

"Let's go," Arth spoke as he parked the car. "We can spend the night here. It is not too big but it is tried and tested, and has no bugs."

Adhira looked outside. They were parked outside a small but neat motel. As they walked inside, Adhira observed that the motel was relatively empty. Good thing!

Arth had a quick chat at the counter and walked to her with two sets of keys. "This one is yours," he spoke, dropping the keys in her hands.

She nodded and followed him.

"Freshen up, we will meet in thirty minutes for dinner," Arth spoke as he pointed at the door for her. "I want to sleep before our day tomorrow."

Adhira nodded and disappeared behind her door.

"How was the journey," Patricia asked when Adhira called her. "And is the driver still alive for calling you a whore?"

"Yes, he is…" Adhira sighed.

"What is it?" Patricia inquired.

"He said something that got me thinking," Adhira spoke quickly. "He said that the address belongs to General Hayat Khan, the leader of Josh faction and he was the mastermind behind Kargil War. He had two grandchildren, whom he had brainwashed since childhood – a girl and a boy. They both are in their twenties now… don't you think that it is too much of a coincidence?"

"Well, it cannot be a coincidence. Josh can certainly devise a plan so deadly, but usually their activities rest around Kashmir. If it is them, then it is very unusual of them to expand their plans to Delhi," Patricia wondered.

"So you think that Pristine is related to Hayat Khan?" Adhira enquired.

"Ava found the address as Pristine's, so Khan must be Pristine's grandfather..." Patricia spoke. "You think the boy is Ikhtiyaar?"

"If I were the mastermind of Kargil war and if I had lost the war, I would hit India on the eve of celebrating the Kargil warriors... It would be poetic, wouldn't it?" Adhira spoke.

"I don't hear any rhymes here, but it does make sense," Patricia agreed. "Well, the good thing is that you have seen Ikhtiyaar yourself. If it is his house, there must be some photos there."

"I hope so," Adhira agreed. "If it is true, we will at least know the reason for these attacks."

"Yes... then all we will need to figure out is how to stop them," Patricia sighed. "By the way, where is Rudhir?"

"Who?" Adhira asked, slightly dazed.

"Umm... Mr R&AW? The man you ditched at the border, who is worried sick for you and is currently looking for ways to enter Pakistan to look for you," Patricia sang.

"Did he find the unmarked truck containing bodies?" Adhira asked, ignoring Patricia's words.

"No, he did not," Patricia replied. "Which is weird because Miranda's intel is never wrong."

"She is the head of Special Ops for a reason, Patty," Adhira agreed. "I think we need to look some more for this bioweapon."

"It is like searching for a needle in the haystack," Patricia groaned.

"We can alert the hospitals at least, so they can report if anyone comes in with the symptoms of Ebola," Adhira suggested.

"And raise panic?" Patricia blanched. "Can you even imagine the havoc it will wreak?"

Knock! Knock! Knock!

"Shoot, it is thirty minutes already!" Adhira whispered as she opened the door for Arth.

"You are not ready?" Arth complained.

"I have no clothes to change into, do I? Just wait for two minutes, I will freshen up," Adhira spoke to Arth. "Patty, I will call you after dinner."

"Dinner with the driver," Patricia commented. "Must have hit something on the journey here."

"Talk later," and Adhira disconnected.

"So," Adhira spoke as they sat to eat. "What's good here?"

"Do you have any specific eating restrictions?" Arth asked her with a flirtatious smile.

"I can eat a human if that's what is needed to survive," Adhira laughed.

"Your humour misses my mark," Arth narrowed his brows and ordered for them.

As they ate in silence, he asked, "No twenty questions?"

"I like to eat in peace," Adhira shrugged as she chewed. "I like to give myself ten minutes to relish the food."

He smiled at her words and ate too.

As they ate, they often locked eyes. Smiled awkwardly. And as the moments progressed, feelings grew uncomfortable. There was a weird pull that Adhira felt towards Arth and it took a lot of self-control on her part to keep her thoughts sane while Arth just looked amused.

Adhira could not be more thankful to the waiter when he came to clear their tables.

"So, you really don't have a handsome hunk waiting for you back home?" Arth asked as they walked back to their rooms.

"Umm…" Adhira's thoughts rested on Rudhir for a second and her feelings eased up a bit. She exhaled heavily and then shook her head, "No. No one."

"Is this your real face or did you not wash the makeup?" Arth asked as she unlocked her door.

"This is not my real face," Adhira laughed as she walked in and made to close the door.

"Good night, then," Arth halted in his steps.

Adhira looked at his face, there was a rawness in his expressions that enhanced his features and made him look irresistibly handsome.

Taking a deep breath, she spoke, "Good night then." And closed the door on his face.

Phew! She exhaled heavily as she slumped against the door.

Knock! Knock! Knock!

Adhira opened a tiny slit in the door and looked at Arth, who was still standing there.

"The sky is purple," she grinned.

"I—" he hesitated and then, without a second thought, he walked forward, swung open the door, grabbed her face in his hands and kissed her hard. The passion with which he kissed her made her melt. It was as if this was what she had been waiting for. Before she knew it, she was against the wall and he had closed the door behind him.

They kissed for long, and when he pulled to draw breath, he paused. "I can go on if you like…" he whispered in her ears. As he wrapped his hand around her waist, Rudhir's face flashed in front of her face, making her exceptionally uncomfortable.

She moved and Arth stepped back.

"So, there is someone," Arth huffed.

"At the moment, I am not sure… anyway this is not the time… I am on a mission, and this… *you*… are a distraction," Adhira panted as she calmed her breathing.

Arth pulled back. "I am sorry then," he spoke, looking defeated. "It's just that I didn't want to let you go without expressing how I felt."

"I got the message," Adhira nodded.

He bent down and kissed her cheek softly. "And it doesn't matter if there is someone back home for you, I too got the message about how you feel," he whispered in her ears with such love that butterflies rose in her stomach for the first time in years.

"Good night then," and raking her red cheeks with his fingers, he left, leaving her standing all hot and bothered.

HAYAT KHAN

"I thought you said you had no clothes to change into," Arth commented as he saw Adhira in fresh clothes at the breakfast table.

"You can tell," Adhira choked on her coffee, "Underneath the *burkha?"* Only her face and hands were visible, every inch of the rest of her body was covered in black.

Arth laughed at this as he sat beside her. "This is a different *burkha.* When you travel like I do, meet so many people every day, you pick up on things."

"Oh really?" Adhira raised her eyebrows at this.

"And you smell fresh… If this was yesterday's then there would have been a staleness around you… I am familiar with that too in my line of work," Arth laughed. "But, you are fresh," and he took a deep breath as if trying to inhale her scent.

"I am fresh… when you have a team like mine, anything can be arranged, anywhere," Adhira winked. "So, do we leave right after breakfast?"

"The house is barely ten minutes away from here, including traffic. So, we will leave in like thirty minutes. You don't go and knock on that door in the wee hours, okay?" Arth spoke seriously.

"Got it," Adhira agreed.

"So, what is the plan, by the way?" Arth asked, picking up his cup of coffee.

"That, I cannot share with you," Adhira smiled mysteriously.

"You won't sleep with that pervert, right?" Arth asked very seriously. "Because I don't think I can take it."

"I don't sleep with anyone…" Adhira scowled.

"What, like ever?" Arth asked with raised eyebrows.

"Not that it's any of your business," Adhira tutted.

"Oh shoot," Arth almost choked on his coffee, "You are a virgin!" he whispered.

"And the status of my virginity is of your concern how?" Adhira asked with crossed arms.

Arth looked at her in disbelief. "No wonder…"

"No wonder what?" Adhira snapped.

"Nothing… *it is not my concern*," Arth whistled to mask his laugh.

They ate in silence and as they were leaving, Arth asked, "Have you kissed someone before or was last night your first one too?"

Adhira's jaw dropped at this.

"Oh my God… I hope I met your expectations," Arth roared with laughter.

"*Hey Bhagwan,* I swear I will shoot you," Adhira warned. Arth stopped and looked at her in shock. "And no, you are not my first kiss. So, don't feel special," she scowled.

"Shut up!" Arth spoke quickly.

"What?" Adhira was taken aback.

He grabbed her wrist and pushed her quickly into the car. He looked around carefully, sat beside her and scolded, "I thought this wasn't your first rodeo? I thought you were an experienced spy!"

"I am, why?" Adhira defended.

"Why?" Arth shrieked, "You are in *Pakistan!* You are wearing a damn *burkha.* How could you utter the word *'Bhagwan'* in here? Do you want to die? Get stripped and raped?" he bellowed.

Adhira shirked at his reaction. He was right, obviously.

"It is *Allah* here… or *khuda*… not *bhagwan, Ishwar, Ram, Krishna*…" Arth continued.

Adhira closed her eyes to compose herself.

"That's why I don't mix business with pleasure or become friends with assets. *You,* Arth, are my asset and you cannot kiss me or talk dirty to me. You distracted me. For the first time ever, I forgot I was in Pakistan, on a mission," Adhira rubbed her face to gain some control. "You made me forget… it won't happen again. Like ever."

Arth raised his eyebrows at her. "I made you forget?"

"Won't happen again," Adhira looked outside to avoid looking at his face. There was a feeling of shame in her stomach that had nothing to do with work! This felt so wrong.

"I—" Arth started again but Adhira interrupted him.

"We need to leave now. I will go in Hayat Khan's house, find out as much I can. Then, you will take me back. If anything goes south, if I am attacked, you will leave me and run. You will not do anything heroic and you will not get caught, because I don't want you babbling about me or my plans," Adhira spoke sharply.

Arth looked taken aback by her words but didn't respond. He started the car and drove in the traffic.

"You meant it when you said that there is no one coming to look for you if you are caught," Arth demanded after a while.

"We all have a role to play, you are just a driver. So, drive away if need be," Adhira spoke curtly.

Arth looked at her sharply but stayed quiet again. He stopped outside the General's house. It was a massive house with a huge garden out in the front.

"Security?" Adhira asked as she peered inside. There was no one around.

"Just one inside," Arth shrugged. "And the guard at the gate will lock the gates and go away, once you enter," he informed.

"What?" Adhira was confused. "Just one man to guard the head of Josh org?"

Arth laughed at this and spoke, "There used to be a lot of security around here, but then, few months ago I think, one of the guards recorded the old troll having sex with a girl. It was a nightmare given how old and powerful he is… Of course the guard and his entire family were executed, but Hayat Khan now keeps his excursions private. Everyone know what he is doing over weekends, but where, when and with whom, that stays quiet. The guard at the gate will return at night, but will stay out of the house. There is just one man who stays with him 24X7, he takes care of the hog. No one else is allowed to enter once the girl has entered."

"Just one man won't be too difficult to handle," Adhira spoke thoughtfully.

"Oh, don't underestimate the man. There is a reason why *just one* is sufficient," Arth shook his head vehemently.

"Who all know he is here, then?" Adhira asked seriously.

"Just handful of people I guess, and me," Arth grinned.

Adhira mulled over this information for a while.

"Ready?" Arth asked her seriously.

"Wait," Adhira ordered and pulled out a small button from her purse. Pinning the button on her *burkha,* she called Patricia, "Can you see and hear?"

"I can see, but cannot hear," Patricia spoke. "Tap the button twice."

Adhira obliged but still, there was no audio.

"I think we have to make do with the video alone," Adhira sighed.

"This is not right. Samuel had tested it," Patricia sounded worried.

"Well, we don't have time to do anything about it, I am stepping out now. The driver will wait outside for me," Adhira informed Patricia.

"Fine. Ask him to stay alert, if anything goes south, he has to bring you back at all costs," Patricia spoke loudly.

"Bye now," Adhira disconnected.

"You will run if things go south," Adhira ordered Arth.

"That's not what your friend just said," Arth spoke grudgingly. "The driver is supposed to bring you back at all costs."

"Things often go south with me and people die. You will leave and won't be one of the people whose blood gets on my hands, okay?" Adhira ordered as she stepped out.

Arth too got out, "Hey," he spoke.

"What?" Adhira looked confused.

"It doesn't matter if I am just a driver… I will never abandon you. I will always come and find you."

Feeling overwhelmed, Adhira turned and walked on.

"As-Salaam-Alaikum," Adhira raised her hand to greet the old man who had opened the door for her.

"Wa-Alaikum-As-Salaam," the man replied as he moved to a side and showed her the way in. "You are late. I was expecting you last night," he was growling in frustration.

"Oh, I didn't know," Adhira replied slowly. "I—"

"Never mind," he raised his hand to touch her shoulder but she stepped back.

His nostrils flared at her movement.

"When did you arrive?" the man asked.

"Are you General Hayat Khan?" Adhira asked quietly.

"Who else, and you will call me *hukum,"* he snapped. "First, take off your *niqab,* I want to see your face."

"*Allah bakshe,*" she whispered softly, shivering slightly.

"Do it," Hayat Khan snapped.

Adhira paused for a moment, then acting way too uncomfortable in doing so, Adhira lifted the *niqab* and exposed her face.

Hayat Khan's face contorted in pleased shock. He murmured something under his breath and moved to touch her, but she moved back again.

"Fine… let me show you around to make you comfortable," and Hayat Khan started to walk inside the house.

Feeling relieved that she could finally get some info on the man, Adhira followed him.

"I have six bedrooms, two halls, seven bathrooms and one kitchen," Hayat Khan spoke with pride, "but you only need to look at one room," and he pointed ahead.

As they passed one of the rooms, Adhira realised it was full of portraits. She paused, not following Hayat Khan, even though he was leading her to another room. She stared at the portraits inside, giving the camera, tucked on her *burkha,* a clear view.

"That is my family," Hayat Khan spoke, making her jump. He placed his hand on her back and pushed her inside the room.

"This is my grandfather," Hayat Khan pointed at a frame. "My father… me… my son… my daughter… my grandson and granddaughter… my family is full of fighters, and all these men *and women*," he paused to point at his granddaughter's photo, "are fighters."

"Your grandchildren are young, are they fighting in the army too?" Adhira asked seriously. Goose bumps erupted on her body as she recognised them. She was in the right house. They were none other than Ikhtiyaar and Pristine.

"No… my son was the last army personnel in my family. My grandchildren are fighting too, but in a different way. Our paths are different, but the goal is the same," Hayat Khan pointed.

"And the goal is?" Adhira asked very seriously.

"Why don't you let our goals remain in this room, let's move on," and Hayat Khan pushed Adhira out.

As they walked ahead, Adhira caught scent of heavy oil and paint. She peaked inside a room and it was full of canisters and paint buckets.

"Again, not your concern," Hayat Khan growled as he saw her stop to peek inside.

"This..." Hayat Khan said, pointing at another door, "Come in, here."

Adhira entered with grave expressions.

"Take it off," Hayat Khan ordered.

"What?" Adhira blanched.

"I need to see what I ordered is right or not. Take it off," Hayat Khan spoke sternly and pointed at her from top to toe.

With fumbling hands, Adhira obliged. She took off her *burkha* and was now standing in front of the old man in her jeans and t-shirt.

"Marvellous," Hayat Khan whispered as he lifted his hands to touch her face, but she walked back again.

"I didn't call you here for you to get away from me," Hayat Khan barked.

"You didn't call me here, I came here to talk to you of my own accord," Adhira took multiple steps back. "Please, stop trying to touch me." Every inch of her body was screaming to punch this man, but she resisted. It was so hard for her to act like a poor helpless girl, who was caught in a corner by a bad man.

"What?" Hayat Khan looked surprised.

"I came to discuss your goals," Adhira spoke seriously.

"My goal," Hayat Khan growled, "is the destruction of your country, from inside out, from every side. My goal is to cripple your country to such lengths that no amount of external aid will help you recover. My goal is mass destruction, complete annihilation... my goal is..."

Adhira gaped at him wide-eyed and covered her mouth with her hands in shock. Hayat Khan grinned victoriously.

"Ya Khuda," Adhira spoke after a long, pretentious pause, "What kind of madness is this... you call yourself a patriot? You fought for our country... and you want to annihilate our *Pak* nation? What kind of man you are?"

"What?" now Hayat Khan looked shocked.

"I will not let you hurt our nation," Adhira threatened. "I will die before you ruin our land. Pakistan is my life. I won't let you damage it." Adhira clutched her chest to show her devotion towards Pakistan.

"Pakistan?" Hayat Khan blanched. "You are not an Indian?"

"NO," Adhira growled and screwed up her face. "Why would you say that? How dare you insult me so?"

"Let's get out of this room then… if you are a Pakistani, then this room is not for you," Hayat Khan narrowed his eyes and walked outside. Adhira, still clutching her *burkha* in her hands, followed him.

"Sit," Hayat Khan showed her a seat and took another one. "Now tell me, who are you?"

"I am Tabassum Khan," Adhira spoke. "I—never mind."

"I am sorry for the misunderstanding. I bring girls from India every week. I like to, well, screw them… fucking young Indian girls gives me the feeling of fucking India as a whole," Hayat Khan laughed like a debauched freak.

Adhira fisted her fingers to control her temper. Her instinct was shouting at her, she wanted to snap the neck of this whore-monger in two, but she resisted.

Hayat Khan's laugh boomed in the otherwise quiet room, making Adhira flinch. "Relax… Relax, my dear Tabassum, I thought you were one of those girls. With beauty like yours, I should have known you are one of us not them… such face could only be carved by *our Allah*," he complimented.

Adhira tried to blush.

"So, my dear, why are you here?" Hayat Khan looked convinced by her fake expressions.

"I heard something and it forced me to come…" Adhira spoke as she twisted her fingers to feign nervousness.

"What did you hear?" Hayat Khan encouraged. "I am very old, my dear. Believe me, you have not heard anything that I haven't heard in my life. So, go on…"

"They... they are launching a memorial for Kargil warriors. They are celebrating men who ruined us... who killed our soldiers, who killed my father," Adhira gritted her teeth.

"Your father?" Hayat Khan raised his eyebrows.

"Yes... *abbu jaan* was in the army. Every time I used to see him in his army uniform, I felt so proud of our nation. I was barely five years old back then, but I still remember the pride in his eyes when he put his uniform on... I knew he was our saviour, he will protect us from the enemy behind the lines," Adhira whispered.

"Your *abbu jaan* died in the war?" Hayat Khan asked sadly. There was a visible droop in his demeanour at these words.

Adhira nodded, tears now leaking from her eyes. "*Ammi* was never the same. Nothing was the same. It was as if something had died in her with him. I don't remember celebrating any *Eid* or *Ramadaan* or anything... every day since was a black day for us, and those days of celebrations were even blacker... and it was all because of those Indians. Those Indians who killed my father... I hate them... *Hukum Saab,* I hate them... and I want revenge..."

"And why have you come to me?" Hayat Khan asked seriously.

"When I heard about Kargil Memorial," Adhira almost spat at the words, "I was beside myself with rage. The man who supports me now, Ashraj Abdul Khan, he told me about you. And how you have a mission. I am ready to do whatever you want. Go where you want. I am ready to kill. I am ready to die... I am ready for anything, on one condition."

"And the condition is?" Hayat Khan asked with raised eyebrows.

"That I get to kill as many Indians with my own hands," Adhira fisted her hands to display her anger.

Hayat Khan laughed at this. "You have come to the right place, my dear..."

"Can I be a part of your mission?" Adhira requested.

"With your kind of spirit, you are already a part of my mission," Hayat Khan laughed even loudly now. "But first, show me the proof of your identity."

Adhira quickly pulled out her passport from her pocket and gave it to Hayat Khan. "I came prepared, in case you want me to leave for India right away… the memorial launch is in less than a week."

"Smart girl," Hayat Khan looked impressed. "Walk with me now."

As Adhira trotted behind him, she realised she didn't have her camera placed properly. Behind his back, Adhira quickly took out the camera from her *burkha* and placed it in her jeans button, hoping that it would capture everything properly.

"This…" Hayat opened another door for her now, and it was full of charts and plans. Adhira stopped at the door, trying to give the camera a good chance to capture everything. She knew it was from a distance, but this was the best she could get. "Is our plan," Hayat Khan continued.

Adhira walked around in the massive room, reading from one board to another. The biggest board had a sketch of the War Memorial that was almost ready for a grand opening in Delhi. And marked around it were four crosses.

"What are these crosses?" Adhira asked, pointing.

"That's irrelevant," Hayat Khan said as he took her to the last board. "This is where you can help."

Adhira studied the board carefully, but it was not clear.

"What is this?" Adhira asked.

"Back-up plan," Hayat Khan laughed. "Earlier, this was my backup plan, but you are a God-send. Now we can attack on all fronts…"

"What is this plan? How can I help? And will this cause some serious damage?" Adhira asked, sounding excited.

"Oh yes, my dear. This will cripple India to the extent they have never even imagined," and Hayat Khan laughed again.

"What would I need to do?" Adhira asked, feigning enthusiasm. She rushed forward to the board and looked at it with delight.

"All you need to do is roam around in the crowd," Hayat Khan spoke seriously. "You need to meet my granddaughter in here," he pointed at a space on the board, but Adhira couldn't make out the exact place on this blurred map. "And she will give you something. You will take it, wait for a while and then roam around the crowd."

"That's it?" Adhira asked, disappointed.

"That will be all. Your movement will do everything," Hayat Khan patted her back.

"But I want to kill them with my own hands," Adhira spoke sadly. "Can't I fire a gun? Make a blast or something?"

"Gun will kill only one… blast will kill a few… but your roaming around will kill thousands, maybe even millions, given how they litter everywhere," Hayat Khan beamed.

"Is it something contagious? Like a virus?" Adhira asked, her mind racing towards the Ebola strain that Miranda had tipped them about.

"Why don't you let us worry about these details," Hayat Khan smiled with fatherly affection. "Let me call Khalid and Khalida, they will be delighted to know that we found you," Hayat Khan beamed.

"Khalid and Khalida?" Adhira asked, confused.

"My grandchildren. They are twins, that's why Haseena named them so…" Hayat Khan spoke with loving affection.

"Haseena?" Adhira looked confused.

"My daughter, she named them… Ikhtiyaar wanted to name them differently, he was wrapped around his whore of a wife. She ran away with another man, good riddance if I might add" and he spat on the floor. "Haseena named them because once she decided something, it had to happen," Hayat Khan's eyes glistened with nostalgic tears.

"Haseena is your daughter?" Adhira clarified.

"*Was*, she passed away years ago, even before the war," Hayat Khan sighed sadly.

"And Ikhtiyaar is your son," Adhira added.

"Yes… my late son. He passed away in the war. My grandchildren are doing everything to avenge his death and fulfil my dream of ruining that country full of animals. My grandchildren will bring me peace. They will bring glory to our family name. And they will help bring peace to you too," Hayat Khan nodded appreciatively.

"Thank you for the opportunity, ***hukum,***" Adhira bowed humbly. She was pretending to stay calm, but her entire being was shivering. What were they planning? What was going to happen? The unveiling was only three days away, how far were they in their plan?"

"Stay here," Hayat Khan smiled as he dialled the number and placed the phone on his ear.

Adhira took advantage of the moment and read through the boards. She couldn't make out any details there… it was all so blurred.

"Tabassum Khan," Adhira heard Hayat Khan take her fake name. "Oh, I see…" Hayat Khan's voice turned serious. She turned in time to see Hayat Khan click a picture of her, flash blinding her for a few seconds.

"Yes, that's her," Hayat Khan spoke on the phone.

Adhira made to step out but she heard a loud voice on the phone, someone was shouting. She turned and saw Hayat Khan pointing his gun at her.

"My grandson believes that you are an Indian Spy," Hayat Khan spoke seriously.

Adhira raised her hand in surrender. She was unarmed at the moment.

"Indian?" Adhira stammered. "I am your kin," she spoke. "I showed you my passport."

"Nothing hard for a spy," Hayat Khan walked to her. "I don't believe a beauty like yours can be Indian. But my grandson believes that the button in your belt is a camera. He saw it reflect in the flash," Hayat Khan looked down at her waist.

Adhira took the opportunity of his gaze on her body and snatched the gun from his frail hands.

"Not so quick on reflexes, are you?" Adhira asked, now pointing the gun at him.

"So, you *are* an Indian Spy!" Hayat Khan spoke impressed. "Didn't know you bastards had it in you."

"Neither did I think that you cockroaches had it in you," and in one swift motion, she hit his head with the back of the gun. He fell to the floor with a loud thud.

Adhira quickly took the pages from the boards and clicked photos of what was written on each board. She was almost at the door when Hayat Khan gained consciousness.

"You can r—u—n…" Hayat Khan croaked. "My children will fuck your country worse than I have fucked your women." And he laughed.

"I will stop you," Adhira spoke seriously.

Ha Ha Ha Ha…. Hayat Khan laughed and laughed. "No amount of deceit will stop us. You think you will leave my country in one piece? You will be caught and sold, limb by limb. You just wait, I will be the first one to disrobe you…"

Adhira growled at these words.

"You cannot run…" Hayat Khan choked. "They are all coming for you. He is sending his best… Ten minutes… you have ten minutes to breathe freely, then you are mine."

Adhira turned and looked at the man who was the mastermind behind everything.

"And you cannot stop us. You can kill me, but it will not stop my children," Hayat Khan spoke softly.

"Let me give it a try," She unzipped the small patch she had on the side of her jeans. It opened not to reveal a pocket but her bare skin and what was strapped around it.

"Don't be a fool, this cannot kill me," Hayat Khan croaked with laugh as Adhira lifted pulled out a small dart from the strap.

"Small dart, miniscule needle, deadly poison, painful death," Adhira spoke venomously. "Take shame in the fact that you escaped tanks all your life, but a 2-inch dart killed you," and putting the dart on her lips, she blew in it. A small needle escaped from its cavity and struck right in the middle of Hayat Khan's brows.

"Ouch!" Hayat Khan winced as he pulled out a tiny needle and dropped it. "Is that it?" he mocked.

Adhira looked at him for a peaceful moment and then Hayat Khan's face started to contort in pain, his face turning pale. Knowing with satisfaction that the poison had started its work, Adhira grinned and stepped out.

She was about to leave the room when she heard heavy footsteps approach her. *Just one guard!*

She hid behind the door that was ajar, and waited. She took out Beretta .22 and tucked it securely in her jeans. She didn't want to shoot and make a bloody mess, but still kept it ready.

A frantic man came and stood rooted just a few feet ahead of her, staring down at the lifeless body of Hayat Khan. He was more than six-feet tall and heavier than the average body-builder. Now Adhira knew what Arth meant by 'just one was sufficient'.

Adhira crouched and readied herself to pounce at the man with full force. Then, in one swift movement, she jumped and hit the man just underneath the nape of his neck, smack on the spine.

He fell forward, disoriented.

She quickly started to collect her things but the man, who was supposed to be unconscious, shook his head like a wet dog to gain composure, grabbed her leg and pulled, making her fall hard. As she came crashing down, she saw him got up and flex his arms and shoulders.

Adhira rolled over in time as his punch landed exactly where her chest was a second ago. She knew one punch, and this man would break her body!

She stood up and realised that her gun was not where she had placed it. It must have fallen when she fell. With no time to pull out another from her jeans, she turned and raised her leg to kick him hard in the side. But on instinct, he grabbed her leg and she came crashing on the floor again. She felt all air getting knocked out of her. He grabbed her hair and made her turn.

As she faced him, he stood on top of her, one hand still tugging at her hair. He lifted his hand to punch her, but she was quicker. She lifted her other leg and her foot met his groin with as much force as she could muster in the moment.

The man's hand, which was balled up in a fist before, opened as he cried in pain and Adhira felt a harsh slap ring on her face. Blood came flying out of her mouth as he fell on her side.

The man grabbed his loins and sat screaming on the floor, right on top of Adhira's leg. Feeling pain all over, especially on her ringing face, and pinned down leg, she looked around for something. And her eyes fell on Hayat Khan's gun.

She kicked the man with her free leg in his face, he fell back in shock, and she crawled to the gun.

The man grabbed her legs and pulled her back, but she got lucky. The gun was already in between her fingers.

She turned, spraining her waist muscles in the process, and fired a shot. The whole house rang with sound as she saw blood ooze from the man's forehead. He let go of her legs and fell. She turned very quickly to protect herself from getting crushed under the weight of the boulder-like man.

RUN!

Adhira saw her blood, hair and saliva spread all over the room. *Ten minutes,* that's what Hayat Khan had said, she had ten minutes. No, now she had seven, maybe six!

Fuck! The entire room was now littered with her DNA.

She rushed to the room that was full of oil canisters and pulled one out. She was drenching the room in oil when she heard Arth shout from the main door, "What happened? Who fired the shot?"

"Take these and go to the car," Adhira ordered as she pointed at a roll of papers from the room on the floor outside. "Just do as I say," she ordered as she continued to douse the room in smelling oil.

She then quickly drew a straight line with oil to the kitchen where she turned on the gas stove, and then spilled it all the way to the main door.

"Are you coming or what?" Arth shouted from outside. He was visibly panicked.

Adhira walked out, turned back and fired the shot that ignited the oil, and before it could blow up the house and kitchen, she ran…

And Adhira ran… she knew that Hayat Khan was right. Khalid, or as the world knew him, Ikhtiyaar, must have informed his people and they all must be on their way now… How much time did she have now? A minute, maybe two.

"Hurry…" Arth shouted from the gate.

"Purple, purple… run…" Adhira came towards him shouting. A huge blast erupted from somewhere in the middle of the house and she knew that her flame must have met the gas cylinder.

Arth rushed to the driver's side and started the engine.

"Faster… faster… drive…" Adhira was not even in the car when she was shouting.

"Come and sit first," Arth barked and the moment Adhira was in the seat, he pressed hard on the accelerator and started driving with full force.

"What the heck happened back there? Why is the house on fire? Where is Hayat Khan? And why are you out of your *burkha?"* Arth demanded as he threw all the documents in her lap.

"Would you fucking drive?" Adhira shouted as she pushed the things she was carrying down the seat and readied her Beretta .22 to shoot when required.

"I am driving," Arth shouted back. "You are bleeding by the way," he pointed at her head.

She wiped her forehead hastily and muttered something about a pain killer.

"Where are we going?" Arth demanded.

"They are coming," Adhira spoke hastily as she looked around. Her phone buzzed and she put in on speaker, "Patty… need extract, ASAP."

"High Commission of India," Patricia spoke quickly. "The driver would know the address."

"I know," Arth spoke as he took a sharp turn around the corner. "Uh-Oh…" he added as he looked in the rear-view mirror.

Adhira turned sharply and she instantly knew her ten minutes were up. They were coming!

"What *Uh-Oh*?" Patricia asked quickly. "What is happening?"

"They are behind us…" Adhira spoke as she saw two jeeps trailing them. "Would they shoot?" she asked Arth.

"Well, this is a highly sensitive area… anything can happen here, but I don't think they know that you are the one they are after," Arth spoke as he drove like a maniac with one eye on the rear-view.

"How are you sure?" Patricia asked.

"We are alive, that's how," Arth growled. "And my worry is not the men behind us, I worry about who might cut us on the crossroads up ahead. Do they have your picture or identity?" Arth pointed ahead and asked.

"Yes, Hayat Khan sent my photo to Ikhtiyaar and that blew my cover," Adhira informed grimly. "But, no matter what happens, don't stop… and if you really need to stop, keep your foot on the accelerator and just be ready to drive when I say so…" Adhira ordered.

"Do you know how many times I have entered Pakistan?" Arth babbled, "Sixty-Seven times… this is my sixty-eighth trip… every time it went smoothly, but you…"

"Well, I am one of a kind," Adhira grinned as she pulled out another gun out of nowhere, a .45, and loaded it under the seat.

"How many guns do you have?" Arth asked, staring from the one in her lap to the one in her hands. "And where are you hiding them?"

"You don't want to know," Adhira grimaced as she looked around in silent panic. This was almost it! "These guns won't help us though; I wish I had my *Dhanno*."

"*Dhanno*?" Arth asked, shocked.

"Yep!" Adhira nodded distractedly. "My MI34 Minigun, firing range 3,280 meters with 2000-6000 rounds per minute," Adhira babbled as she turned in her seat.

"Wow," Arth whistled, impressed. "Bullets?"

"7.62×51mm NATO, it is a beauty like no other," Adhira sighed. "Don't have it though, can't carry it inside Pakistan!" She was muttering aimlessly.

"Why do you call it *Dhanno?* It is not a horse," Arth spoke as he pressed hard on the accelerator.

"Oh, you should see its speed and precision. It is nothing short of that beautiful horse," Adhira replied.

"Still!" Arth spoke aimlessly. Her chatter was helping him from not panicking.

"Well, I am no short of *Basanti* myself," Adhira laughed.

"Oh my God!" Patricia screamed on the call. "Are you guys fucking insane? You are smack in the middle of a catastrophe and you are talking about *Sholay* movie."

"Right," Adhira shook her head and focused.

Arth was about to comment but instead spoke, "We have to stop." Arth slowed down as he peered at a distance. The road was barricaded and men carrying HK G3 - 7.62 mm calibre assault rifle and HK MP5 - 9 mm calibre sub-machine gun were patrolling the area and checking each vehicle. "They will blow us up if we don't stop. And if we stop, they will shoot us!"

"Turn right," Patricia spoke quickly on the phone.

"It is a dead-end there," Arth barked.

"Trust her and take the turn," Adhira shouted.

"Adhira, get ready to run," Patricia spoke.

"Oh shoot," Adhira hurriedly pulled her bag from the backseat and shoved all the documents and things in it.

"Stop right outside the yellow and green building. It is an opening to the other end of the road," Patricia informed. "You have to cross it on foot, then find your way to the roof of any house on the opposite street. Climb to the roofs and you will see High Commission of India from there," Patricia continued.

"Oh, is that right?" Arth mocked. "You think it is easy with ISI, ISIS and whatnot behind you, in the fucking Pakistan?"

"You have a better idea?" Patricia snapped.

"Put on your damn *burkha*," Arth shouted.

"It will come in the way," Adhira muttered as she put it on. "I should have taken the form of a man. It always helps me navigate. Men here have such liberties."

"You can convert into a man?" Arth looked abashed as he saw the yellow and green building. "This is it..." he pointed.

"She can look like anyone, it is her gift," Patricia spoke quickly.

"You should use your gift right now... they are looking for a woman... if you *can* change into a man now, we can move easily," Arth spoke in a matter-of-fact tone.

"Do you have what you need?" Patricia asked.

"Yes, of course, I have. As he said, we are in fucking Pakistan," Adhira snapped.

"Let's go," Arth spoke as he ditched the car at a corner. "You owe me a car, by the way," he spoke to Adhira.

"I will buy you a showroom of cars if we escape from this wretched country in one piece," Adhira grunted, jumping out of the car. Arth took out her bag from the trunk of the car and entered the building.

"We need someplace for me to change," Adhira spoke hastily. "And I need a kurta. I have things for a makeover, but no clothes."

Arth looked at her in shock.

"What? I need clothes. I cannot be a man and wear jeans and a girl's top," Adhira rolled her eyes.

"Oh, in here," Arth pushed her in a bathroom and she wrinkled her nose. "I thought you said you have been to worse bathrooms?" Arth snorted at her expressions.

"Yeah, but men's toilet is shittier in every place," Adhira spoke as she threw her burkha at him and pulled out her vanity bag from her small bag.

"Some space please?" Adhira requested.

"I am not going out there to die," Arth looked at her in disbelief. "Do whatever you want in here, in front of me."

She sighed and got to work. As she took off her existing mask, revealing her true face, he just gaped. His eyes popped open when she washed her face finally.

"Holy Shit!" Arth gasped. "That's your real face?"

"Uh hun," Adhira nodded as she got to work again. She placed tape after tape on her face to change her features... she pulled out her makeup kit and wondered where to put them.

"Don't just ogle at me, make yourself useful," Adhira spoke hastily, grabbed his hands and placed her makeup kit in his hands. "If you drop anything in this super unsanitary bathroom, I will remove one car from your future showroom."

"What?" Arth looked confused.

"You know, you are now the only living person who is seeing me change my face," Adhira spoke as she put contour all over her face.

"All others are dead?" Arth demanded with raised eyebrows.

"Only situation when someone had to witness my change was dire, life-threatening one. And well, yeah, they are dead!" Adhira shrugged.

"That's very comforting," Arth mumbled.

"I need a change of clothes, you know," Adhira demanded as she quickly swapped one thing after another in Arth's hands.

She worked for a few more minutes, then she was done. She placed a beard and moustache on her face and turned.

"What do you think?" Adhira asked Arth.

"Great, but you know, men don't have breasts," Arth pointed at her chest.

"Yeah, right," Adhira spoke quickly and pulled out a very small belt from her bag. She pushed the belt in his hands and placed her makeup kit in her bag.

Adhira took off her shirt, Arth's eyes popped open again.

"Again, the only man," Adhira grinned as she undid the skin coloured strap from underneath her breasts and pushed it in Arth's arms. She then took the small belt and tied it around her chest. It took her a while to zip it, but she did it in the end.

"See, no breasts," Adhira laughed at Arth's expressions. "Now help me with the tape," and she started placing silver tape around her chest to mask the bulge. He helped her with dead shock on her face. Once she was done, her chest, though a little muscly, was entirely flat.

"How are you doing this? Are you okay?" Arth looked at her in disbelief.

"I am fine," Adhira rolled her eyes. "Now, where are my clothes?"

"Oh yes," Arth took out a kurta pyjama from his bag. "I wore it last night, so it is not fresh."

"It will do," Adhira spoke as she took it from his hands and wore them. "Don't just stand there, shove my clothes in the bag," she ordered.

Arth did the needful.

"Are you able to breathe? Doesn't it hurt?" Arth asked seriously.

"Better than dying here, isn't it?" Adhira spoke. "My hair!" she commented as she took out a small white cap from her bag. She tied her hair in a knot on top of her head and covered it all with the cap.

"Works?" Adhira asked. Arth's kurta was hanging way too loosely on her tiny frame.

"Will do," Arth shrugged. "You are brilliant…" he couldn't stop himself.

"Let's go," Adhira shook her head and looked around. "Make sure we don't miss anything," she instructed, scanning the dingy bathroom.

"We are good," Arth too looked around.

"I just don't have a male's passport. I can't believe I missed bringing it," Adhira groaned.

"Let's see what will happen," Arth peered outside, the coast was clear. "Let's go."

And they walked out together.

"Wow," Arth spoke as he saw Adhira walk beside him. "Your shoes. Those are female slippers."

"Oh God!" Adhira quickly picked them up and shoved them in the bag hanging on Arth's back.

"Here," Arth whispered as he saw a pair of sandals outside an apartment. "Gents' sandals! Should fit you, hopefully," and he stole them. Wearing the stolen slippers, which slipped a lot, Adhira and Arth made way to the opposite side of the building.

Adhira called Patricia once they were out of the building. There was a lot of commotion on the street. "High Commission is opposite these houses," Arth pointed.

"Let's go then," Adhira spoke, almost slipping on the floor.

"These houses are occupied," Patricia informed Adhira, who passed on the message to Arth. "So, make sure no one spots you."

"Why does she want us on the roof if it is on the opposite side?" Arth demanded as he went inside the main gate of one of the houses and went through the narrow passageway beside the house.

"And Adhira," Patricia spoke, but Adhira was not listening to her anymore because they quickly found out why Patricia wanted them to go to the roof. The backside of the house was walled up. And it seemed all the houses had their backyards walled.

"What? Why is this walled?" Arth looked confused.

"Hence the roof," Adhira whispered and pointed at the staircase that was visible from where they stood.

"It is going inside the house," Arth babbled.

"We have to take that chance," Adhira exhaled heavily. "I saw them rounding up women on the streets. They are taking every woman in… we have to get away and soon."

Arth nodded and tried to unlock the door while Adhira waited with bated breath.

"Who is it?" someone asked from the inside. It was a woman.

"Please help me," Adhira pleaded in her own voice. "Some men were trying to rape me, so I ran and hid here. Can you please help me?"

The woman opened the door hastily and stood rooted at their sight. Adhira lunged forward and clasped the woman's mouth before she could shout.

"I won't hurt you," Adhira spoke. "I am a woman and some Indians are chasing me, so I made myself look like a man. Please help me…"

The woman looked frightened, but nodded.

"Are you alone?" Adhira asked quickly.

The woman shook her head.

"I am removing my hand, I really don't want to hurt you, but if you scream, I will have to. I don't want to be captured and raped by those men, do you understand me?" Adhira threatened.

The woman nodded again. Her eyes flickered towards Arth. "He is my friend. He helped me escape," Adhira added. "Don't scream, for your own sake, please don't scream," Adhira begged and removed her hand from the woman's mouth and stepped back.

"What do you want?" the woman asked quickly.

"Who else is in the house?" Arth asked seriously. All the curtains were drawn and the house was in darkness.

"My son, he is asleep. Please, he is only six. Please don't hurt him," the woman begged.

"Where is your phone?" Adhira asked. The woman showed it to them. Adhira took it and placed it in the kitchen. "Go to your son's room and stay there. Don't come out for thirty minutes. We won't take a thing from your house, we just need to lay low and escape. Please…"

The woman hesitated.

"Or we can kill you both and stay here for as long as we like," Arth shrugged.

"I will go, please don't hurt us," the woman begged with folded hands.

"We won't hurt you, just stay there and stay quiet..." Adhira insisted. "You will not find a thing upturned, please believe me."

The woman nodded and left without a backward glance.

"What if she has another mode of communication? What if her son has another phone?" Arth asked, worried.

"A Six-year-old?" Adhira asked curiously.

"Yeah?" Arth looked shocked. "Have you met this generation? They are brats!"

"Let's go," Adhira spoke quickly as she walked to the stairs. "I'll go check it out," she started to climb.

"Stay down, I will go and check," Arth looked shocked. He muttered something on the lines of 'bloody woman would be the death of me' and climbed the stairs.

Adhira waited for a few minutes, then saw Arth come down.

"Let's go, I can see a way to the High Commission," Arth whispered.

"One sec," Adhira rushed to the main door, unlocked it, made a sound as if it has been opened and closed, and ran back up the stairs.

She was on the fourth step when she heard the woman creep out of her room to check if they had left. Her full attention was towards the main door and Adhira climbed to the roof, unnoticed.

"Why did you do that?" Arth demanded as they crouched down on the roof and jumped from one house to another.

"So that she can tell whoever she calls that we have left from the main door and nobody will come to look for us here," Adhira replied.

"Genius," Arth looked impressed.

"Not my first rodeo," Adhira smiled. "But she can tell that I am dressed as a man, so we should speed up," her smile faltered.

"That's right," Arth nodded.

They were looking for a way to the High Commission when Adhira's phone buzzed.

"Hey Patty, can't talk right now," Adhira spoke quickly.

"Where are you?" Patricia demanded.

"In the line of sight of the High Commission, but there are forces around it now. We need to find a way into it safely. Once we are in, we can look at our extraction options," Adhira rushed on.

"You cannot," Patricia cried. "High Commission of India is closed for a week now."

"What? They cannot close it," Adhira shrieked. Arth shushed her.

"They can, actually. There are various threats on the Indians working there so all of them were extracted last week. It is closed," Patricia spoke quickly.

"Why?" Adhira couldn't believe it.

"Because of the Kargil Memorial. The way PMO is showcasing, it has hurt many sentiments there... so..." Patricia trailed on.

"We are out in the open, we need to get away," Adhira snapped. "If we cannot go to High Commission, we need to go somewhere."

"Find a place to lay low, then try to get out of Islamabad, we will get you picked up very soon," Patricia spoke quickly. "Keep me posted, okay!"

"Yeah, yeah," Adhira spoke and disconnected. She explained the situation to Arth, who looked very worried.

He peeked down the lane and many military vehicles were circling them.

"This is not good," Arth whispered.

"Is that a chopper?" Adhira asked, baffled as the sound of a helicopter got louder.

"Yes, and we should move. They will shoot us for crouching like this, believe me," Arth grabbed her arm and dragged her to a shed, hiding them from sight.

"I think both ISI and ISIS are looking for us," Arth hissed. "What did you do? What was that blast?"

Adhira shrugged and muttered, "As if there is a difference between ISI and ISIS. Though one is government-run and another is terrorist run, their *mai-baap* are one and the same!"

"This kind of retaliation can only mean one thing," Arth groaned as he saw the chopper fly overhead, "You killed Hayat Khan."

"Like I said," Adhira twisted her mouth sourly, "Not my first rodeo."

"Oh fuck," Arth shouted. "They won't let us get away. Hayat Khan was literally their *mai-baap.*"

"Good thing then that he is out of the way, isn't it?" Adhira shrugged.

"How are we going to get out?" Arth demanded.

"I have an idea," Adhira thought quickly and dialled on her phone. "Ava, SOS."

"I know," Ava's worried voice came from the other side. "*Tu es dans un tas de merde.*"

"English darling," Adhira smiled. "And yes, I am in a deep pile of shit!"

Arth looked confused so Adhira added, "She always brings out French when she is panicking!"

Arth looked even more confused.

"How are you so calm?" Arth asked, baffled.

"What do you need?" Ava asked quickly.

"I need a distraction. Can you leave a false trail? Something that says we are on the other side of the city? It has been around four hours since I left Hayat Khan's place. So, put us somewhere that would look genuine for three hours approximately. That will give us some space to move and think," Adhira asked.

"Sounds great, let me do it. What were you wearing when you ran out?" Ava asked.

"Maroon top, blue jeans," Adhira informed.

"Make it two hours, we left my car two hours ago, didn't we?" Arth supplied.

"Then two hours it is," Ava added quickly. "I will call you when I know something. And we are working on an extraction. Our assets in Pakistan are not coming forward at the moment. Hayat Khan was a big deal, you shouldn't have shot him!"

"What's done is done…" Adhira groaned and disconnected.

"See! I told you so," Arth growled as he sat back in his corner.

"What's done is done… one bastard less," Adhira too slipped on the ground and tried to get a bit comfortable, though noises around didn't let her. They were being hunted!

EXTRACTION

"Fake trail is in place," Ava messaged Adhira. "Stay away from the route to Lahore..."

"Thank you," Adhira replied and informed Arth.

"You know what?" Arth spoke, peeking outside. "ISI and ISIS have an army, and I mean it... an army. So, they won't abandon the High Council. They will leave men here."

Adhira groaned and looked down, he was right. There was no change whatsoever downstairs. The helicopter was gone, but the crowd below was still there.

"Maybe, we wait it out," Adhira suggested.

"I don't think we should stay here for much longer. They will know it is a fake trail, so they will soon start searching from house to house," Arth continued.

"I feel we should enter High Commission of India. It is Indian soil in there. They, technically, should stay away from that. Entering the Indian embassy is an act of war," Adhira spoke.

"And you think they care about war at the moment?" Arth snapped. "You killed their hero. You killed the man who was behind everyone. You have started a fucking war!"

"Yeah, whatever," Adhira shrugged.

"You don't feel remorse? You don't feel sorry?" Arth glared at her.

"We are already at war here, okay," Adhira snapped at his tone. "They forced Indians out of the embassy, they are planning a fucking bio-attack on our country. They are planning to shoot us with radioactive material, we are at war, Arth... Hayat Khan was the mastermind behind it all. He and his bloodthirsty grandchildren. You think that my killing Hayat Khan has instigated a war? By killing him, I have prevented all the future wars. All I need to do is also kill his bloody grandchildren and it would bring peace, well, for the time being at least," Adhira ranted.

Arth's jaw was hanging at this news. His expressions made her realise how much she had let out.

"And all this, by the way, is confidential information. One word to anyone, and I swear to God, I will kill you," Adhira threatened.

Arth laughed at this.

"You think I won't hurt you?" Adhira roared.

"I think that you like me too much to kill me," Arth laughed again. "I think you are a little bit in love with me too."

This time, it was Adhira's turn for jaw-dropping. Arth closed her mouth with his finger.

"And if it is any consolation, I think I have already fallen in love with a badass like you," and he kissed her cheek, burning her face. "Your fake beard tickles," he snickered. "I have never kissed anyone looking like a man before. If we manage to survive this, I will marry you."

Adhira looked thunderstruck at these words.

"Well, you cannot get away with such experience and not spend the rest of your life together, now do you?" Arth laughed.

"You are insane," Adhira shook her head and looked away. "I need eyes out there," she groaned as she peered down.

"I have seen your real face, your man face, your fake face... I have seen your multiple sides and I am fascinated. I don't think I have ever met another person like you. So, will you marry me?" Arth insisted. "I am alone, you are alone... maybe we belong together."

"I am not *alone!*" She barked.

"You said so last night, you are now and forever alone… so, let's be alone together," Arth grinned.

"You are a bloody transporter. You smuggle people across border," Adhira accused.

"Excuse me," Arth screwed up his nose, "I am the future owner of a world-class showroom of XUVs. My future wife has promised me a showroom of cars if we survive this…"

Adhira couldn't help but laugh at his words.

"Just keep laughing, alright," Arth smiled at her. "And I will take it as a 'yes'."

Adhira blushed at the words.

"You are crazy, and it is not a yes, so don't get your hopes up," Adhira rolled her eyes and sneaked a peek downstairs. "Why are they not moving?"

"You didn't say 'no' either, I take it as a positive sign," Arth laughed as he too looked down. Adhira looked shocked at his resilience. "The crowd is thinning, though," Arth assessed. "Maybe we can sneak out in the middle of the night."

"Yes, maybe, if we stay alive until then," Adhira spoke.

"What do you mean?" Arth asked seriously.

"I am famished, we have been on this roof for hours now… if we don't eat anything soon, we will die…" Adhira groaned.

"Humans can survive without food for days, it is water that is a necessity," Arth spoke as he crawled to a water tank and filled his small water bottle.

"I know," Adhira smiled, "I once lived without food for forty hours."

Arth's jaw dropped at these words.

"What the heck did you do?" Arth spoke, handing her his water bottle.

Adhira smirked as she drank her fill.

"You are just distracting me, aren't you?" Arth asked with raised eyebrows.

"Well, yes… and I *am hungry.* I can live without food, though I don't prefer it," Adhira sighed and looked longingly at the High Commission's building. This building was supposed to be her safe haven, but currently, it was empty.

"On my mark, Ava," Adhira spoke softly in her phone a few hours later as they got ready to make a run for it.

"Extraction is in place. Use the cover of darkness and make to the extraction point, Adhira. I… we want you alive," Ava spoke hastily in the call.

"Right… 3… 2… now…" and Arth and Adhira started running.

A lot of noise and commotion followed them. Though it was well past midnight now, their sentry were not asleep.

"Damn it," Arth spoke as he panted. It was clear to Adhira that his job as a transporter didn't require a lot of exercise.

"Keep running," Adhira spoke quickly. "Just keep running. We need to get over the fence. We need to enter the premises."

"Are they after us…?" Arth cried.

"Just a few more feet, just a little more," Adhira spoke, as she raced towards her destination. Her freedom.

"Yes…" Arth almost choked in exhaustion. He stopped, clutching a stitch in his side.

"You are too heavy for me to carry," Adhira spoke as she raced back and pulled at his arm. "Let's go," she cried.

Arth ran with her again.

"THERE THEY ARE…" somebody shouted at a distance.

"Oh! Fuck," Adhira cursed and they ran harder.

"Almost there," and Adhira jumped over the wall to enter the premises.

"Come on," Adhira cried as she saw that Arth didn't follow her.

"I can't," Arth groaned from the other side. "You go on… I will hold them off."

"Oh, shut up," Adhira cried. She hopped on the wall and stretched out her hand. Arth grabbed it, and while she tried to get Arth on the other side, everything was brightened up suddenly.

A blinding flash, a loud bang, and the Indian Embassy was lying in ruins, completely drowned in fire.

DIVERSION

"What are you doing? Let's go," someone shouted at Adhira. She looked up and saw the High Commission of India enveloped in flames opposite the road.

Adhira, still dangling by the wall, looked back.

"Don't just stand there, help me," she shouted.

Three men rushed forward to help. Two of them leaned against the wall and pulled Arth to the other side.

"It was a big play," the third man spoke from the shadows. "Using the mask of darkness, planting fake information about you running to Indian Embassy… Big and brave play!" Adhira looked astounded as she recognised the voice. "Are you okay?"

"Is that her?" one of the men who pulled Arth up asked.

"Yes, that's her," Rudhir smiled at her.

"Let's go, ma'am, it is not safe," they pushed Adhira and Arth in a black SUV and drove away. Two men sat in front, while Rudhir sat beside Adhira, Arth on her side.

"Stop… Stop… Stop…" Arth shouted at a turn.

"What?" the driver spoke.

Arth pulled out a small remote from a zip line of his bag and pointed it at a lane. As he clicked the button, a small explosion took place.

"What was that?" Adhira asked, shocked. Her face reflected in the flames.

"My car… too much evidence to leave behind," Arth smiled at her. "Let's go."

And they drove ahead.

"Do you always keep a bomb in your car?" Adhira asked, intrigued.

"Yes… you have no idea how much information they can pull out from that car. I always build a safe keep," Arth shrugged.

Adhira nodded, impressed.

"And given that they blew High Commission a lane down, nobody would suspect a thing, I guess…" Arth shrugged.

"Yeah, they blew the Indian Embassy," one of the men spoke from the front. "Bloody fucking Pakistanis, this means war."

"Let's see what Adhira has discovered so far," Rudhir spoke calmly. "By the way, it was a clever ruse. How did you manage to fool them? How come they believed you were in the Embassy?"

"Ava…" Adhira shrugged. "They wanted to believe I was there, so when we faked it, they took the bait."

"How did you fake it?" Rudhir asked.

"Ava arranged for multiple calls, three people called, one after another, with information," Adhira informed.

"Accent?" Rudhir was confused. "Ava is French."

"And how hard is it to find a Pakistani out of Pakistan? All Ava needed to do was pay three people and make them say on the call that they saw someone climb the East wall of the Indian embassy," Adhira laughed.

"Plus, the dark helped," Arth added, feeling left out.

"Arth, you really need to work out," Adhira laughed at him. "You work in such a dangerous environment and yet you couldn't even run a mile."

"Never needed to. All my missions have been smooth… no issues ever… but you… well, you are one of a kind," Arth panted still.

"That I am," Adhira nudged him in the ribs. He complained but laughed.

"You could have told me, you know," Rudhir interjected. "I could have helped you."

"I don't need your help," Adhira rolled her eyes. "Why are you even here?"

"To extract you. I would never leave that to anyone… I needed to ensure that you were safe," Rudhir shouted. "You are insane. You run away on missions like these… you are crazy."

"That I am…" Adhira shrugged. "And I am very uncomfortable at the moment… so will you just shut it."

"Do you need help taking it off?" Arth asked, pointing at her chest.

Rudhir looked at him in disbelief.

"Oh, yes please," Adhira cried and Rudhir's jaw dropped. "But first, men, look away," she ordered, pulled out her t-shirt from her bag, took off her kurta and switched it with her t-shirt.

"It's better. No offence Arth, but I feel much better in my own clothes," Adhira laughed at him.

"I understand, it was way too baggy for you anyway," Arth took his kurta and pushed it in his bag.

"But it saved my life, so I am forever grateful," Adhira grabbed his hand and squeezed it.

"Now," and Adhira started to clear her face. She took off her moustache, beard and tapes on the face. She cleaned her face with multiple wipes and when she was done, she felt the air fill her sodden pores.

"Beautiful," Arth whispered as she opened the window of his side and let the fresh air brush her face. "Would it be way too inappropriate if I kissed you again?" he murmured in her ears.

"Yes, always," Adhira whispered back, looking uncomfortably at Rudhir.

"Fine," Arth laughed.

Next, Adhira pulled out a pocket knife from her bag, handed it to Arth, turned her back to Arth, lifted her t-shirt from behind and waited.

Slowly and carefully, Arth cut the tape while Rudhir and Adhira stared at each other. His expressions were completely unfathomable.

"There," Arth spoke as he removed the tape from her back and she pushed her hand inside her shirt and took it off from the front, crying in the process. As she rolled the tape and pushed it down her bag, tears leaked from her eyes.

"Should I undo the skin strap as well?" Arth asked.

Adhira considered him for a moment. For the first time, she was in so much pain that she didn't even wish to shift slightly, let alone move her hands to unzip the strap that was stuffing her breasts in her chest. Eyes still locked with Rudhir's, she nodded. She felt Arth's fingers graze her back as he felt the zipper on her side. Slowly, Arth unzipped the strap and Adhira felt relief flood all over her body. It had been more than twelve hours since she had to keep her breasts tucked in… longest ever!

"Does it hurt?" Rudhir asked quickly as she finally dumped the strap back in her bag as well.

"Nothing I cannot tolerate," Adhira crossed her arms on her chest and closed her eyes. She wanted to massage her super-sore breasts, but couldn't when surrounded by four men.

"Here," Rudhir covered her with his jacket and she nodded appreciatively. "I am glad you are okay," he wiped her face.

Adhira felt Arth move at this.

"Thank you for coming for me," Adhira whispered. "Though, you didn't need to."

"I will always come for you," Rudhir stressed. "You should know it by now."

"Who are you?" Arth demanded rather curtly.

"This is Rudhir, the head of the R&AW, the man who hired me. He is also the man who left me at the altar six years ago…" Adhira replied without opening her eyes. And though she couldn't see the two men, she could feel their shock and resentment for each other.

"And who are you?" Rudhir demanded.

"He is Arth, ex-military personnel, now my asset. He is the man who transported me to Pakistan. He saved my life a few times. He—" Adhira stopped abruptly. "I owe him a showroom full of high-end cars," she smiled despite her pain and tensed situation.

"Why?" Rudhir demanded.

"So that I can turn into a world-class businessman and marry this gorgeous woman here," Arth added sharply.

"What?" Rudhir shouted in shock.

"For the record," Adhira finally opened her eyes and looked at both men. "I am not marrying anybody. I have loved once, been betrayed once. And that was it… I will not marry, like ever… so, whatever games you both wanna play, play it with someone else because in my line of work I don't have time to play 'House' with anybody."

BACK HOME

"How long will it be?" Adhira asked the man driving the car. She was getting sick of the hostility that was prevailing in the car now.

"It will be a few hours, ma'am. We have to take a longer route to ensure that they don't catch up to us. We have a chopper waiting at a secure location," the man replied.

"What's your name?" Adhira asked politely.

"Major Raj Shukla," the driver replied.

"Major Aman Verma," the man sitting next to Raj replied and nodded at her. "It was an honour to rescue you, ma'am."

"Thank you for saving us, Major and Major," Adhira smiled.

"You found some incriminating intel on Pakis. That is worth more than hours of drive," Major Aman laughed. "You should rest, it will be a while. We will not reach the chopper until dawn," he added.

"Thanks, guys," Adhira yawned, sat back and closed her eyes once more.

"Did you take your pain meds in the past two days?" Rudhir asked her. "I can feel your pain at this very moment. How much does it hurt?"

"I have barely eaten since yesterday, let alone a pain killer," Adhira sighed, moving in her seat.

"Here ma'am," and Aman handed her a bag full of sandwiches. Both Adhira and Arth took it gratefully, mumbled quick thank yous and started eating.

"Wow, I have never been this hungry before," Arth spoke with his mouth full of bread.

"Eh!" Adhira shrugged and kept on eating.

"Here," Rudhir pulled out medicines from his pocket and gave them to Adhira. "I kept spare, in case you misplaced them on the mission."

Adhira took the medicines without sparing Rudhir a second glance and gobbled them with water.

"You never told me how you got so brutally injured. I mean you have bruises all over your torso. And I could see your blackened ribs yesterday," Arth spoke quickly. Rudhir moved as if he wanted nothing more than grabbing Arth and throwing him out of the car.

"Who do you think helped her tape herself?" Arth asked Rudhir seriously. Apparently, Rudhir's move didn't go unmissed by him.

Rudhir fumed and sat back. "You should have taken me with you," he spoke through gritted teeth. "You are so stubborn. Always have to do things alone. You could have died."

"She was not alone," Arth added angrily but Rudhir ignored him.

"First UK, then Tehran, then Pakistan, you have a death wish, don't you?" Rudhir continued, still fuming.

"Tehran?" Arth looked shocked.

"My current wish is to sleep, so shut your faces and let me sleep," Adhira yawned broadly now.

"You too should sleep, you look like a corpse," Rudhir spoke to Arth.

Arth looked at him seriously, then spoke to Aman and Raj, "Hey man, wake me up when we have to board the chopper alright. I don't believe this Romeo to wake me up," he laughed.

"I am a man of honour," Rudhir growled at his words, then added, "Sleep man, you need your sleep."

Next when Adhira opened her eyes, she was being carried in somebody's arms. A loud noise had woken her up. She looked up and saw a helicopter ready to leave.

"Here," Adhira heard Arth's shout. Rudhir passed her to Arth at a height and Arth placed her in a seat.

"Let me," Rudhir spoke, quickly hopping inside too. He buckled her and sat beside her. Adhira was drifting on and off in sleep.

"What did you give me?" Adhira asked, eyes still closed. "Why can't I wake up?"

"Just a pain killer, you are severely sleep-deprived," Rudhir spoke and before Adhira went back to sleep again.

"Are we there yet?" Adhira was in the car now, again between Rudhir and Arth.

"Yes, almost home," Rudhir informed.

"Is Arth okay?" Adhira asked clumsily. "We didn't leave him behind, did we?"

"I am here too," Arth squeezed her hand. She smiled and continued sleeping.

"What is happening to her?" Arth demanded as they entered Adhira's house.

"Major sleep deprivation," Rudhir spoke as he placed her on her bed. "She has slept for less than twenty-four hours in the past ten days. Are you not leaving?" he asked Arth, who was looking around Adhira's room.

"I think I am going to stay and help mitigate this threat. This is going to get nasty. The memorial launch is in two days and we need to stop Hayat Khan's grandchildren."

"What?" Rudhir asked sharply.

"She told me bits about what she discussed with Hayat Khan," Arth spoke. "Who are you calling?" He asked as he saw Rudhir dial on his phone.

"A nurse. She needs cleaning up and IV fluids. Seeing how she is sleeping, she needs nutrition," and Rudhir talked to someone.

"Why do I always find her like this," a woman in her forties came around an hour later and sighed. "What did you people do this time?"

Rudhir shrugged.

"Fine, keep your secrets but someday I would like to know," the nurse snapped and pushed both men out of the room.

"Here," Rudhir showed another room to Arth, "You can clean up here and sleep."

Arth nodded and started to go to the room, but stopped abruptly, "Where do you sleep?"

"In my own home, but lately here," and Rudhir pointed at Adhira's room.

"What the hell," Adhira woke up with a start. "Again!" she shrieked as she realised what was going on.

"Morning," Rudhir smiled as he kissed her bare shoulders.

"Am I naked?" Adhira demanded.

"Ummhmm," Rudhir muttered in his sleep.

"And you are naked!" Adhira added. "Pressed against my naked body."

"Yes…" Rudhir spoke, rubbing his nose on her neckline.

"Get the fuck away from me," Adhira shrieked and Rudhir jumped back. "How dare you?"

"I am sorry," Rudhir spoke, finally snapping out of sleep. "I was dreaming, I am sorry."

Knock! Knock! Knock!

Rudhir wrapped his towel around his body, ensured that Adhira was well covered and opened the door.

"I heard noises, so came to see if you are awake," Arth spoke before the door was even opened. His expressions darkened as he saw Rudhir standing in the doorway in his towel.

"Come in," Adhira spoke from the bed. Rudhir stepped aside and Arth walked in.

"I ordered breakfast," Arth said, standing uncomfortably between Adhira and Rudhir. "I hope I was not…"

"Yes, you were," Rudhir snapped.

"Shut it," Adhira shouted. "Will you help me take out the IV?" she spoke to Arth. He moved forward and helped her get free.

"Are you feeling better?" Arth asked seriously.

"Yes, comforts of my bed," Adhira smiled.

"You owe me an explanation," Arth muttered as he gave a quick sideway glance towards Rudhir, who was still standing in his towel.

"I don't need to explain anything to you. There is nothing to explain," Adhira replied.

"The tattoo on his shoulder says differently," Arth sighed. "Am I like the third wheel here?"

"Yes," Rudhir spoke and went to get dressed.

"Do you love him?" Arth asked as he stared at the bathroom door behind which Rudhir had disappeared.

"We all have a past, don't we?" She muttered.

"So, he is your *past and present*, and I can be your *present and future?"* Arth asked seductively.

Adhira grinned and was about to say something when a loud snap behind them. Rudhir was walking out of the room, fuming.

"I think I will get dressed now," Adhira sighed.

"Sure," and with one soft kiss on her lips, he walked out.

PLAN FOR TOMORROW

"They are ready for you," Rudhir spoke mechanically after their quiet, awkward breakfast.

"Who is waiting?" Arth asked suddenly.

"My team, you should meet them," Adhira beamed and led Rudhir and Arth to her work room.

"Sneaky," Arth grinned appreciatively as Adhira opened the secret door. "And wow!" his jaw dropped as he saw the interior. "You are rich."

"Richer than you can imagine," Adhira laughed loudly as she dialled her team.

"Money at the cost of bruises and near-death experiences," Rudhir snapped, standing a little too far behind. Adhira rolled her eyes at him.

"And there she is…" Franc spoke jovially as, one by one, her team popped on their respective screens. "And who is that?"

Adhira waited for a few seconds for everyone to join, then introduced.

"Ah, so you are the French," Arth spoke to Ava and Patricia.

"Yes, they are… well, Patty is Canadian," Adhira laughed.

"You hired me," Arth spoke to Patricia, who nodded. "Forever grateful, milady," Arth bowed in front of Patricia's screen.

"He is cheesy," Patricia snickered, "I like him."

"And how is Mr R&AW taking the cheesy?" Franc asked sourly.

"Shouldn't we work? Isn't the attack, like, tomorrow?" Rudhir snapped.

"Yes," Ava spoke and put up various photographs on the screen. Everyone turned deadly serious at this. "These are the pictures we could capture while you were with Hayat Khan," Ava continued. "What is their plan?"

"Hayat Khan has two grandchildren, Khalid and Khalida. Ikhtiyaar and Haseena were Hayat Khan's children. Khalid and Khalida are using their names in their terrorist organisation. I don't know if they are doing it out of respect or what, but Pristine or Haseena's real name is Khalida," Adhira informed, pulling out the sheets she had snatched from Hayat Khan's house and placing them on board around the room.

"Ikhtiyaar was Hayat Khan's son?" Rudhir asked.

"Yes, but Ikhtiyaar is dead. And Khalid has taken the name of his father while forming the organisation Ikhti-Baksh," Adhira nodded.

"So, they are related," Patricia gasped. "You were right Adhira. Everything is linked."

"Yes, and the final piece is this Memorial," Adhira pointed at the chart. "I couldn't make out much, but it seems that they plan to shoot the crowd with XRS bullets from these four locations."

"The memorial is near the Embassy area," Rudhir added, "There are no high-rise buildings in the vicinity."

"And they need high-rise buildings to shoot," Franc spoke.

"The speed," Samuel spoke for the first time, "needed for the bullets to break is 3300 kmph, the speed is provided by the custom-made rifles, but it is not possible in close proximity. I studied the bullet you sent, these specific bullets need to travel for some distance to gain that kind of momentum… they will either shoot from the sky, or they will shoot from a distance of more than 500kms."

"They can't shoot from 500kms away," Rudhir added. "Delhi is way too crowded, in no way they will get a direct range to the crowd around Memorial if they shoot from that kind of distance."

"Drones," Arth added. Everyone turned towards him. "Pakis have been testing drones on the border for months now. They are putting guns on drones and shooting at our villages, haven't you heard about it?" he asked, surprised.

"I have heard of drones carrying bombs," Rudhir looked at Adhira in surprise, "but never guns."

"Is it possible?" Adhira asked Samuel.

"Difficult, but not impossible," Samuel spoke thoughtfully. "There were some tests with handguns. Though I won't be surprised if it has graduated to rifles."

"Oh damn!" Rudhir almost cursed. "This just keeps getting better and better."

"If not drones, then what?" Adhira asked the group.

"Paragliders?" Patricia spoke thoughtfully. "Last year, there was a murder in Canada where the killer was on a paraglider. But he accepted that it was mere luck, the wind made it way too unpredictable."

"What else?" Adhira asked.

"Airplanes?" Franc suggested.

"Due to Memorial, the entire area is being declared as a No-Fly zone. If any plane takes the route over the area, it will be shot at, PMO is very strict about it," Rudhir informed.

"I think we should investigate if any high-rise building falls in direct trajectory to the Memorial," Adhira spoke thoughtfully. "Hayat Khan spoke a lot that day, but he didn't utter the word 'drone'. It could be deliberate but I am still apprehensive about the drones. Call me hopeful, but a part of me is scared to think of drones carrying guns and shooting at will, without any witnesses."

"Yes, it would be catastrophic," Samuel nodded. "But if you find one in the field, would you mind keeping it for me?" he asked hopefully.

"Why Sam?" Patricia laughed. "You want to replicate it?"

"I don't think it would be such a bad idea, seeing how dangerous it is getting for this girl. Especially on this mission. We almost lost her twice and if I can stop a third, I would be delighted," Samuel spoke with fatherly affection.

"I will get it for you," Rudhir added before anybody could speak.

"So that's sorted," Adhira spoke quickly. "Ava, Franc, you have two tasks. First, look for high-rise buildings from where they can shoot. Also, look for any manufacturers who can produce drones, even prototypes, which can carry and shoot using custom-made rifles. Ask Samuel to give his input here so that we don't waste any time."

"Got it," both Franc and Ava spoke in chorus.

"Now, they are planning twin attacks," Adhira exhaled heavily and everybody moved in shock. "Yes, two parallel attacks."

"What do you mean?" Rudhir asked quickly.

"Hayat Khan asked me to go somewhere, take something from Khalida and walk back to the crowd. All he wanted me to do was take that thing and roam around in the crowd," Adhira spoke, trying to remember.

"What was that thing?" Franc asked.

"He wouldn't say, he only laughed. He just said it was something that would annihilate India, kill millions in one go," Adhira sighed. "I think that it is some kind of biological weapon."

"Oh my God!" Ava cried. "What if it is that strain of Ebola?"

"Zaire ebolavirus?" Patricia added.

"Yes, Miranda's info is never wrong. What if there really was a truck smuggling Ebola in India?" Ava cried.

"There has been no movement on LOC in the past two days," Arth supplied.

"And how do you know that?" Rudhir demanded.

"Because that is my job to know!" Arth replied curtly. "But, there was a consignment entering India last night," he added.

"Consignment? What kind of consignment?" Adhira asked quickly.

"I don't know. I declined it as I was supposed to be bringing you back to India in my car, wasn't I? I don't take two jobs in one go," Arth shrugged.

"How large was the consignment?" Adhira asked.

"A small box," Arth informed. "All I was supposed to do was take the box across the border and dump it at a designated area."

"What designated area?" Rudhir asked sharply.

"Don't know now. Didn't take the task so didn't get the memo, did I?" Arth dismissed casually.

"Didn't Miranda say something about a truck?" Ava asked the group.

"Not if they harvested the virus and planned to smuggle it in vials," Samuel wondered. "It is always easy to carry small vials and break them in populous than carrying dead bodies."

"That's a valid point," Adhira nodded. "What would they need to harvest the virus?"

"A State-of-the-art Bio-Lab," Samuel spoke. "And high-end equipment."

"What is a bio-lab?" Arth asked seriously.

"Consider it a highly restricted lab where they develop, mutate and harvest viruses," Adhira spoke quickly.

"And, do they wear those hazmat suits in it?" Arth asked.

"Yes," Adhira nodded.

"They built one such facility two months ago near the airport, I saw it… a small but fortified facility. It is restricted and is always guarded. I have seen it multiple times," Arth informed.

"Can you give the coordinates to Ava?" Adhira spoke quickly.

"I can, let me search for it," and Arth started looking it up on his phone.

"How can we know if any consignment entered our borders last night?" Rudhir asked.

"You cannot. Once it is across the border, it can be anywhere," Arth shrugged.

"Just awesome," Rudhir fumed in rage.

"The grand memorial launch is tomorrow," Adhira spoke softly. "They must be setting up now, they won't risk any delays."

"Delhi is massive," Ava supplied.

"Yes, but as per Hayat Khan, I was supposed to meet Khalida at a walking distance from the memorial," Adhira spoke. "We would need to search every single vendor tomorrow, every single booth and every single house in the vicinity of the memorial."

"It is very risky," Franc added.

"They could break the vial the moment they realise that you are searching for them," Patricia spoke. "Ebola, even if not exposed in the heart of the crowd, is still very contagious. Only one person needs to be exposed, the rest will follow."

"Who has a better plan?" Adhira asked, defeated.

There was dead silence in the room at these words.

"We need a plan, I won't let them infect our people with dirty bombs and Ebola without a fight," Adhira shouted.

"Calm down," Arth tried to console but she raised her hand to quiet him.

She turned to Rudhir and spoke, "You will rally all the forces and make sure that every nook and cranny of this city is searched," she ordered. He nodded. "But first, start a mass-vaccination drive for Ebola."

"I don't think they would have enough supply," Patricia sighed. "But at least Arth should get a shot urgently as well. I will arrange for it right now," and she vanished from the screen.

"I will see how many doses can be arranged at the moment," Rudhir spoke in a worried tone.

"What about the mole? Won't the person know if you rally everyone?" Franc asked.

"The mole must have already fled the country," Ava spoke.

"No sane person, who is aware of the plan, would stay back when there is a huge threat of radiation poisoning and Ebola," Samuel added.

"Unless the mole is not aware," Rudhir informed. "I have been keeping tabs on all movements across all agencies and Home Ministry since we discovered that there is a mole. Daily attendance is shared with my department. And PMO has made attendance mandatory in the weeks leading up to the launch. No one has fled the country."

"Maybe, the person is brain-washed," Adhira supplied. "Hayat Khan believed I was willing to die for the cause and he was happy to find me."

"Maybe," Rudhir nodded.

"Look for families," Arth spoke. "Even if your mole is willing to die, he or she would want to save their family. Look for the families who fled the country recently."

"Or those with no family at all," Ava added.

"Too much work," Rudhir rubbed his face.

"I will do it," Ava rolled her eyes. "It is a matter of minutes, an hour max, I will do it for you…"

"Thank you," Rudhir nodded. "I need to update the Home Minister about this," he started to walk out.

"Anything else?" Adhira asked her team. Everyone shook their heads.

"Call if anyone needs anything, just call," and with one nod, they all disconnected.

"What should I do?" Arth asked Adhira as they walked out. Rudhir was packing his things there.

"I will see you in a while," Adhira spoke to Arth and literally pushed him out.

"You need a calm head for this mission," Adhira spoke to Rudhir. "Don't be rattled, you will mess things up."

Rudhir threw his shirt from last night that he was folding and glared at her.

"I have always loved you, never been with another woman ever. Only you," Rudhir spoke harshly.

"What I do is my business," Adhira replied simply. "Who I do it with is also my business."

"And your business is that driver?" Rudhir growled. "He only wants to—only –"

"What? Fuck me?" Adhira asked with a roll of eyes, "I am thirty-plus, I think it is high time someone did that," she laughed. "I have almost died numerous times in the past week alone. I may die tomorrow and it makes me think that I shouldn't die a virgin."

Rudhir looked at her in disbelief but she just shrugged and walked to her wardrobe to take out her clothes.

"You want me to come to the Home Minister's office with you?" Adhira asked with her back to him but he didn't reply.

He forced her to turn around, pushed her inside her wardrobe and kissed her. Before she knew it, she was against the wall and he was kissing her intimately and passionately. He pushed her on the bed and started kissing her all over, starting from her neck to her cleavage, to her stomach.

She pushed Rudhir away and got up.

"I love you," Rudhir spoke, pushing her back on the bed. "I made a terrible mistake in the past, but I love you, only you. And you are mine… I have waited years for you. I am not going to send you off to the horizon with another man without a fight."

Adhira's eyes filled with tears at these words.

"You love me as much as I love you," Rudhir spoke. "You and I are meant to be together. I will make it up to you for the past years with all my life, but right now, get dressed, we have a meeting with the Home Minister." And with this he got up and stepped out.

PORTRAIT ON THE CEILING

"I still can't believe that he won't budge," Adhira cursed as Rudhir drove away from the Home Minister's office. "Despite everything, they won't."

"Well…" Rudhir started.

"I mean, there is a radioactive threat, bio threat, and God knows what else, and yet your ministry won't postpone the damn launch," Adhira continued angrily.

"Home Minister wants to, it is the PMO that won't budge," Rudhir informed. "He tried his best, but PMO wants to send a statement to Pakistan, especially after they blew up our embassy there."

"Where are Pakistan's embassy people?" Adhira asked.

"Holed up in their own embassy, waiting for evacuation," Rudhir informed.

"Don't you think that they would bring their people back before the attack?" Adhira wondered.

"They were planning to leave today, but your involvement has changed things. Indians are rallying outside the Pakistan embassy, demanding an eye for an eye. All of them are holed up inside," Rudhir laughed.

"Good for them," Adhira snorted.

"Ava called with a list of nine people who are potential moles, all of them have been detained. The rest are getting briefed for the search," Rudhir informed.

Adhira nodded.

"What's next?" Adhira called Patricia from the car to fill her in regarding the meeting with the Home Minister.

"What's next?" Rudhir asked both Adhira and Patricia.

"Good night's sleep, tomorrow is going to be a big day," Patricia spoke. "Is your team searching every area?"

"Yes, nonstop," Rudhir informed.

"Good," Patricia spoke.

"Call us if anything is needed," Rudhir spoke and Adhira disconnected.

"Let's go," Rudhir spoke as he parked the car outside a house.

"This is your house or your dad's?" Adhira demanded as she stared at a two-storeyed house in the heart of Delhi.

"Mine," Rudhir smiled and dragged her inside. "A place where we can spend the potential last night together."

As they stepped inside, she was shocked to see the interior of it. It was completely opposite to hers. Where her house was barren and void of any emotions or personal touch, Rudhir's entire house was covered in photographs. And not of his family, but hers!

"I remember that you loved capturing moments, I didn't know…" Adhira was speechless as she saw the one where he had proposed to her and they were laughing.

"I never stopped loving you," Rudhir sighed.

"I don't want any boundaries or limitations on me," Adhira shrugged as she walked around in his house and her jaw dropped as she walked in his bedroom.

There was a life-size portrait on his ceiling, *her portrait.*

"Are you fucking insane?" Adhira demanded, lying on the bed and gazing at her own face. "This is creepy."

"My Adhira," Rudhir lay beside her and stared at her.

"I dread to think all that you do while staring at my photo," Adhira screwed up her face.

"So much… I did so much," Rudhir spoke as he pressed his lips on hers.

"Good?" Rudhir panted as he slipped on her side and tried to focus.

"Painful," Adhira panted too. "But good," she added.

"I have read that it is painful the first time," Rudhir nodded at her. "Maybe next time…"

"You mean if we have a next time," Adhira spoke as she got up and got dressed.

"Where are you going?" Rudhir demanded, pulling at her clothes. She felt smitten, standing naked in his room, next to him.

"I like this colour on your skin," Rudhir spoke, caressing her cheeks and kissing her back.

"Do you love me?" Rudhir asked pushing her back on the bed.

"I don't know," Adhira replied. "I—I have hated you for a very long time, but I don't think I love you now."

"Hmm," Rudhir groaned. "Maybe now, you will," and without any further words, he climbed on top of her.

Adhira was fast asleep in Rudhir's arms when her phone buzzed and she answered it on speaker, like always, without looking at the caller.

"Yes," Adhira spoke groggily.

"What are you doing in Rudhir's bedroom?" Patricia demanded.

"*Sleeeepping*… what else?" Ava giggled but Patricia shushed her angrily.

"How do you know?" Adhira asked sharply, covering herself with sheets.

"We have done quite a few video calls with him in the past weeks to know what is on his ceiling," Patricia informed. "Is he with you?"

"I am here," Rudhir spoke from Adhira's side.

"Good, romance and sex aside, we are only a few hours away from the big showdown. So, here is an update," Patricia spoke matter-of-factly. "As you both have been vaccinated for Ebola two days ago, I have arranged for the doses of SARS and flu vaccine for you. They have been delivered to your doorstep, Rudhir. Please administer them ASAP"

"How will we administer them?" Rudhir asked, surprised.

"I can do it, it's no biggie," Adhira shrugged.

"Also, Ava had an update," Patricia added and gestured Ava to begin.

"I found a facility that made drones to carry rifles and handguns. But they sold two to someone in Pakistan... so I am assuming that those two drones will be carrying the rifles," Ava informed, trying to mask her glee.

"Four bullets... Drones can circle," Rudhir spoke seriously. "They can fire once and then be reloaded."

"Or it is two drones and two humans. If I were Hayat Khan, I won't risk all four bullets in drones. What if it fails," Adhira wondered.

"Are we sure it is only four bullets?" Rudhir asked.

"If it is more, then we are royally screwed by her-highness," Adhira groaned.

"Her highness?" Rudhir asked.

"The Duchess Pristine Dawson, aka Khalida aka Haseena aka Hayat Khan's granddaughter," Adhira sang.

"Have you informed the queen?" Rudhir asked Ava.

"I will, once we have mitigated the threat, let's not get ahead of ourselves and tip them off," Ava supplied.

"Fair point," Rudhir nodded.

"So, two drones, two humans with rifles, and Ebola virus in vials. That's what we are looking for tomorrow," Rudhir concluded.

"Easy-peasy, isn't it?" Patricia added sarcastically.

"Drones, we can tackle as we can monitor airspace properly, humans are a problem," Rudhir spoke.

"And even bigger problem is the Virus," Ava added.

"Yes, my main concern is the virus," Patricia agreed.

"There you are…" Arth smiled as Adhira entered the house sometime in middle of the night.

"Here I am," Adhira tried to smile back.

"Someone gave me this but I have no clue as to how to inject in myself," Arth showed her an icebox.

"I will do it," Adhira spoke and took the icebox from his hands. "Roll up your sleeves."

He took off his shirt instead. Adhira sighed and injected him in his arm.

"We are taking these but these are not going to take effect until ten days minimum. We are all at high risk of contracting Ebola tomorrow," Adhira informed him very seriously. "And I have an update," and she informed him of what Patricia and Ava had said about drones, high-rise etc.

"Just a few hours and it all will be done," Arth groaned at the information.

"Just a few hours," Adhira nodded and went off to sleep.

"Are we ready?" Franc asked when Adhira, Rudhir and Arth connected with the team on VC the next morning.

"Yes," Adhira nodded. She was dressed in a skin-tight shirt and trousers with guns and gadgets poking out of various pockets. "I just need to do a final touch."

"What is the status of the high-rise?" Rudhir asked Ava.

"Narrowed it down to three, they can be in any one of them, so, you would need to search each and every one," Ava informed. "But…" she added as she pulled up the maps on-screen, "You should start from here. It has least occupancy, so this becomes highly likely."

"Got it," Rudhir nodded.

"Where do you need me?" Arth asked Adhira.

"Rudhir, you are with drones or high-rise?" Adhira asked.

"Drones," Rudhir informed.

"Then I need you at the high-rise, I need you to go door to door and look for anomalies. I will be on the virus and deadly vials," Adhira ordered.

"Ava, hack into the camera feeds of these buildings and see if anything out of ordinary has happened," Adhira spoke. "Give the feed access to Samuel, Franc, Patty and just shuffle through them as quick as possible."

"We are already on it, there is nothing out of ordinary but the building with least occupancy has no cameras," Ava supplied.

"Then they are there," Rudhir spoke. "No cameras, no records."

"Arth, go and search these buildings," Adhira ordered. "You guys should go through the feed dating at least a week back. Sometimes they plant themselves long before to avoid detection."

"Will do," Ava nodded.

"Let's roll, then," Adhira clapped as she walked out to get dressed.

"I will get going," Arth spoke to Adhira.

"You will meet Captain Vir on the ground. Say 'Rudhir Singh Rajput' sent you," Rudhir spoke.

Arth nodded and started to leave.

"Arth," Adhira spoke as she rushed to him. "I am sorry for everything, but please, don't do anything stupid. Come back alive, okay," she insisted.

Arth nodded and she hugged him tightly.

"Good luck," and kissing his cheek clumsily, she let him go. He walked away without sparing her a second glance.

"He will be fine," Rudhir spoke, rubbing Adhira's back consolingly. "We all will."

Adhira turned and hugged him.

"I love you," Adhira choked at the words knowing she may never get another chance.

"Ah, finally…" Rudhir smiled in tears. "I love you too."

ARTH

Dressed in baggy jeans and a loose shirt, Adhira made way to meet the person in charge of the Vial search. At the same time, Rudhir made way towards the van searching the skies for drones. And Arth made way towards the least occupied building.

9:00 AM – Arth's location.

"Captain Vir?" Arth asked a constable standing at a distance.

"There he is," the constable pointed at a man in civilian dress, looking at the surroundings seriously.

"Captain Vir?" Arth asked. Captain nodded. "I am Arth, Rudhir sent me to find you."

"Yes, he told me that someone would join me in the search. Which team do you belong to?" Vir asked politely.

"Don't have a team, just that we are here to save our country," Arth laughed.

Vir nodded at him and looked around. "You have intel on which buildings to search?"

Arth handed over the names with priority status.

"Alright," Vir spoke as he called his men. He assigned ten men to each building and asked them to search house by house, look for anybody scared or panicked and report back.

"Do not engage," Arth spoke, "Let's make a list of flats that look compromised, then search them together."

Vir didn't look convinced with this but nodded. "You heard the man. Our job is to identify homes where the terrorists may be hiding. They are armed so our priority is to protect the civilians and neutralise the threat. I don't want any casualties, neither of civilians nor of our men. Understood?" he shouted the last word.

"Understood," everyone reciprocated and went in their respective directions.

"Let's go," Arth spoke as he led the way. "They can only be on top ten floors," he informed.

"And why didn't you say this to my team before?" Vir looked horrified.

"We will start from the top, but we will search till the ground floor. They need to shoot from high ground, but it doesn't mean that they couldn't take hostages on lower floors," Arth rolled his eyes at Vir. Vir looked slightly convinced, yet he called his teams and informed them to start from the top!

"Let's not withhold information, okay," Vir requested.

"Sorry, sure," Arth shrugged and walked forward.

"Why do you think that this is the building?" Vir asked as they took the elevator with Arth. Four men were with them, rest were to come in the next round as only one elevator was working!

"Because this one does not have any cameras, which is weird because all high-rise buildings have cams these days. Also, this one is the least occupied. Ideal for such crimes, isn't it?"

"True," Vir spoke as they stepped out and sent the elevator back to the ground floor for the remaining team to come up.

"Let's go to the roof," Arth spoke leading the way.

"I will wait for my team," Vir spoke.

"Fine, follow me when they are here," Arth looked at Vir in disbelief and walked up the stairs.

"Wow, this is high," Arth swore as he looked down.

He called Adhira and informed about the same.

"Can you see the memorial from there?" Adhira asked.

"Yes, from the left view," Arth informed. He looked through the binoculars and could see tiny forms of humans gathering.

"Then, that's the series of the flats they may aim from. Or from the adjacent ones if there is any window or balcony opening to the area," Adhira informed.

"Yes, I gathered that..." Arth spoke.

"Start searching then. Arth, if we miss," Adhira spoke.

"I know... I know..." Arth disconnected. He was well aware of what would happen if they missed!

"It's already 9:10," Arth spoke to Vir as he went down. "Where is your team?" he demanded.

"Very slow lift," Vir shrugged and the elevator opened finally, reuniting the entire team.

"There are six flats on each floor, isn't it?" Arth asked.

"Yes," Vir nodded.

"First we need to identify which of them have a clear view to the memorial, and then we need to prioritise those," Arth whispered.

Vir nodded again and divided his team into pairs and started to knock on the doors.

Arth took one alone, and Vir took alone too. The rest went in pairs.

"Hello ma'am," Arth spoke as he peeked inside.

"Yes?" The woman asked. She was incredibly beautiful and Arth was reminded of Adhira at the sight of her.

"I am Captain Vir," Vir interjected and showed his badge to the woman. "May we come in, please?"

The woman looked confused but let them inside.

"Are you alone in the house, ma'am?" Vir asked seriously.

"Yes, why?" The woman looked scared.

"Have you noticed anything unusual around here recently?" Vir continued.

"No, why?" The woman replied simply.

While Vir chatted with the woman, Arth looked from the balcony. The house had a clear view to the memorial ground and it was so high that nothing was visible without binoculars.

"Well, if you notice anything unusual, please let us know," and Vir handed over his card to the woman.

The woman nodded and they took her leave.

"Sir, only series 2 and 3 have visuals of the Memorial ground," one of the team members reported.

"Then that's what we will search on priority," Arth spoke. He turned to look at the door they had just come out of and saw some movement from underneath the door. The woman was listening.

"Maybe she is just scared," Vir spoke, patting at Arth's back.

"Or she is the one," Arth raised his eyebrows at him.

"Did you pick something on her?" Vir asked seriously.

"No, but still. This will be the ideal place," Arth spoke as they climbed down and started searching and interrogating people.

9:40 AM

"I have searched the entire premises, well houses that face the ground and no one is there," Arth spoke to Adhira on call.

"Wait, I will take others on the line," Adhira spoke and Arth heard the automatic voice telling him to hold the line. The voice annoyed him, yet he waited.

"Yes, we have everybody on the line," Adhira spoke quickly.

"Searched the entire building, found none," Arth repeated in a disinterested tone. "Adhira, where are you?"

"Juggling from place to place, looking for Khalida," Adhira informed. "Anyway, no one looked out of the ordinary?"

"Well, none… just that the woman on the top floor looked a little fishy," Arth made a *meh* like sound.

"How fishy?" Franc demanded.

"Didn't answer properly, you know. Only yes, no and why… and there was something off about her," Arth spoke as he tried to remember.

"What was off, how was her home? Was it cosy? Dirty? Was she alone?" Franc asked.

"Searched all houses, no news," Vir informed Arth.

"The other buildings are normal, no sign of any terrorist activity," Arth informed.

"Let's circle back to the lady on the top floor," Franc said.

"Well, she was clean, but her house was not, wasn't it so?" Arth tried to remember. "Shoot! We went through so many, I don't remember that well."

"The lady on the top floor?" Vir spoke. Arth nodded. "It was not as per the girl who was occupying her, don't you think?"

"A little less clean, we can say," Arth repeated.

"Had a feeling of abandonment?" Franc asked seriously.

"Oh shoot," Arth cursed and started to run towards the apartment, Vir following at his heels. "I knew that the lady looked fishy," Arth shouted, pressing the button hard on the elevator panel.

"If she realised who you are, she would have changed places," Franc spoke.

"Oh! Shut up," Arth spoke, irritated, and disconnected.

All ten officers squeezed in the elevator and the alarm rang. "Out... all those who can climb the stairs, out," Vir bellowed. "And call all other teams here. I want everyone in this building, inside and outside. Set a parameter of ten and I want all the rest inside, searching."

The door closed and the elevator started to climb.

"Oh... come on..." Arth jumped on his heels as the elevator moved very slowly. Even Vir was agitated beside him.

"Finally," Vir muttered as they all barged out of the elevator and rushed to the apartment door.

Vir lifted his fingers to indicate silently– 3... 2... 1... and Arth and Vir pushed the door hard and it came off its hinges.

"She is not here," one of the men, who rushed inside to check, shouted.

"How on earth did we miss this?" Arth snarled, looking around. "Where is she?"

"Someplace other than here," Vir commented as he peeked out of the balcony and craned his neck to see on the roof and floors below.

"Let's go," Arth dragged him back before Vir could fall. "Let's fan out and search."

Vir ordered his team to start looking for each house in the building. While Arth stared at the hallway.

"She must be carrying a heavy gun," Arth muttered. "They said something about a very heavy rifle, able to shoot with the speed of 3000 KMPH."

"Open the windows," Vir ordered his team members. They did the needful and as the sun rays fell on the floor of the hallway, they saw footprints reflect in the sunlight, dusty footprints headed towards the roof.

"She is on the roof," Arth whispered.

"Let's go, very quietly," Vir hushed as he loaded his gun and started to climb.

Arth took out his Glock too and loaded it.

"You have a licence for it?" Vir asked sarcastically.

"Bite me!" Arth snapped as he peeked on the roof through the gap in the door. "There she is..."

The woman, in all black, was sitting on the floor where a big rifle was placed on a tripod-like stand, facing the memorial. She was fully focused on setting the rifle in the right direction.

"Don't spook her..." Arth whispered as he stepped on the roof. Vir followed, while his team fanned out quietly.

Arth kept his Glock pointing at her head, ready to shoot if she placed her finger on the trigger, but all she did was adjust the scope. She then took out her cell and called someone, "I am ready... there was a hitch, but now I am ready."

"No... no... it is all fine. These Indians are dumber than I had thought," she laughed on the call.

"Right... I will wait for the signal, I'll wait for it, then bang!" laughing still, she disconnected and turned.

"Not so stupid now, are we?" Arth said as he hit her on the head with the back of his Glock, rendering her unconscious.

"Nicely done," Vir nodded, impressed.

Arth ignored him and took the rifle out of its stand. "It's heavy," he commented and inspected it. "No place to keep bullets though."

Vir searched the woman and found a box full of long, slender bullets.

"I was told to look for glass bullets," Arth spoke as he checked the bullets that Vir handed over to him.

Vir looked confused, "Glass bullets?"

"I know, I was shocked too," Arth pouted while Vir searched the woman more thoroughly. "Nothing..." he informed.

"Sir," one of the men spoke, "I saw in a movie once, bullets were hidden in the stand," and he walked forward and searched the stand properly. "Nothing," he spoke defeated.

"What if they are in the barrel or inside the rifle?" Vir suggested. "She was ready to pull the trigger. What if the rifle holds one or two somewhere inside?"

"But there is no space to hold the bullets," Arth groaned and started to take it apart, piece by piece.

Vir rattled each part to listen to its contents.

"Something is inside this," Vir spoke excitedly.

Arth halted and listened too. He was right, something was inside the midsection of the rifle.

"What model is this?" one of the men commented.

"Something custom made," Arth shrugged and pried open the part from where the sound was coming.

"Wow!" Vir laughed as he punched Arth on the shoulder.

Arth called Adhira quickly as he held two glass bullets in his hands.

"I found the bullets, two of them," Arth spoke in the phone. "And the transparent liquid turned sterling white when I shook the bullet."

"Good job," Adhira's muffled voice came from the other side of the line. "Keep them safe. If I don't meet you later, give them to Rudhir. If he too doesn't meet you, keep them safe and hand them over to one of my team, only to my team, and no one else, alright?"

"Where are you?" Arth asked, concerned.

"It is almost 10 AM, at the climax of this thing," Adhira panted.

"I am coming to you," Arth spoke as he disconnected the call. He pocketed the bullets while Vir handcuffed the woman.

"By the way, what did she mean by she'll wait for the bang?" Vir asked seriously.

"She said she'll wait for the signal, then bang!" Arth corrected. "Didn't she?"

"Hope so… I seriously hope we stopped the bang," Vir commented, looking down at the ground. Hundreds of thousands of people were gathered around the memorial… Waiting for the Prime Minister to make the speech and do the big unveiling.

It was 9:55 AM…

RUDHIR

9:00 AM - Rudhir's Location

"I am on my way to the van," Rudhir spoke to Adhira on call. "Almost there. Where are you?"

"Somewhere," Adhira sounded lost.

"Stay safe, okay? I need you back in one piece, okay?" Rudhir stressed.

"You too," and she disconnected.

"I love you," Rudhir spoke to the dead line and stared at the phone in his hand. "Crazy woman," he sighed and entered the van.

"Any sign?" Rudhir asked. There were two people inside, a boy and a girl, both in their early twenties.

"No sir," the boy spoke, slurping at his coke.

"Neha, please tell me that you have everything in place," Rudhir asked seriously.

"Yes boss, Joy here has some questions though," Neha smiled as she clicked away on her keyboard. The boy, Joy, stood straight.

"What do we do once the drone is in sight?" Joy asked.

"You will gain access to it," Rudhir spoke.

"Then?" Joy persisted.

"Hold on," Rudhir made a face and called Ava.

"Hello Mr R&AW, or should I now say, Mr Rogue Spy," Ava laughed on the call.

"I am with my team, Ava, and they have questions," Rudhir spoke, trying hard to supress his laugh.

"Rogue Spy? Are you going rogue, sir?" Joy asked hastily.

"Don't they call that other spy Rogue? I have read all about her, she is really mysterious and nobody has seen her real face. Is it true that she can change into a man?" Neha asked quickly.

"Yes, it is true," Ava spoke on the call. "And she is more mysterious than you can even fathom."

"Your question, Joy?" Rudhir glared as he saw Neha and Joy get all excited about Adhira.

"Oh yes, ma'am. I can hack into the drone, what's next?" Joy asked Ava.

"I will take control, upload a virus and direct it to a pre-decided, contained location. From there, we will bring it down and Rudhir will disarm it," Ava informed.

"Why can't I control it? I mean I am here," Joy retorted.

"Because for that I need to give you my virus. And one slip can make the virus affect your entire network and all our plans go down the drain," Ava informed.

"I am not—" Joy started but Rudhir stopped him.

"We all have our parts to play Joy, you do yours and we will do ours," Rudhir interjected.

"You have two Joys there, right?" Ava asked seriously.

"Joy and Neha, both are excellent hackers," Rudhir assured. "Each will tackle one drone…"

"And what if there are more than two? Shouldn't you have kept a third and a fourth on backup?" Ava asked.

"I have one more, he is roaming the streets presently," Rudhir rolled his eyes at the phone. "If need be, he will be summoned."

"Fine… you know why I am like this, you don't need to roll your eyes at me," Ava snapped.

"How?" Rudhir was shocked and so were Joy and Neha, who were listening.

"I know you Mr R&AW, though we have met briefly, I am an excellent hacker, of computers and of minds," Ava spoke proudly.

"I believe you," Rudhir laughed. "Talk to you when we have something."

"You all know the plan, right?" Ava asked seriously.

"Yes…" Rudhir sighed and pointed at Joy and Neha to speak. Neha took the lead and spoke, "The moment we spot the drone, we will point it with a beam. The beam is connected to the jammer we have installed on top of our van, the jammer will block the signals it is receiving from outside and will initiate a refresh sequence. As the refresh sequence goes live, we will gain access to it. In a fraction of a second of gaining access, we will link it to you. You will upload the virus and we will be able to navigate it. We will then steer the drone to the contained area marked by Rudhir Sir. We will follow by the van and safely bring it down in the contained area. Once it is de-weaponised by Rudhir Sir, we will dismantle it."

"Perfect," Ava clapped on the call. "Now, don't mess it up."

"We won't, ma'am," Neha assured.

"See you later then," Rudhir spoke and disconnected.

9:25 AM

"We have detected the drone," Rudhir informed Ava.

"Drone or drones?" Ava asked.

"Just one for now…" Rudhir informed. "I can see it. It is not that high, you know. It is like a crow flying at a distance. Why is it not very high? Shouldn't it be?"

"It should be high but this is good news for us… we can hack it easily," Ava replied.

"Can Joy or Neha point it with the beam?" Ava asked.

"Already on it, you should get the signal at any second," Rudhir spoke, still staring at the drone. He pulled out his binoculars and started looking at it.

"Got the access," Ava spoke on call, "I am uploading the virus now."

"This is not a rifle, it is a handgun," Rudhir spoke as he focussed on the drone. "What if this is not it?"

"We still have to dismantle it, we don't know what they did. You have to take it to the contained area," Ava ordered.

"I know but this is weird," Rudhir spoke. "I will leave one of the hackers with the van here and go on with the other," he spoke as he entered the van. "Neha with me. Joy, stay here and wait for the next drone. Do not approach it, it is very dangerous, okay?"

"Yes sir," Joy looked very unhappy but didn't comment on being left behind.

"Keep searching, and don't mess it up," Rudhir ordered as Neha hopped out of the van and they ran together to Rudhir's car.

"Keep it in sight," Rudhir spoke to Neha as he started to drive.

"Ava," Rudhir spoke, "What is the probability of contamination?"

"The XRS bullets don't go off that easily. Even if the drone falls now, unless the gun is fired at a precise speed, the bullet won't break. Masterpiece, really," Ava smiled.

"Yet, what will happen if it does… I would like to be prepared," Rudhir said as he entered the contained area.

"India Gate?" Neha shrieked.

"Only place big enough to contain the spread. We will land it right in the middle. The whole place is closed off, so no casualties, *hopefully*" Rudhir informed.

"Liking your optimism," Neha muttered but Rudhir ignored her.

"Ava, answer me. What will happen?" Rudhir insisted.

"Well, you know first-hand what XRS does," Ava spoke gravely. "If there is any leak or contamination, run, run as fast as you can."

"Can running help?" Rudhir asked very seriously as he parked the car and started to walk to the centre point.

"It can save your life, the half-life of XRS is very small in the air, so the radiation is going to die out very quickly. It is a danger when it mixes in water, and pandemic if it is mixed in blood. Iron in blood fortifies it, so it becomes deadly and almost impossible to kill. So, if there is any leak, in any way, make sure that it is not in water or blood. And run, okay, run like hell," Ava stressed.

"And the spread will be equal around the leak? I mean in a circle?" Rudhir asked.

"The virus will spread in circle, but it will spread faster in the direction of the air, so run opposite to the breeze," Ava sighed. "But it will spread. The worst will be closest to leak, and least will be on the edges, do you get what I mean?"

"Yes, I do…" Rudhir spoke as he stood inside the circle marked as the boundary. He looked at his team standing outside the circle to man the boundary.

"Okay, it is coming down…" Rudhir spoke as he looked at the drone right on top of him. "Ava…" Rudhir sounded scared now. "It is a handgun and it is wet…" he gulped. "I think it is leaking, Ava. Yes… it is white… and looks a lot like XRS. Is it possible that they changed the bullet and it started leaking? They tried to fit it in the handgun and it got contaminated."

"Oh God… Run Rudhir RUN…" Ava screamed on the call as the drone touched down with a small thud and a lot of white stuff leaked on the grass.

"BOMB… RUN…." Rudhir shouted and started to run in the opposite direction. He saw his team run back, and he glanced backwards and saw grass dying… in a circle and diagonally.

Rudhir ran and changed track, it was as if the contamination was following him.

He ran and ran…

50 meters…

"It is following you," Neha shouted from the van.

100 meters…

"Run…" Neha encouraged.

The wind was picking up and so was the speed of radiation.

"Sir, you are in the circle," Neha yelled and Rudhir looked down, the grass ahead of him was already dead…

He sped up, adrenaline in his body working hard. He pushed himself to his limit and fell.

He looked back, scared… Adhira's laughing face flashed in front of his eyes… He felt burning sensation on his skin, he felt pain… serious pain… and he passed out.

ADHIRA

9:00 AM Adhira's location

"I am on my way to the van," Rudhir spoke on the call. "Almost there. Where are you?"

"Somewhere," Adhira felt overwhelmed by the extent of the area that she had to search. She couldn't help but feel lost.

"Stay safe, okay? I need you back in one piece, okay?" Rudhir stressed.

"You too," and she disconnected. She was now looking at the team that she was supposed to work with.

"Adhira Shekhawat," she introduced herself to a police officer.

"Inspector Rathod, ma'am," the officer shook hands. "Have heard a lot of about you. It is an honour to serve beside you."

"Honour is mine," Adhira replied, looking around. "How many hazmat suits do you have?" she asked.

"We cannot roam around in hazmat suits, it will cause panic," Inspector Rathod spoke with a shrug. "We do have gas masks, it should give us initial protection. We have NCDC on standby. They will take actions and precautions if we find the location."

"Good, we need National Centre for Disease Control to ensure that there is no spread," Adhira nodded and the inspector handed her a backpack.

"This contains basic requirements - your gas mask, sanitiser, towel and spare clothes and shoe covers, in case of exposure," inspector informed. Adhira nodded and placed the bag on her back.

"Shall we?" Adhira asked and they started searching, one by one.

They searched for around fifteen minutes when the Inspector asked, "Ma'am, why are we concentrating only in this area?"

Adhira concentrated to recall what Hayat Khan had said.

"I saw this area in their plans, the west of Memorial, this is where the virus is," Adhira informed.

"How did you manage to get hold of their plans?" the Inspector was shocked.

"Not relevant," Adhira shook her head. "Are there any abandoned warehouses in the vicinity?" she asked.

"Ma'am, this is the heart of Delhi, every single place is full," the Inspector laughed. "But," he looked grave now, "There are a few shops which closed down few months ago… they are only a few blocks down. We can check them…"

"Why don't your team continue searching this area, while you and I go and look at those shops?" Adhira suggested. "Time is of the essence here, we need to work fast."

The inspector nodded and ordered his team members to continue searching. He then led her to his jeep.

"Let's go in my car, little less conspicuous," Adhira smiled and led way to her Volkswagen. "Drive," she handed him the keys and sat in the passenger seat. "I need to think…"

The inspector looked confused, but obliged.

They reached the shops in minutes but all of them were empty.

"No joy, ma'am," the Inspector shook his head. "Sorry to have wasted your time."

"Not a waste, really," Adhira spoke as she grabbed the inspector's hand and pushed him beside the door. "I have seen this man…" she pointed.

Inspector peeked outside, there was a man standing opposite the road, talking on phone.

"Are you sure?" the Inspector hissed.

"When you are beaten mercilessly by someone, you don't forget their faces easily," Adhira growled.

"What?" the Inspector almost jumped in shock.

"Shut it," Adhira snapped. "I need to know where he is going. And it doesn't seem like he has the vial."

The Inspector clicked the man's photo and sent it to his team, "We need to keep an eye out for him."

"He is moving," Adhira hissed, "but not towards the Memorial."

"Maybe we'll get lucky," Inspector spoke.

"Or, it is a trap," Adhira groaned. "I don't like it when things are easy."

"Ma'am," Inspector sighed, "It is 9:35 am already. We don't have time to think if it is easy!"

"You are right..." Adhira nodded. "Let's follow him."

They followed at his heels silently and saw him enter a small building. The paint was peeling on the walls and there was a sense of abandonment there.

"Let's go," Adhira started to walk to the door but the inspector stopped her.

"We need backup," the inspector called for it. "They will be here in a few minutes."

"And it will be 9:55 by then. I need to be at the memorial soon... I have to be there..." Adhira sighed.

"So, what do we do? Enter, guns blazing?" inspector looked impressed.

Adhira pulled out two guns from her pockets and loaded them, "Exactly!" and she entered.

"We should wear the mask," Inspector hissed behind her.

"The man didn't, maybe there is no virus here," Adhira replied as they crept in, slowly.

The house was covered in dust and darkness and there was no sound whatsoever.

"There," the inspector hissed. Adhira saw his profile in darkness and saw that he was pointing ahead. She too looked in the direction and saw a thin beam of light peering from under a door.

"Let's go," Adhira spoke as she made way. It was a very difficult task to navigate in darkness. She led the way, while the inspector followed her quietly.

Once by the door, they tried to listen but no sound came.

"Damn it!" Adhira cursed.

"What do we do?" the Inspector asked.

"Go outside and knock hard. Someone will come out, then take him down. It will give me a moment's time," Adhira ordered.

"Ma'am, you should go out while I tackle them," the Inspector suggested.

"Really, no time to play hero or assume the male role. Just go and do as you are told," Adhira ordered.

"I—" the inspector started, it was evident from his tone that he didn't like taking orders from her. But Rudhir and the Home Minister had given her authority.

"Just go and knock, exactly after a minute, okay?" Adhira hissed and the inspector retreated.

Adhira placed her phone right in front of the door, hiding it with a board and then hid herself on the side, crouching beside a dingy chair.

Inspector went out and banged the door. The sound echoed loudly in the silence.

A few seconds later, the man emerged from the room. He didn't notice Adhira, nor her phone that was capturing the inside of the room when the door opened.

She heard the man interacting with the Inspector, then a tussle. By the sound of it, she knew the inspector was successful in over-powering the man.

Adhira picked up her phone and checked it.

It was mostly empty but there was a large plastic wall dividing the room. *The Virus was here*...

Adhira messaged the NCDC contact with her location and barged in.

The room was empty, except for one woman inside the plastic wall and she looked sick, epically sick. The plastic wall enclosure was like a small room within the room, which was keeping the woman isolated.

The woman looked at Adhira and staggered towards the plastic wall.

"Who are you?" The woman croaked.

The plastic wall was making the woman's face hazy, but Adhira recognised her nonetheless.

"Pristine?" Adhira gasped. "You got infected? Oh my God! You are infected."

Pristine's eyes widened in shock.

"I know you... how are you alive?" Pristine croaked.

"It is not that easy to kill me," Adhira laughed as she looked at the sick woman.

"You are the bio weapon and Hayat Khan was so happy to have infected you? His own granddaughter? Oh my God! You people are monsters..." Adhira swore.

Pristine didn't react to these words.

"You are Khalida, aren't you?" Adhira asked seriously.

Pristine's expressions darkened. "You killed my *bade-abbu*, you are the same woman, aren't you?"

Adhira shrugged.

"You will pay," and Pristine started to unzip the plastic enclosure in which she was kept. "Where is Ahmad? I think it is time for me to go."

Adhira quickly extracted the gas mask and placed it on her head.

"There are no vials, you are the weapon. You are the bio-weapon. You are infected with Ebola and you are planning to roam around amongst the masses to infect others," Adhira gasped.

"Very quick on the uptake," Pristine spoke as she slowly crawled out of her safe bubble. As she came out, Adhira realised how weak Pristine was. She was literally crawling on the floor, her nails were brittle and dark, her skin was patchy and she was almost bald.

"What happened to you? Ebola doesn't do this..." Adhira asked as she took multiple steps back.

"You killed him..." Pristine cried as she moved closer to Adhira.

"He killed you! Don't you see what he did to you? And he was happy... so proud and laughing," Adhira couldn't believe the dedication this woman had for Hayat Khan.

"He didn't kill me. He could never. He never knew that I was infected. I was experimenting with the viruses and I got infected. *Bade Abbu* died without the knowledge of my infection," Pristine sighed. The movement and effort of speaking was taking a toll on her body.

"Hayat Khan died two days ago... are you telling me that you have mutated Ebola virus so drastically that it does this in two days?" Adhira blanched.

"This is not Ebola any more... Ebola is not airborne or water borne," Pristine laughed throatily. "Why don't you take off your mask, I will show you exactly what it is!"

"What have you done?" Adhira moved back, scared.

"We have made it deadlier... more potent... and more dangerous. Now, one breath from me will kill you all..."

"What?" a shiver ran down Adhira's spine. What did they do!

"This will reach Pakistan too... how you are not worried?" Adhira tried to stall her, praying for NCDC and back up to arrive soon.

"My country is aware… they have already barricaded the borders. We have been planning this for years. We have made ourselves self-sufficient enough to live in isolation. Virus from India will not enter my nation," and though Pristine was very weak, her will was very strong. "I will avenge my father and grandfather. I will avenge all those who have died in the war. I will bring peace to their souls…"

"Stop," Adhira pointed a gun at her. But Pristine didn't stop. She found enough strength to stand up and lunged at Adhira. Her nails dug into Adhira's arms, tearing the shirt that she was wearing.

Aaahhhhhhhhhhh, Adhira cried. She was not in pain, pain she could bear, but it was the fear of getting infected.

The gas mask was heavy, it was making Adhira lose balance, she tripped and Pristine fell on her. Pristine tried hard to undo her gas mask but before she could, members of NCDC, inspector and others entered and pulled Pristine away from her.

"Are you okay?" the inspector asked Adhira. He too was wearing the gas mask and looked very worried.

"I am fine," Adhira shrugged.

"She is infected," Adhira informed the NCDC members. "And it is not Ebola, it is something custom, far more lethal and contagious."

They injected Pristine with something and she was rendered unconscious. They pushed her back in the plastic bubble and looked at Adhira.

"She scratched you," one of the NCDC member spoke.

"No," Adhira took off her shirt and showed them her untouched black suit.

"Still, you need to stay in quarantine," the NCDC member spoke. "We cannot predict how much this gas mask will stop the virus, especially since they modified it."

"Doesn't it take a while for the infection to kick in? You know, for someone to become contagious?" Adhira asked quickly.

"Yes, but intubation period can be as low as two hours in some cases," the NCDC member warned her.

"Well, then I will come find you before my two hours are up," Adhira patted his shoulder. "National emergency here…"

Her phone rang, it was Arth, "I found the bullets, two of them," Arth's voice brought relief to her. Now, just Rudhir's part was left. Maybe she would call him or Ava and get an update.

"Good job," Adhira spoke through the gas mask. "Keep them safe. If I don't meet you later, give them to Rudhir. If he too doesn't meet you, keep them safe and hand them over to one of my team, only to my team, and no one else, alright?"

"Where are you?" Arth asked, concerned.

"It is almost 10 AM, at the climax of this thing," Adhira sighed.

"I am coming to you," Arth spoke and disconnected. It was 9:50 AM… It really was the climax.

Pristine moved in her plastic bubble.

"What do we do with her? And why is she gaining consciousness so soon?" The Inspector asked, staring at Pristine's moving hand. The NCDC member looked shocked too. The drug should have kept her unconscious for hours.

"She did something to herself," Adhira muttered, "The extent to which their hatred for us goes…"

She looked at the crowd at the room and decided the next action on the spot.

"I want you both to turn around," Adhira spoke to the NCDC member and the Inspector.

"Why?" the Inspector retorted.

"Be my guest," Adhira shrugged, went inside the plastic bubble with the gas mask on her head and shot Pristine four times in the head.

Inspector took out his gun to stop her, but it was too late.

Adhira walked out with raised hands, and spoke, "If you had heard what she was planning for our country, you too would have done the same thing… now burn her…" and she started to walk out.

"Hey! Wait," the NCDC member shouted. "Your clothes are infected."

Adhira took off the layer on top of geared clothes on her way out and threw them back inside for them to burn.

The inspector followed her but he was only wearing his undergarments now. He quickly got dressed in the spare clothes in his backpack.

"You cannot walk out like this… you look like terminator on a mission. The crowd will panic," the Inspector pointed as he stared down at her. Her entire body was strapped with various weapons. "You really need a bomb?" he asked, pointing at her thigh to which a grenade was attached.

"Always prepare for the worst," Adhira shrugged as she also put on the spare clothes. "Damn, now I cannot get to my guns."

"Shall we?" The inspector asked, and together they walked out.

THE GRAND UNVEILING

"Talk to me…" Adhira spoke as she dialled Ava and Rudhir on their way to the memorial.

"This is Neha, ma'am," another woman's voice came.

"Okay, what is happening Neha? Where are Ava and Rudhir?" Adhira demanded.

"I—" Neha sounded shocked and disconcerted.

"What happened to the drone?" Adhira asked, getting to the point.

"There was only one drone, but as per the conversation between Rudhir sir and Ava ma'am, it seems that both bullets were in this drone," Neha informed.

Why is she hyperventilating? Adhira wondered but she decided to focus on the mission.

"Is the drone neutralised?" Adhira asked.

"Yes ma'am," Neha confirmed.

"Fine, ask Rudhir to call me the moment he is able to," and before Neha could reply, she disconnected.

"We are here," the Inspector spoke as he got out of the car. "So, is it done? Are we safe?"

"Yes… Arth took down the sniper, Rudhir took down the drone… and well, we took down the bioweapon," Adhira sighed as she looked at the crowd gathered at the big unveiling.

It was 10:00 AM now… and the crowd was going crazy.

"It's time for the Prime Minister to address the nation," the Inspector informed Adhira, and the Prime Minister's voice boomed. He was standing right next to the memorial, which was covered with a long cloak.

My dear Indians… my brothers and sisters,

My humble salutations to you all.

And I salute all the warriors of Kargil again, their families, their friends and everyone who is associated with them in any way.

Today, we are celebrating those who were there, who fought for us… and not just those who gave lives in the war… we celebrate every human who suffered at the hands of our enemy, dead or alive!

War… war is humanity's worst enemy, but sometimes it is unavoidable. We have been trying to avoid war for decades because we understand and value the lives that have suffered on the border ---.

"Something is amiss," Adhira spoke quickly in between the speech.

"What do you mean?" the inspector asked, perplexed.

"Today we are not just commemorating martyrs, but also the ones who survived the horrors of the war…"

"There were four 'X's," Adhira spoke as she turned around.

"What 'X's?" The Inspector asked.

"One was the high-rise, one was the house with the bioweapon, one was the drone, and another… right above the memorial," Adhira recalled.

"The memorial you are going to witness today, it is made of glass… highly pressurised black glass that is unbreakable. It depicts our nation's strength… our valour, our gallantry…"

"Oh my God…!" Adhira gasped as she started to run forward with Inspector following at her heels.

"It shows that we will not break down… we will stand tall and strong, no matter what, and let it be a message to our enemy, we will not go down quietly. And no matter what darkness they throw at us, our

Sun i.e. our army, our navy, our air force… our people will always break it… our Sun will always break the darkness they throw at us…"

"MOVE…. MOVE…." Adhira shouted as she made way to the crowd. She dialled the Home Minister, who answered with a grudge.

"I now will ask the honourable Retired General Meher Allhuwaliya, the man who has witnessed it with you all, the man who had suffered with you, who felt your pain ---"

"Not the right time, Ms Shekhawat," the Home Minister growled.

"A bomb… bomb in the Memorial… evacuate, right now…" Adhira shouted as she rushed ahead, but the crowd didn't let her.

She pushed through but it was the Inspector's voice that helped clear the path for them… "Police business, let us pass… Police business…"

"Are you sure?" The Home Minister hissed on the phone.

"Yes Sir, PLEASE EVACUATE…" Adhira shouted.

The home minister rushed down from the make-shift stage and spoke hastily to the security around.

Adhira was now at the foot of the memorial. There were at least twenty steps up ahead, over which the memorial was built.

Security rushed forward to secure the Prime Minister, and they all hurried down the stairs as Adhira looked around… However, to great shock and sudden applause from the crowd, the Prime Minister halted for a second and unveiled the memorial suddenly. The black glass glowed in the July sun, almost blinding everyone around. Despite the situation, she wondered why they had made such a tower. Won't it impact traffic? Or was it not visible from the road?

"Where are you?" Adhira whispered as the bomb scare and panic started to spread through the masses. She had to shield her eyes as the reflection from the black glass was practically blinding her.

The Police started to push the crowd behind, and the Inspector started to drag Adhira away from the memorial.

"I am not sure if I should hope for you to be right or wrong about this," the Inspector muttered.

"There he is..." Adhira pointed in the opposite direction. While everyone was panicking and running, only one man was standing at a distance, smiling at the chaos. He was beardless now but Adhira recognised him nonetheless.

"Who?" the Inspector stopped dragging her and stared where she was pointing.

"Khalid, Ikhtiyaar, whatever name he goes by... the mastermind behind this all..." Adhira roared as she pulled out her Beretta .22 and took aim.

Khalid aka Ikhtiyaar tilted his head towards her as he tried to recognise her. Then, a huge smile spread on his face. *He recognised her.*

He gave her a thumbs up, showing his approval at what she had accomplished so far, and waved.

Adhira stopped dead in her feet.

Khalid looked at the memorial and his expressions hardened. Adhira knew what this memorial represented to him. Hayat Khan was very clear about it and so was Pristine aka Khalida.

Khalid looked at Adhira once more, waved goodbye and before Adhira could shout 'RUN'

B – L – A – S – T

And with shards of glass piercing her entire body, Adhira felt herself flying... flying in very slow motion... as the memorial... representing the Sun... came shattering down around her...

...THE END...

ACKNOWLEDGEMENT

First and foremost, I thank all the beautiful readers. It is because of your love and motivation that I have written something entirely new and I hope you find it as good as my other works.

My special thanks to my beloved husband, ***Rajat Sharma***, for your love and evergreen support.

Big thanks and shout out to my beautiful kids, ***Vihaan*** and ***Vanya.*** You are so understanding and patient, and always allow me time to write and fuel my passion.

My lovely nephews, **Dwij** and **Aadit**, your cheery smile and sparkling eyes always light up my day.

To my parents, ***Dr. R. N. Gupta & Dr. Rekha Gupta***, ***Justice Anil Sharma & Manju Sharma,*** for supporting me, motivating me, and making me what I am today.

My brothers and sisters, ***Anmol, Juhi, Shalabh, Kavita, Navendra, Harshita, Vipul, Arsh, Arushi and Arpita,*** thank you for being there for me at any time of the day.

My loving thanks to my friend, ***Shubham Sharma***, for your suggestions in this novel. Thank you for having endless discussions with me patiently, they have helped me make this book what it is today.

My big and special thanks to ***Anuj Kumar***, my publisher and a very good friend, for all your support and encouragement.

To my editor, ***Priya***, for your suggestions and support.

And last but not least, a big thanks to the almighty for guiding me, blessing me, and making me what I am today.

ABOUT KRITIKA SHARMA

Kritika Sharma is a proud mother of two beautiful children. She is also an author, blogger, reviewer and a dreamer. Besides her writing career, she is also a marketing professional with more than a decade of experience.

She loves to read, write, and cook Indian delicacies for her foodie husband. Her every waking second is dedicated to her family, and yet she finds time for her passion, i.e., her books. She has published 10+ books across genres – Romance, Thriller, Non-Fiction etc. She loves to connect with her readers and is always available at

Email: kritikawrites@gmail.com

AuthorKritikaSharma

AuthorKritika

AuthorKritika

www.kritikasharma.in